Praise for

the memory book

★ "Sammie's narrative voice is sardonic, distinctive, wildly
intelligent, and sometimes hilarious.... Indelible."
—*Kirkus Reviews* (starred review)

★ "Fans of John Green's work and Jennifer Niven's
All the Bright Places will be reaching for the tissue box at
the book's tear-inducing end." —*SLJ* (starred review)

★ "An emotionally charged story about a young woman who
has kept her eyes trained on the future, only to learn that all she
has is now.... Avery's novel stands out for its strong characters, a
heartbreaking narrative that shifts to reflect Sammie's condition, and
a love story that will leave many readers in tears."
—*Publishers Weekly* (starred review)

★ "Teens will be inspired by Avery's heart-rending story about
a special and intelligent young woman coping with a devastating
disease—a story buoyed by the strong love of family flowing
through Sammie's narrative and by an exquisite love story."
—*VOYA* (starred review)

"Things you will probably experience while reading this
wonderful book: gut-wrenching hope, ugly-crying, the joy of finding
beautiful moments in the midst of difficult times. Enjoy."
—Adi Alsaid, author of *Let's Get Lost* and *Never Always Sometimes*

"In Sammie McCoy, Avery has created a character that completely
vibrates with energy. Such a moving read." —Geoff Herbach,
author of *Stupid Fast* and *Fat Boy vs. the Cheerleaders*

"Lara Avery's brilliant novel about a girl who learns that her
life might be ending—just when it feels like it's finally getting
started—will open your heart and very possibly break it. Fierce
Sammie McCoy is an unforgettable heroine, and as soon as I closed
this book, I started to miss her. I still do." —Emily Raymond,
co-author, with James Patterson, of *First Love*

the memory book

the memory book

LARA AVERY

POPPY

LITTLE, BROWN AND COMPANY

NEW YORK   BOSTON

Copyright © 2016 by Alloy Entertainment
Excerpt from *A Million Miles Away* copyright © 2015 by Alloy Entertainment
Cover photo copyright © 2016 by Maksim Shirkov
Cover design by Elaine Damasco

Poppy
Hachette Book Group
1290 Avenue of the Americas, New York, NY 10104
Visit us at lb-teens.com

Poppy is an imprint of Little, Brown and Company. The Poppy name and logo are trademarks of Hachette Book Group, Inc.

The publisher is not responsible for websites (or their content) that are not owned by the publisher.

Originally published in hardcover and ebook by Little, Brown and Company in July 2016
First Trade Paperback Edition: May 2017

alloyentertainment
Produced by Alloy Entertainment
1325 Avenue of the Americas
New York, NY 10019
www.alloyentertainment.com

Book design by Liz Dresner

The Library of Congress has cataloged the hardcover edition as follows:
Names: Avery, Lara, author.
Title: The memory book / Lara Avery.
Description: First edition. | New York : Little, Brown and Company, 2016. | "Poppy." |
    Summary: When a rare genetic disorder steals away her memories and then her health, teenaged Sammie records notes in a journal to her future self, documenting moments great and small.
Identifiers: LCCN 2015029157| ISBN 9780316283748 (hardback) | ISBN 9780316283779 (ebook) |
    ISBN 9781478909712 (audio book)
Subjects: | CYAC: Memory—Fiction. | Genetic disorders—Fiction. | Terminally ill—Fiction. |
    Love—Fiction. | Friendship—Fiction. | BISAC: JUVENILE FICTION / Love & Romance. |
    JUVENILE FICTION / Social Issues / Dating & Sex. | JUVENILE FICTION / Social Issues /
    Death & Dying.
Classification: LCC PZ7.A9515 Me 2016 | DDC [Fic]—dc23
LC record available at http://lccn.loc.gov/2015029157

ISBNs: 978-0-316-28376-2 (pbk.), 978-0-316-28377-9 (ebook)

Printed in the United States of America

LSC-C

10 9 8 7 6 5 4

To Tidsch and Sherry Baby

THE MEMORY BOOK

If you're reading this, you're probably wondering who you are. I'll give you three clues.

Clue 1: You just stayed up all night to finish an AP Lit paper on *The Poisonwood Bible.* You fell asleep briefly while you were writing and dreamed you were making out with James Monroe, the fifth president and arbiter of the Monroe Doctrine.

Clue 2: I am writing this to you from the attic at the little circular window, you know the one, at the east end of the house, where the ceiling almost meets the floor. The Green Mountains have just recently turned green again after a freakish late-spring dump of wet, sloppy snow, and you can just barely see Puppy in the early dark, doing his morning laps up and down the side of our slope in his pointless, happy Puppy way. Sounds like the chickens need to be fed.

I guess I should do that. Stupid chickens.

Clue 3: You are still alive.

Do you know who you are yet?

You are me, Samantha Agatha McCoy, in the not-so-distant

future. I'm writing this for you. They say my memory will never be the same, that I'll start forgetting things. At first just a little, and then a lot. So I'm writing to remember.

This won't be a journal, or a diary, or anything like that. First of all, it's a .doc file on the tiny little laptop I carry with me everywhere, so let's not get too romantic about this. Second, I predict that by the time I'm done with it (perhaps never) it will exceed the length and breadth of your typical journal. It's a book. I have a natural ability to overwrite. For one, the paper on *The Poisonwood Bible* was supposed to be five pages and turned out to be ten. For another, I answered every possible essay question on NYU's application so the admissions committee could have options. (It worked—I'm in.) For another, I wrote and continually edit Hanover High's Wikipedia page, probably the longest and most comprehensive high school Wikipedia page in the country, which is funny because technically I'm not even supposed to go to Hanover High because as you know (I hope), I don't live in New Hampshire, I live in Vermont, but as you also know (I hope), South Strafford is a town of five hundred and I can't go to the freaking general store for high school. So I bought Dad's old pickup on an installment plan and found some loopholes in the district policy.

I'm writing this book for you. How can you forget a thing with this handy document for reference? Consider this your encyclopedia entry. No, consider this your dictionary.

Samantha (proper noun, name): The name Samantha is an American name, and a Hebrew name. In English, the meaning of the name is "listener." In Hebrew, the meaning of the name is "Listen, name of God."

Listen, name of God, this isn't supposed to be a feelingsy thing, but it might have to be. We tried emotions in middle school and we didn't care for them, but they have snuck back into our life.

The feelings came back yesterday in Mrs. Townsend's office.

Mrs. Townsend (proper noun, person): A guidance counselor who has allowed you to test into all of the advanced classes you wanted to take even if they didn't fit your schedule, and has made you aware of every scholarship known to woman so that you don't have to bankrupt your parents. She looks like a more tired version of Oprah, and with the exception of Senator Elizabeth Warren, she is your hero.

Anyway, I was sitting in Mrs. Townsend's office, making sure that I hadn't missed any deadlines because Mom and I had to go to the geneticist in Minnesota two times in the past month. I didn't even get a real spring break. (I type that as if I've ever had a spring break, but I was hoping to get some major prep in with Maddie, Debate Nationals being just a month away.)

I will try to reconstruct the scene:

White walls covered in old MILK: IT DOES A BODY GOOD posters, left over from the last guidance counselor because Mrs. Townsend has been so busy since she started five years ago, she hasn't had the chance to replace them. Me, on a carpeted block that was supposed to be a cool, modern version of a chair but is really just a block. Across from me, Mrs. Townsend, in a yellow sweater, her hair jetting out in thick black curls.

I was asking her to get me a twenty-four-hour extension on the *Poisonwood Bible* paper.

Mrs. T: Why do you need an extension?

Me: I've got a thing.

Mrs. T (*staring at her computer screen, clicking*): What thing?

Me: Google "Niemann-Pick Type C."

Mrs. Townsend types, and begins to read.

Mrs. T (*muttering*): What?

I watched her eyes move. Right, left, right, left, across the screen. I remember that.

Me: It's very rare.

Mrs. T: What is it, Neeber Pickens? Is this a joke?

I had to laugh in spite of her face scrunching up, still reading.

Me: Niemann-Pick Type C. Basically, it's dementia.

Mrs. Townsend takes her eyes off the computer, her mouth hanging open.

Mrs. T: When were you diagnosed with this?

Me: Two months ago, initially. It's been a back-and-forth process to confirm. But yeah, I have it for sure.

Mrs. T: You're going to have memory loss? And hallucinations? What happened?

Me: Genetics. My great-aunt died of it when she was much younger than I am now.

Mrs. T: Died?

Me: It's common among French Canadians, and my mom's originally French Canadian, so . . .

Mrs. T: Excuse me, died?

Me: I'm not going to die.

I don't think she heard the part about me not dying, which is probably for the best, because at this point it is a statement I can neither confirm nor deny. What I do know, which I forgot to tell Mrs. Townsend (sorry, Mrs. T), is that people my age who exhibit symptoms (without having it when they were younger) are extremely rare. Usually kids get it very young, and their bodies can't handle the strain. So we're looking at a "different timeline," the doctor said. I asked if this was good or bad. "At the moment, I believe it's good."

Mrs. T (*hand on forehead*): Sammie, Sammie.

Me: I'm okay right now.

Mrs. T: Oh my god. Yes, but . . . are you seeing someone? How are your parents handling this? Do you need to go home?

Me: Yes. Fine. No.

Mrs. T: Tell them to call me.

Me: Okay.

Mrs. T (*throwing up her hands*): And you told me this by asking for an extension on your AP Lit paper? You don't have to write it, for god's sake. You don't have to do anything. I can call Ms. Cigler right now.

Me: No, it's okay. I'll write it tonight.

Mrs. T: I'm happy to do it, Sammie. This is serious.

Yes, I guess it is serious. Niemann-Pick (there are three types—A, B, and C—and I have C, commonly called NPC, the only C I've ever gotten, ha ha ha) happens when the wrong kind of cholesterol builds up in the liver and spleen, and as a result, blockage collects in the brain. The buildup gets in the way of cognition, motor function, memory, metabolism—the works. I don't have any of that yet, but I have been exhibiting symptoms for almost a year now, apparently. It's interesting the names they put on stuff I thought were just weird tics. Sometimes I get this sleepy sensation after I laugh: That's cataplexy. Sometimes when I reach for the saltshaker, I miss it: That's ataxia.

But all of that is nothing compared to losing my memory. As you know (ever hopeful!), I'm a debater. Memory's kind of my thing. I wasn't always a debater, but if I hadn't become one four years ago, no joke, I would probably be addicted to weed. Or erotic fan fiction. Or something like that. Let me tell you the story:

Once upon a time, Future Sam, you were fourteen, and you were tremendously unpopular (still true) and felt alienated and like there was not a place for you in high school. Your parents wouldn't buy you cool clothes, you were the first one out in dodgeball, you didn't know you were supposed to say "Excuse me" after you burped, and you had become a human encyclopedia of mythical beasts and scientifically impossible space vehicles. Stated simply: You cared more for the fate of Middle Earth than actual Earth.

Then your mom forced you to join a club, and debate team was the first table at the club fair. (I wish it were more epic than that.) Anyway, everything changed. The brain you used to employ memorizing species of aliens you used instead to memorize human thought, events, ways of thinking that connected your tiny house tucked in the mountains to a huge timeline, one just as full of injustice and triumph and greed as the stories you craved, but one that was real.

Plus, you were good at it. After all those years of devouring books, you could glance at a passage and repeat it verbatim ten minutes later. Your lack of politeness was to your advantage, because politeness isn't necessary in getting your point across. Debate made you realize you didn't have to lose yourself in invented worlds to experience life outside the Upper Valley. It gave you hope that you could be yourself and still be part of the real world. It made you feel cool (despite still being unpopular). It made you want to do better in school, so that once you reached the real world, you'd be able to actually work on all the issues you debated.

So yeah, ever since then, I have counted myself proudly among the people who roam the halls of high schools on a weekend, talking to themselves at a million miles an hour about social justice issues. Yes, the weirdos who decide it might be a fun idea to read an entire Internet search yielding thousands of articles on Roe v. Wade and recite them in intervals at a podium across from another person in a battle to the rhetorical death. The ones who think they are teenage lawyers, the ones who wear business suits. I love it.

Which is why I haven't quit, even though I'm now kind of stuttery at practice, and I make excuses when I miss research sessions for doctor's appointments, and I have to, you know, psych myself up in the mirror at tournaments. Before this happened, my memory was my golden ticket. My ability to memorize things got me scholarships. My memory won me the Grafton County Spelling Bee when I was eleven. And now it's gonna be gone. This is, like, inconceivable to me. ANYWAY.

Back to the office, where I can hear people in the hallway, yelling at one another about stupid shit.

Me (*over the noise*): It's fine. Anyway, can you give me the name of that NYU pre-law mentorship thing again? I know only college juniors are eligible, but I think I could—

Mrs. T makes a choked sound.

Me: Mrs. T?

Mrs. Townsend pulls Kleenexes from her drawer and starts wiping her eyes.

Me: Are you okay?

Mrs. T: I just can't believe this.

Me: Yeah. I have to go to ceramics now.

Mrs. T: I'm sorry. This is shocking. (*clearing her throat*) Will you have to miss more school?

Me: Not until May, right around finals. But it will be a quick trip to the specialist. Probably just a checkup.

Mrs. T: You're very strong.

Me (*starts packing up stuff, in anticipation of leaving*): I try.

Mrs. T: I've known you since you were a little fourteen-year-old with your (*puts fingers in a circle around eyes*) little glasses.

Me: I still have glasses.

Mrs. T: But they're different glasses. More sophisticated. You look like a young woman now.

Me: Thanks.

Mrs. T: Sammie. Wait.

Me: Okay.

Mrs. T: You are very strong, but . . . But considering everything . . . (*begins to choke up again*)

At this point, I began to feel an uncomfortable tightness in the back of my throat, which at the time I attributed to a side effect of my pain medicine. Mrs. T really had been there for me since I was a freshman. She was the only adult that actually listened to me.

Sure, my parents tried, but it was only for five minutes, between their jobs and feeding my younger siblings and fixing some hole in our crap house on the side of a mountain. They don't care about anything I do as long as I don't let my siblings perish and I get my chores done. When I told Mrs. Townsend I was going to win the National Debate Tournament, get into NYU, and be a human rights lawyer, the first thing she said was, "Let's make it happen." She was the only one who believed me.

So for what she said next, at the risk of being melodramatic, she might as well have stuck her hand down my esophagus and clutched my heart in her hands.

Mrs. T: Do you think you can even handle college?

Explosions in head.

Me: What?

Mrs. T (*pointing at computer screen*): This—I mean, I will read up on it more, but—it seems like it affects everything. It could do serious damage.

Me: I know.

And here's the thing. The health stuff I could take, but don't take away my future. My future I had worked so hard to set up so nicely. I have worked for years to get into NYU, and now I was in the homestretch. The very idea that Mrs. Townsend would even consider that I would give it up filled me with rage.

Mrs. T: And on top of that, your memory is going to suffer. How are you going to go to class with all of this? You might—
Me: No!

Mrs. T jumped back. Then it was my turn to begin weeping. My body wasn't used to crying, so the tears did not come out in clean, clear supermodel drops like I thought they would. I shook a lot and the saltwater pooled up in my glasses. I was surprised by the strange whine that came out of the back of my throat.

Mrs. T: Oh, no. No, no. I'm sorry.

I should have accepted her apology and moved on, but I couldn't. I yelled at her.

Me: I am NOT not going to college.
Mrs. T: Of course.
Me (*sniffling*): I am NOT going to stick around Strafford, riding around on four-wheelers, working at a ski resort and smoking

pot and going to church and having tons of children and goats.

Mrs. T: I didn't say that . . .

Me (*through snot*): I pushed my way into Hanover, didn't I? I got into NYU, didn't I? I am the valedictorian!

Mrs. T: Yes, yes. But—

Me: Then I can handle college.

Mrs. T: Of course! Of course.

Me (*wiping snot on my sleeve*): Jesus, Mrs. Townsend.

Mrs. T: Use a Kleenex, hon.

Me: I'll use whatever surface I want!

Mrs. T: Sure you will.

Me: I haven't cried since I was a baby.

Mrs. T: That can't be true.

Me: I haven't cried in a long time.

Mrs. T: Well, it's okay to cry.

Me: Yeah.

Mrs. T: If you ever need to talk to me again, you can. I'm not just an academic resource.

Me (*exiting*): Yeah, cool. Bye, Mrs. T.

I walked out of Mrs. Townsend's office (perfectly normally, thank you) and skipped ceramics and went straight home to work on my paper until the feelings went away. Or at least until the feelings and me got some miles between us.

I cried because I have never been more scared in my life. I fear that Mrs. Townsend has a point. I envision a vague gray shape that is supposed to be my brain inside my head, but instead it's this blob outside of me, empty, that I won't be able to use.

And I'm tired.

It's like, take my body, fine, I wasn't really using it anyway. I've got this enormous butt on ostrich legs, the hair of a "before" picture, and weird milky brown eyes like a Frappuccino. But not my brain. My true connection to the world.

Why couldn't I wither slowly and roam around on an automatic chair, spouting my brilliance through a voice box machine like Stephen Hawking?

Ugggggghhh. Just thinking about it makes me—

g;sodfigs;ozierjgserg

I don't know how else to say it right now. And I don't like not knowing. Anything. I don't like not knowing in general. I should always be able to know.

And that's where you come in, Future Sam.

I need you to be the manifestation of the person I know I will be. I can beat this, I know I can, because the more I record for you, the less I will forget. The more I write to you, the more real you will become.

So: I've got a lot to do today. It's Wednesday morning. I've got to read seven articles on living wage conditions. I've got to call Maddie and remind her to read these articles, too, because in her three-year tenure as my debate partner, she has had a terrible habit of "winging it" because she thinks she's God's gift to affirmative speeches. (She is, sometimes.) The dumb chickens still need to be fed. The window is cracked open. I smell dew and cool air coming off the Green Mountains. No one else in my house is up yet, but they will be soon. And look, the sun is rising. At least I know that.

FUTURE SAM

- goes by "Sam" or "Samantha"
- eats only nuts and berries
- wears fashionable glasses (or maybe contacts?)
- wears tailored outfits, only in solid neutrals, blue, or black
- laughs only on occasion and always in a low register
- gets cocktails every week with group of witty, professionally competent women
- reads the *New York Times* in bed in a soft white robe
- is recognized by people on the street and told that her op-ed on international development changed their life

CURRENT SAMMIE

- goes by "Sammie" because no one will adjust to addressing her as Sam—except for Davy, but with lisp it sounds like "Tham"

- eats anything put in front of her, including fake fruit by accident at a church function
- glasses are okay, just way too "gold" and "huge" and possibly disco
- wears whatever free school-function T-shirts haven't been visibly slobbered on by one of the smaller organisms in the house
- laughs at SpongeBob and fart jokes even when stupid people make them (I can't help it, it's actually so funny)
- closest female friend is Maddie, but I'm not sure if we're really friends or just that she and I spend so much time in the government classroom that we are friends by proxy, and between you and me, her ego is way too off the charts
- reads the *New York Times* at Lou's when other people throw it out because Mom and Dad refuse to pay for it
- gets high fives from debate team, so at least that's a start

WHAT MRS. TOWNSEND
WAS PROBABLY LOOKING AT

From the NPC Wikipedia page:

Neurological signs and symptoms include cerebellar ataxia (unsteady walking with uncoordinated limb movements), dysarthria (slurred speech), dysphagia (difficulty in swallowing), tremor, epilepsy (both partial and generalized), vertical supranuclear palsy (upgaze palsy, downgaze palsy, saccadic palsy or paralysis), sleep inversion, gelastic cataplexy (sudden loss of muscle tone or drop attacks), dystonia (abnormal movements or postures caused by contraction of agonist and antagonist muscles across joints); most commonly begins with turning of one foot when walking (action dystonia) and may spread to become generalized, spasticity (velocity-dependent increase in muscle tone), hypotonia, ptosis (drooping of the upper eyelid), microcephaly (abnormally small head), psychosis, progressive dementia, progressive hearing loss, bipolar disorder, major and psychotic depression; can include hallucinations, delusions, mutism, or stupor.

From Wikipedia, after I edited the NPC page:
Your shit is fucked.

(Was taken down shortly after and all my Wiki editing privileges were suspended, but it was worth it.)

WHITE MALE PHILOSOPHERS WHO (BASED ON THEIR PORTRAITS) I/WE WOULD MAKE OUT WITH

- Søren Kierkegaard: those lips
- René Descartes: I've never said no to a man with long hair
- Ludwig Wittgenstein: the coiffe, the straight nose, the sunken, knowing eyes
- Socrates: that beard though

SHAH DOLCE VITA

When I told you that this wouldn't be feelingsy, I lied. You probably knew that, Future Sam, but maybe you've been able to put a lid on them by the time you read this.

I want Stuart Shah. I want Stuart Shah so bad.

Stuart Shah (proper noun, person): Oh, screw it, I'll just tell you everything.

Picture this: It's two years ago. As a critique of capitalism, you have taken to wearing a lot of vintage (fine, *used*) clothing, mostly your dad's oversize T-shirts, cutoffs, and your mom's gardening clogs that you took without permission. You are reading a lot of *National Geographic* articles about how the ice caps are melting and polar bears are being pushed from their usual habitats, and watching a lot of your mom's old DVDs of *The West Wing*. On this particular day, Ms. Cigler (then your Advanced Sophomore English teacher) has asked you to complete the short-answer questions at the end of a Faulkner story, "A Rose for Emily," about an old lady who sleeps with her dead husband's corpse. Anyway.

Suddenly, a figure passes by your desk. This person has that smell like they have just been outside, you know what I mean? It's a combination of sweat and humid air and grass and dirt, and when you've been inside air-conditioning all day, you can tell from just one whiff they've been outside doing something.

You look up and you see it is Stuart Shah.

You have seen Stuart around before—he's a senior while you're a sophomore, one of those kids who's always eating a sandwich while walking, on his way to the next thing. He's tall and has an old-fashioned, guy-in-the-fifties haircut and dark, wet eyes like two river stones. It appears that he wears the same thing every day, just like you, except he wears a black T-shirt and black jeans and he looks amazing. He's friends with everyone and no one in particular. He played Hamlet in the spring play.

Now he's bending down next to Ms. Cigler, telling her something in a low voice. The corners of his lips turn up in a smile while he's talking. You watch his long fingers twitch from where they prop up his lean arms on the desk.

Ms. Cigler gasps and claps a hand over her mouth. The class looks up from their work. Stuart straightens and folds his arms, eyes on his feet with a shy, half smile still on his face.

"Can I tell them?" she asks, glancing up at him.

Stuart shrugs, looking up at the class, and then at you, for some reason.

"Stu just got a short story published. In an actual literary magazine. A high schooler. I mean . . . my god."

Stuart lets out a little laugh, eyeing Ms. Cigler.

"*Ploughshares* is a publication I wish *I* could publish in, folks. Give this young man a round."

People clap halfheartedly, except for you. You don't clap. Because you are staring at him, your hand holding a strand of your hair. You shift in your chair, leaning toward him. You catch your eyes running up from his lace-up shoes, to his jeans, across his waistband, to his brown neck, his smooth lips, across his eyebrows like black brushstrokes, down to his eyes, which meet yours again.

You turn hot and look down at your to-do list.

He leaves the classroom, and instead of listening to Ms. Cigler, you find yourself tracing a letter *S*.

Later, you wonder aloud to Maddie about him at debate practice, and she notices your drifting eyes, your fingertips playing on indiscriminate surfaces, your little sighs.

"Sammie McCoy is crushing," Maddie says.

"I'm just curious. You know, like professionally. I wonder what it's like to be published." That word, *published*. It comes off the lips like an adult drink, like sweet cherry liqueur. It means that Stuart's way of seeing the world is so complete, so sharp, so fascinating that important people want to spread it around.

You want your words to be like that. I mean, not in a fictional story, you could never do that, but in general. You want to be a debater (and then a lawyer) so you can look at the world from above, so you can cut it into neat, manageable pieces and fit problems and solutions together like a puzzle, making it fair for everyone. You want to tell people what is correct, what is real. Stuart is already doing that in his own way, and he's only eighteen.

Over the next year, wherever he goes in the halls of Hanover High, he glows. You make excuses to switch lunch periods so you can watch him pop rolls of sushi into his mouth with his fingers from Tupperware he brought from home, his other hand holding *The New Yorker* or other publications with important names like *The Paris Review* or small, worn novels of every conceivable color. You make note of their titles and read them, too, so you can know what scenes are passing through his head. Once or twice he catches you reading the same book he is, in the cafeteria or elsewhere, and gives a little nod of recognition, which sends your lunch swirling.

But eventually he spends less and less time in the halls, and more in the backseats of Jeeps headed to the swimming hole or Dartmouth parties or trips to Montreal with his friends. As he should, you think, because he's *cool.* You get to school early to study, and you stay late to do your homework. You are not at the parties where he is, or joining Hanover's literary magazine where he's the editor, or making friends with groups of girls who laugh loudly and wear revealing clothes, which might catch his attention.

On his graduation day, you watch him from the bleachers, standing between his parents, wearing sunglasses, shaking hands with all the teachers, smiling bigger than ever, trying to keep his cap from falling off. Last you heard, another magazine, *The Threepenny Review*, had seen his work and picked up a second story. Ms. Cigler told your class that he had been writing short stories since he was your age, and he's hoping to publish a collection, and then a novel, then who knows? He's off to New York now, because his parents have an apartment there anyway. He won't go to college. He's just going to write, because he's found what he wants to do and what he's good at, and he'll stop at nothing to keep doing it. The thought of him still sets a fire in you, and before he leaves for good, you catch one last sight of him, taking off his robe and draping it over his arm, then disappearing into the crowd.

That is, until this morning. That's right, Future Sam. It's been two years, and I saw him this morning.

I was feeding the stupid chickens with Harrison and Bette and Davy (because even when it's one of their turns to do chores it automatically becomes my turn), and suddenly Puppy jets up from whatever he was doing in the backyard and runs around the house past us, down the front slope. I followed the dog for a bit and watched him head toward the main road. He started trotting alongside a person walking, which wasn't unusual. Our twisted little two-lane highway is too tangled and nestled among the mountains to allow for cars to go very fast, and people bike and jog and walk along it all the time, sometimes from as far as twenty minutes away, in Hanover. But this person was wearing a black T-shirt and black jeans. This person had dark hair and brown shoes. I squinted but I couldn't be sure.

Then Puppy came back, and Davy and Harrison and Bette and I piled into the pickup and set off toward the elementary school, where I would drop them before I went into town. On the way, we passed the guy in black walking along the road. I slowed down and we all craned our necks backward. Stuart waved behind his sunglasses. All my siblings waved in reply. I just stared forward and tried not to scream.

I have held the scream in my throat all day and am now having trouble keeping it in while Maddie goes over her opening. Okay, I'm swallowing it, but I keep seeing his face against the Upper Valley morning, his hand up in a wave, his mouth lifting in a smile, as if he recognized me.

Stuart Shah is back.

THE WAITING ROOM

Two days, no sign of Stuart anywhere. I looked for him again on the drive to and from school, around the bend at Center Hill, up every winding driveway into the oaks, birches, maples, in every car we passed along the Connecticut River. I looked for him on the streets of Hanover coming out of Lou's, or maybe sitting on a bench near the Dartmouth campus, reading a book. There aren't too many guys of Indian heritage wearing black jeans in this town, but I managed to find two, and neither of them was him.

Now my family's at the doctor's office, minus my dad, who's at work. Specifically, we're at the office of pediatrician Dr. Nancy M. Clarkington at 45 Lyme Road, and I've drunk five Dixie Cups of water from those little water machines. There's a possibility I will leave here and clean out my locker, living the rest of my days as a homeschooled inpatient. Unless, that is, I get the doctor's note required by Principal Rothchild. I don't even want to think about the possibility of walking out of this office without Dr. Clarkington's signature on that godforsaken note.

Mom is next to me, reading a garbage magazine about garbage people. An enlarged photograph of a jungle scene covers the walls. Bette and Harrison and Davienne are all on their knees in front of the aquarium watching the fish, because they are still children, and they don't know what it feels like to have their whole lives hang in the lotioned hands of a small-town pediatrician.

Mom (proper noun, woman, 42): short, wispy-dark-haired person who birthed you. Looks like a Tolkien elf with laugh lines. If she is not at work, find her at home in mud boots in the yard, weeding vegetables, cursing at rabbits for getting into her garden, caulking cracks in the shed and/or house, or throwing a stick for Puppy. In winter, find her in the leather La-Z-Boy, wrapped up in a blanket.

Harrison (noun, brother, 13): enormous boy-man with skinny limbs good for climbing trees, thick brown curls like mine, and a potbelly full of macaroni and cheese. Find him in the sixth grade, playing Minecraft, or sulking in the outdoors because he can't play Minecraft.

Bette (noun, sister, 9): a miniature version of Mom, but for all we know was deposited by aliens to examine our species. Find her at the tree line building weird structures out of sticks, in the back of her fourth-grade class making beeping noises, or doing Harrison's math homework for caramels as payment.

Davienne (noun, baby sister, 6): another Mom miniature, but with Harry's and my sturdy build. Find her as the most popular girl in first grade, sticking jeweled stickers to everything, and still blissfully unaware that her siblings' habit of yelling "Surprise!" whenever she enters a room is the result of an unfortunate case of eavesdropping on Mom and Dad when they found out they were pregnant again.

We're all here because Dr. Clarkington has to determine whether or not I'm healthy enough to go on an overnight trip to Nationals in Boston next month, and to finish out the school year.

The answer is obviously yes, because, like, look at me. I mean you can't look at me, Future Sam, but there's nothing grossly wrong. Sure, I have to shake my hands and legs out sometimes because they fall asleep. And my eyeballs hurt. But I think that's just from reading too much. Besides, no one needs hands and legs at a debate tournament. Just a memory and a voice.

If Dr. Clarkington says I'm too sick, there are two major consequences:

(1) If I don't go to the debate tournament, I can't win, and (2) if I can't win, then my NYU essay (about working steadily toward winning) was a lie, and I go into NYU a liar. Not to mention the fact that my entire high school career would have been a waste. If not for spending hours in the government classroom after school and on weekends, I could have been a popular, sex-positive hottie by now. Plus, I was just born with that steely blood, man. I always want to win. The first time Harrison beat me at chess (this year) I banished myself to only playing checkers in self-punishment. Anyway, that's not the end of it.

If I don't get to finish out the school year, my grades go down.

If my grades go down, Hanover will reconsider my valedictory status.

If they take away my valedictory status, my parents will realize

I'm losing control of things . . . and they might not let me go to college in the fall.

If I can't go to college, I . . . actually haven't even considered this possibility. I can't imagine what I'll do. Probably walk up the Appalachian Trail with nothing but a coat and some jerky, hoping to start a new life somewhere in Canada.

It's because there's this part of me that wants to be extraordinary. Like I want to believe that if you work hard and you have good ideas, you can be who you want to be. Like Stuart, for example.

Imagine the horror if I were to be banished from school, and I run into him somewhere, and by some miracle speak to him without going into psychedelic reverie.

Sammie: Oh, hey, Stuart. What is that, Zadie Smith's new novel?

Stuart: Hello, Sammie. Wow, yeah. It's amazing. And you! You're stunning. You've really grown into your glasses.

Sammie: Thank you. You don't look so bad yourself.

Stuart: What are you up to these days? You're debating in one of the most prestigious competitions in the country, right?

Sammie: No. No, I'm not.

Stuart: Oh really? What a shame. What are you doing instead?

Sammie: Oh, just, you know, diseasin'. Diseasin' around.

This cannot happen.

I just proposed popping down to the Co-Op to buy a large bouquet of flowers to give to Dr. Clarkington, but Mom just looked at me like, *Aren't you supposed to be the smart one?*

I also feel really dumb because we're all in our nice clothes since we have to go to Harrison's confirmation after this. I told Mom that we look like we got dressed up to go to the doctor and that's dumb.

Mom sighed. "Just let me be out of my scrubs in public in peace."

"But it's as if you're wearing pajamas all day, that seems nice," I said.

And she was like, "Have you ever had an old man show you a mole on his lower back while you're in line at the grocery store because he thinks you're a nurse?"

"Touché."

Mom's not a nurse yet, by the way, Future Sam. She's still working reception at the Dartmouth Medical Center.

Still waiting.

Text from Maddie: Where are you?
Me: Be back in time for practice

I vaguely remember this quote from one of my favorite theorists, Noam Chomsky—something about optimism as a strategy rather than just a feeling. If you don't believe the future is going to be better, then you won't take action to make it better. It sounds cheesy, but there's another word for cheesy: It's called *sincerity*.

And besides, Maddie already used her birthday money to buy us both National Debate Tournament pantsuits in corresponding colors, navy for me, mauve for her, and they are *bangin'*. (I will pay her back when I've sold some of my Plato to any stoned-looking Dartmouth freshmen who I can convince that it's necessary for Philosophy 101.)

We also got a write-up in the school newspaper. The newspaper makes it official. What are they gonna do, issue a correction that Sammie McCoy will no longer be competing and instead will be replaced by Alex Conway?

Yes, that is exactly what they'll do.

Oh god, I want to put my fist through a wall.

East Coast Debate, the premier blog and newsboard for East Coast high school debate, called Maddie and me "the team to beat." That's Maddie and ME, not Maddie and Conway.

Alex Conway didn't even *start* doing policy until last year! Little bitch was doing Model UN as *Denmark*.

I told you I'm competitive.

Oh my god, the nurse just called my name. Bye.

(Harrison, I love you, but if you take my laptop and read any of this, I will tell Mom and Dad that you wake up at two a.m. every night and play Minecraft.)

NOT TOO SICK, OR HOW TO
AVOID BEING ON A WEBSITE
IN A TROPICAL SHIRT

Hi.

Right now we're driving to the church and Mom is completely quiet.

After taking my vitals, Dr. Clarkington put the Minnesota specialist on speaker while we talked about the future. The specialist is a geneticist. He's a man, middle-aged, Minnesotan, mild and forgettable as mayonnaise. Or maybe that's what I tell myself because I want to forget him. His voice came over the speaker like one of those recordings at the airport talking about safety.

We all looked at a website together for families who have to deal with Niemann-Pick Type C. They have clubs for the little kids who get it, where they do fun things. I saw pictures of their happy, twitchy faces at a meetup in Pennsylvania, everyone wearing shirts with palm trees on them and drinking tropical drinks, some of them in wheelchairs.

I was kind of an asshole about it, because I told them that didn't look very fun, and what would be fun would be to win the debate tournament, thanks. Then they practically put me through a spy-level interrogation to determine if I should even be allowed to continue at school.

What if slurred speech prevents you from speaking in class? The inability to form words is among the neurological risks of NPC.

I'll write. Did you know poet Tomas Tranströmer was going to give a Nobel Prize acceptance speech in the form of playing the piano because a stroke had left him without the use of his frontal cortex?

What if you can't remember how to get home from school?

A two-year-old can use Google Maps.

What if you start experiencing seizures?

No comment. No, wait, I'll put a wooden spoon in my mouth.

Epilepsy?

Do I look like a person who would go anywhere near a strobe light?

Symptoms of liver failure?

Come on, that could happen to anyone. I'll call the authorities.

And what if it happens at the debate tournament?

Aren't there doctors in Boston?

et cetera

et cetera

They compromised by saying that everywhere I went, including school and the tournament, there had to be a first responder present. Most of the symptoms—muscles twisting and legs aching (and, according to a video I saw on the website, not being able to judge the distance of a glass of water two feet in front of me so that I'll knock it over like a bad actor in a school play who has been instructed "knock that glass over, try to make it look like an accident")—anyway, all of that will be gradual over the year. However, I could "seize" or "fit" at any time (as if my participation in high school society wasn't already hard enough) and might need immediate medical assistance. At school this will be easy, since every school nurse is a first responder. Elsewhere, he monotoned, "You take a risk."

"Like an EMT with a fluorescent vest? All the time?" I asked, laughing. I imagined getting them to guard my spot at the library with their defibrillator pads, or getting them to use the ambulance to clear the summer bed-and-breakfast traffic that happens when New Yorkers go on vacation.

"No, just someone who is trained in CPR," the specialist said.

It's like every time we go to the doctor there's a new thing I have to deal with. I wondered if any of these droopy kids had to go through this, or if they were too far gone before the doctors could do anything. It was exhausting, like trying to justify my own goddamn existence.

On top of it, he reminded us: *NPC is always fatal.* The majority of children with NPC die before age twenty (many die before the age of ten).

(Let us pause to soak in how utterly and completely tragic all this is.)

Okay, neat. What are people who are completely screwed supposed to do? Look forlornly out the window? I'm not good at the feelingsy things. Let's move on.

So. So, here's where it gets interesting. The specialist said: Late onset of symptoms can lead to longer life spans. It's extremely rare for someone my age to have it. Or, at least, he hadn't treated any cases yet. This means that because I'm older, my body can fight it better. Even the less-specialized doctors agreed with that. Jackpot. I mean, he had already told Mom and me the life span thing at the Mayo Clinic. I just wanted Dr. Clarkington to hear it straight from the horse's mouth.

Before we came back to the waiting room where the kids were, Mom and I hugged very tightly in the hallway. I squeezed her with all my muscles. And then, ironically enough, I threw up. Not because of NPC, I don't think, probably because I was so nervous.

But anyway, we got the approval. We got the note. We're back on track. Longer life span, baby! What now, huh? Whatcha got? BRING IT.

I've really got to pull through this thing until I get to NYU. If I'm the only one in my immediate household who believes I can recover, then I need to get away from their negativity. My parents are thinking small, Future Sam. Mom's asking the doctor about "in-house nurse" options and prescription plans. They're preparing for the worst. As Mr. Chomsky says, optimism yields responsibility. I'm not delusional: I know I'm sick. But I'm not going to set myself up for failure.

I'm going to ace everything, win the tournament, go to New York, and figure it out from there.

And you've got to help me.

THE REVENGE OF COOPER LIND

Our Lady of Perpetual Help is in Bradford, just a thirty-minute drive from Hanover, in one of the flatter parts of the Upper Valley. It's angular and beautiful and white, like most of its parishioners. There, on this very night, Harry declared himself a soldier for Christ for the rest of his life, which makes *a lot of sense* for a thirteen-year-old to decide (not).

Especially a thirteen-year-old who chose Saint James (aka Santiago) as his patron saint because Santiago is the main character from Rainbow Six, a tactical shooter game. So Christlike.

Little Taylor Lind took her place next to him on the velvet kneeling-thing for the sacraments ceremony, her flaxen strands bundled into a delicate ponytail next to Harrison's curls, side by side, on the fringes near the shelf full of Virgin Mary candles, just like her brother, Cooper, and me five years ago. As I watched Father Frank touch the ceremonial cheeks of all the tween St. Cecilias and St. Patricks, confirming their Catholichood, Mom reached for my hand and squeezed.

It made me think of my own confirmation—

I had worn one of Mom's old dresses from when she was a teen in the '90s, lime green, short, collared, and patterned with daisies. My hair was peeking out of several randomly placed metal clips. My old glasses sat low on my nose, the ones with the rectangular frames that were too small for my round face and made my eyeballs bulge.

Cooper had chosen St. Anthony of Padua because it was the first name of a list of suggested patron saints.

I had chosen St. Joan of Arc because duh.

I was beginning to wonder which saints Bette and Davy would pick when it became their turn, and suddenly the hymn version of "Bless Us, O Lord" sounded from the enormous pipe organ from the corner, and I could see my dad standing in the front row with all the other sponsors, a blazer over his City of Lebanon employee shirt, and all the what-ifs from the doctors began to float in my head, like *what if something goes wrong before Bette and Davy even get to this point*, and my throat released a tension I didn't know it had, and the saltwater pooled in my glasses again. I had to bow my head to keep the crying quiet, but the tears just kept coming, so I excused myself to the bathroom, and there in the lobby, speak of the devil and St. Anthony of Padua, was Coop.

Cooper Lind (noun, person): was once practically my brother, but is now more like an estranged brother—no, more like just a regular neighbor. Adonis with a perpetual windburn. Find him on the other side of our mountain, in a cloud of weed smoke, or in bed with any given female age fifteen to nineteen. Coop is the only other person from Strafford who worked the system and goes to Hanover High, but only because they wanted him to play baseball.

I gave him a cursory nod and brushed past him to the bathroom, got rid of the last gut heaves, and washed my face.

When we first went to Hanover, Coop and I carpooled together, clean and prepared and nervous out of our goddamn minds, sitting side by side in his mom's car, and I don't know. Something happened, gradually, and all at once. Maybe we had nothing in common besides the imaginary games we used to make up about magic. Maybe we grew apart because Coop pushed out long, muscular legs from where his chubby Band-Aid-covered knees used to be, and broad shoulders came out of his Batman shirt, and cheekbones poked out of his cheeks, and none of that growing ever happened to me. I was too weird and ugly to be around him, a little scrub bush to his mighty oak. Coop became a star pitcher and made friends with the popular kids; I became a debater and made friends with no one. It was meant to be, probably. I used to read fantasy books during his Little League games.

His freshman year, Coop made All-State after pitching four no-hitters. Then, shortly before the State championship, he was kicked off Hanover's varsity team for smoking weed. I'm pretty sure I'm the only person who knows that. The day it happened, I found him on the border between our two properties, playing a video game on his little Nintendo thing, still wearing his Hanover cap. I could tell he'd been crying.

"What happened?" I asked.

He pulled out the disciplinary letter from his pocket.

"Well," I said. "That's what you get," like I had told him when he broke his leg after jumping off a high wall when he was seven. I laughed as I read the letter, as if we would forget about it the next day and we would play again.

But when I looked for his eyes to say, *Hey, just joking, no big deal, I'm really sorry*, I remember I couldn't find them. His eyes were there, but it was like something had sunk behind his pupils.

I even said aloud, "Hey, just kidding, you'll be fine . . ."

But he had already started to turn away. I remember thinking, *We aren't good enough friends to joke like that anymore, I guess.*

"This is yours!" I called out, still holding the letter. "You probably need to give it to your parents."

He turned back and snatched it, then walked away to the other side of the mountain and didn't answer when I called him, so I stopped calling.

At school, the general rumor was that he quit, and I kept it that way. Our silence grew and grew, he moved desks in the one class we had together, and pretty soon he got his Chevy Blazer and I got Dad's truck and we didn't have to carpool anymore.

When I came back out of the church bathroom, I did not expect to find Coop waiting for me.

"Are you okay?" he asked, and I almost wasn't sure he was talking to me. His eyes were on his phone.

"Yeah! Totally."

I kept walking, but he didn't return to the sanctuary. I threw a quick "Thanks!" over my shoulder.

"Hey, wait," Coop called. "I'm gonna get some air. You wanna come?"

"Oh, um . . ."

I froze and looked at him. Coop looked out of place at church—I mean, so did I, but it's different. At least I wore my dress (that really just looks like a huge shirt)—he was wearing a tank top emblazoned with THAT GOOD GOOD (who knows what "that good good" even is?) revealing his Mr. Clean arms, and it appeared he hadn't brushed or cut his shoulder-length honey hair in a while. But it was the same Cooper whose house I used to go to for lunch after we played all day in the summertime, swimming in our underwear at the Potholes, fighting over the last Cherry Vanilla Dr Pepper in the Strafford general store.

"We've got about"—Coop looked at his phone—"about twenty minutes."

"Cool."

I followed him outside into the spring night, where we landed in the center of a circle of benches out front, in the shadow of OLPH's enormous white cross. Coop pulled a spliff out of his pocket.

"In the name of the Father, Son, and Holy Spirit . . ." I began.

"Amen," Coop finished, and sparked the tip, and we laughed a little.

We stood in silence while he smoked.

I didn't really know what to say.

"So how the hell are you?" he asked after an exhale.

"Uh . . . fine."

"Want some?" he asked, leaning the spliff in my direction.

"No!"

"Okay, fine, I don't know, maybe you started to relax a little, I don't know . . ." Coop said, laughing from that place between his chest and his belly like he does when he knows no one else thinks his joke is funny.

"I don't need weed to relax," I told him, straight out of a PSA, but also, straight out of my heart.

"What *does* Sammie McCoy do to relax?" he asked.

"I watch *The West Wing*. I also like to clean my room. Sometimes I'll—"

"Why were you crying?" he interrupted.

"First of all, don't interrupt me. You, of all people, should know that."

"What is that supposed to me—" he started, then caught himself and shut the hell up.

"As for your question, I was crying because . . ." I thought of how I had seen him in the halls earlier today, at the bottom of a human pyramid made of sophomore girls. "You don't want to know."

"Yes, I do."

"Okay . . ." I tried to read his face. "But I can't tell you."

"Why?"

"Because for all you care I'm, I don't know, getting my period or something."

Coop snorted. Even in the shadow of floodlights, I could tell he was blushing.

This is why I don't make friends easily. Small talk, among many other things, makes me want to punch a hole in the wall. So when I do talk, I want to make it count. I don't know if after four years, Coop actually wanted to know why I was crying, or just the small-talk version. But I wasn't going to do the small-talk version. Not today.

"Now I made it awkward," I said.

"I live with women. I know what periods are like."

"I'm not getting my period."

"You don't have to tell me."

"I don't have to, no."

"But I asked."

"Why?" I asked him.

"Because something's going on."

"How can you tell?"

Coop shrugged and smiled.

Maybe he could tell because he'd seen me pee my pants in this very church, when the homily went too long. Maybe because I'd seen him pee his pants once, in our car on the way back home from Water Country.

Or perhaps it was that I had come from the doctor's office, where someone had just pressed on every part of me so hard that I could feel her cold wedding ring against my skin, and I had to tell her that yes, it does hurt when you press there, and there, and there. Dr. Clarkington touched my neck and my spine and my butt and my boobs and my belly button and the soft part between my hip bones, and told me how each part would dissolve or melt or harden, like Play-Doh left out too long, and she could already see my body changing.

I said, "Let's sit. Can we sit?"

"Of course we can sit."

We sat down, our backs against the cross.

I told him about today.

I told him about two months ago, when I found out I couldn't turn my eyeballs upward and went to the doctor for what we thought was some sort of migraine. I told him about six weeks of medical tests, reading AP Euro while waiting on the freezing tarmac because the Mayo Clinic has to be all the way in Minnesota, and telling Maddie I had to miss debate practice because my great-aunt was dying, because it seemed closer to the truth: My great-aunt *did* die and she *did* have what I have, which is another reason Maddie can't know that I'm sick, because if she thinks I'm going to die it will throw her off, and she'll start telling me I'm doing good work even when I'm not, and she's one of the only people whose opinion about debate I can trust. I told him that watching Harrison get confirmed brought back all these memories and, in turn, curiosity and fear about the future, which looked narrow and hard but not impossible, and how now I feel more determined than ever to get what I want and get it now.

Coop's eyes were blazing red by the time I was finished. To clarify: not from getting emotional, but from getting high, I'm pretty sure.

"Shit, man," he said. To his credit, he hadn't interrupted once.

"So, yeah," I said. I felt like I had just thrown up. I may have been sweating. But I was empty and calm.

Coop nodded for a second, forming words. "Sammie, I am so sorry."

He stared at the ground. His phone lit up in his pocket and he pulled it out. I caught the name "Hot Katie" on the screen. He ignored it. But it was already enough of a reminder of who we were now. He would not have ignored the call if I wasn't here. We would not be standing here if he hadn't wanted to smoke weed. This was not how his night was supposed to go, or mine. We were just space rocks bouncing off each other temporarily in this strange little Upper Valley void, but our trajectories were still separate. We were not friends.

"It's cool." I wanted him to go then. I wanted Coop to take with him everything I had dumped on him so I would never have to talk about it again. Hot Katie lit up his phone a second time.

I pointed to his pocket. "You can take that."

"'K," Cooper said, unlocking the screen. "Be right back," he added, and flicked the butt of his joint forward so I had to jump to avoid it.

"Sorry!" he said, darting back, phone to his ear. He ground the tip with his Adidas.

While he cooed to Hot Katie, I ducked inside for the conclusion of the service, and when we came back out, Cooper was gone. Good to see him, though. Good ol' Coop.

Oh, fuck. I really hope he doesn't tell anyone about the disease thing.

He won't.

Oh well.

He won't.

AFFIRMATIVE CASE FOR ATTENDING ROSS NERVIG'S PARTY FRIDAY NIGHT: AN EXPLORATION INTO TEEN SOCIAL HABITS UNDER THE GUISE OF DEBATE PREPARATION

Good afternoon, Future Sam. The topic for debate is that Sammie will attend a party at Ross Nervig's house, Friday, April 29. We define the topic as follows: A party is a gathering of adolescents in a residence where no parents are present and alcohol *is* present. "Sammie" is an eighteen-year-old who has not previously attended a party. "Ross Nervig" is a former student at Hanover who regularly facilitates parties as they have previously been defined. We, as the affirmative team, believe this statement to be true, and that Sammie will attend her first party.

As the first and only speaker, I will be discussing the professional benefits of attending said party, the feasibility of Sammie's parents allowing her to attend, and the likelihood of the presence of Stuart Shah at said party.

My first point addresses the conditions under which Sammie's attendance at the party was requested, and how Sammie's fulfillment of this request will further her professional goals. Sammie aspires to win the National Debate Tournament in two weeks. At debate practice, Maddie Sinclair mentioned the party as a reward for their hard work.

We define "Maddie Sinclair" as Sammie's debate partner of three years, a regular attendee of parties at Ross Nervig's house, and a future student at Emory University. Find Maddie in every school play, as the head of the Queer Union, and in the center of an orbit of theater kids and film kids. (She once told me she's like Rufio in that old Peter Pan remake *Hook*, and all of her friends are the Lost Boys. For the record, I Googled it, and her hair, currently a bright red Mohawk, is pretty close.)

Today, Maddie and Sammie were trying on their National Debate Tournament pantsuits in the girls' bathroom next to the government classroom. I will now relay the transcribed exchange verbatim, in support of the affirmative:

Maddie: My butt in this pantsuit makes me want to jump my own bones.

Me: It's like I finally know what people mean when they say "hourglass figure."

Maddie: So true! Looking good, Sammie.

Me: I was talking about you. I look like a box.

Maddie: Whatever.

Me: Your affirmative rebuttal is killer now. Alex kept pretending to have to sneeze but you know she was just killing time.

Maddie: Right? (*facing Sammie*) Your closing is airtight, too. We're set.

Me: We're not set . . .

Maddie: We're as set as we're going to be at this stage. I say we cancel Friday practice.

Me (*cautionary*): Maddie . . .

Maddie: Fine.

Me: You can. I'm not.

Maddie: No, it's fine . . .

Me: Why, you have somewhere to be?

Maddie: Ross Nervig's having a party and I want to pregame.

Me: It's cool. You go. I can work on other stuff tomorrow.

Maddie: You want to come?

Me: Nope.

Maddie: Come.

Me: No, thanks.

Maddie (*narrowing her eyes at me, thinking of an argument*): We need to bond as friends.

Me: This is friendship.

Maddie: This is a bathroom at school, next to a government classroom at school. We need to be less institutionalized. We need to be on each other's *level*. We need to feel each other's *rhythm*.

Me: . . .

Maddie: You disagree?

Me: I don't disagree, but my parents would never let me go.

Maddie: What if they did?

Me: They won't.

Maddie: Ignore the conditions, acknowledge the desire.

Me: You sound like an inspirational quote poster.

Maddie: See? This! Your zingers. You're secretly fun.

Me: I'm not secretly fun. I am openly fun.

Maddie: People who have to label themselves as "fun" are not fun.

Me: That's not true.

A silence passes between us wherein both of us acknowledge that this is true.

Maddie: I want to see you drink! Seriously, you probably don't believe this, but smart people are the best partiers.

Me: Prove it.

Maddie: No! You know why? (*pretending to brush dirt off her shoulders*) I just want to rela-a-a-x with you. I just want us to *relax* so I don't have to feel like I always have to be top of my game around you. You know what I mean?

Me: I think. Like I stress you out?

Maddie (*pauses*): Kind of. You're just really intense.

Me: That's not my problem.

Maddie: It will be if I start hating you and want to quit debate.

Me: This is true.

Maddie: Plus, I can tell my mom that I'm spending the night with you so I can break curfew.

Me: Just tell her you're staying with Stacia!

I go into a stall to change out of the pantsuit.

Maddie (*from outside*): You know I can't tell my mom I'm spending the night at Stacia's because she'd never believe me. Stacia's like a little mouse who lives in a little mouse hut, and I don't think she's even come out to her parents.

Me: Oh.

Maddie: You don't have to go to the party. I was just saying.

I emerge. Maddie has never asked me for this kind of favor. I'm curious, and I don't want her to hate me or feel stressed out around me. (Note: I just hope forced social interaction doesn't worsen this effect.)

Me: Okay, we'll go.

Maddie: YES.

Maddie smacks her own ass, and then smacks mine.

END SCENE

As was evidenced, Maddie desires Sammie's presence in order to make their partnership stronger, therefore making them better debaters. Sammie's acquiescence in this matter will make her a more effective debater, thereby moving her closer to her goal of winning Nationals, therefore she will go to Ross Nervig's party.

My second point asserts that Sammie's parents will give her permission to go to the party because Maddie is a first responder as well as a fellow debater. Because of Sammie's medical situation, in order to go anywhere with her parents' permission, Sammie has to think about the conditions and prevention of her own death (thanks, Dr. Clarkington!).

Sammie can also tell her parents she's going to a debate party. Historically, debate parties mean root beer and Trivial Pursuit in Alex Conway's basement, which does not pose as much of a threat of death as a traditional "alcohol and no parents" party. However, because Sammie will attend Ross Nervig's party with Maddie, technically it is a debate party, so she would not be lying.

Because she will be in the presence of a trained saver of lives, and attend, for all intents and purposes, a "tame debate party," Sammie will have her parents' blessing, and therefore, Sammie will go to Ross Nervig's party.

My third and final point is simply a screenshot of the text Maddie sent just minutes ago:

Maddie Sinclair: Anddddddd
Maddie Sinclair: Guess what I heard?
Maddie Sinclair: Your old flame is gonna be there
Me: Who?
Maddie Sinclair: Stuart Shah

Therefore, Sammie will go to Ross Nervig's party on Friday, April 29.

THE UNEXPECTED PARTY

So here's why I'm regretting this:

Stuart Shah is coming here, to Maddie's house, to this very room, before we all go to the party. She just decided to drop that little bomb when her mom pulled out of the driveway.

Stuart is a friend of a friend, Maddie told me.

Stuart had become super close with Dale when Dale played Rosencrantz to Stuart's Hamlet.

And Dale's friends with Maddie.

And Dale and Stuart are coming here.

My stomach is a washing machine.

Earlier we picked up my siblings after school and waited until my dad got home from trimming trees. While I made us a quick dinner of spaghetti, Maddie played with my sisters out in the yard.

Bette roamed around the perimeter, yelling her questions, and Maddie yelled back answers while throwing a Frisbee to Davy and/ or Puppy, whoever got to it first.

Then came the whole CPR-certified thing. Maddie still didn't know I was sick, and at the risk of her thinking I couldn't handle Nationals, I had to keep it that way.

So I did some James Bond shit. As Maddie was outside, I asked her for some gum. She pointed to her bag and invited me to dig around. I dug. Instead of gum, I pulled her Red Cross CPR-certified card out of her wallet and slipped it into my jeans. While the spaghetti boiled, I went to the family desktop, scanned it, printed it, and then returned it.

Dad came home. I followed him into my parents' bedroom, told him my plans, and showed him the scanned certificate.

He pretended to examine it really closely like he actually knew what he was doing. He even put on his bifocals and took it to the desk where they pay bills and held it under the lamplight. I was like, *Cute, Dad.*

After leaving a message on my mom's cell, we came here to Maddie's place in Hanover, where I told Maddie's mom, Pat, that yes, Maddie would be spending the night with me and therefore would not be home at curfew.

Maddie stood behind her in my sight line, giving me a quiet thumbs-up, which made me feel cool and rebellious. Pat gave us both a kiss on the cheek and went out to eat with her book club.

Maddie's room smells like how I think Lothlórien, the elf realm from Lord of the Rings, would smell. Like burning wood and lavender and kind of like dirt. She has leafy plants hanging from every corner, succulents in little glass terrariums in rows along her windows and desk and dresser, a skinny tree in a big ceramic pot. Her stereo speakers take up almost a third of the wall, blaring synthesizers, and she roams back and forth from the bathroom in her bare feet, wearing boxers and a tank top, hair in a towel.

The plan was that we would pregame and leave for the party before Pat got home at ten. That was the plan. Stuart was not part of the plan. I was just going to watch him from a distance at the party and if he saw me, wave, and that would have been enough for me. And now he'll be in the same room as me. Where I am one of four people. Where I can't just hope he'll notice me, where he will have to notice me, and where I will have to acknowledge that he notices me. I will have to pretend like I haven't wanted him since the first time I saw him. Maybe I'll even have to figure out if I actually want him to want me back, or just want to add him to a list of smart people with whom I would make out if given the chance.

Once, shortly after he had gotten published for the first time, I had stayed late to talk to Ms. Cigler about an assignment, and Stuart came into the classroom for the following period. He had sat down and scrawled something quickly on a piece of notebook paper, looking back and forth from a novel held open, doing his homework at the last minute.

I could have said something so simple. Like *hi*. Or *congratulations*. Instead, I said loudly to Ms. Cigler, "Thanks, Ms. Cigler. I didn't consider that passage that way before."

I guess I hoped he would have looked up and said, *What passage?*

And I would have told him which one, and he would have said, *You have an unconventional beauty. Let's talk about it sometime.*

But I had wanted him to think I was smart before he thought I was beautiful, because I knew no one would think I was beautiful, so I just kept talking, louder and louder, about the book, until Ms. Cigler said, "My next class is about to start," and he never looked up from his homework.

That was about how much I was prepared for an interaction with Stuart. Talking loudly to other people while he was in the room. Oh god.

THE DEATH DRIVE

When Maddie was done in the bathroom, she came back with wet hair and a green glass bottle of gin.

"What color is your hair now?" I asked.

"Just a little darker red," she said. "Less Ariel, more *Loud*-era Rihanna."

I bunched my curls into a ponytail and looked past her to her mirror. "What music is this? This isn't Rihanna."

Maddie laughed. "No, it's not." She toweled off her hair and tossed the towel aside. "It's the Knife."

I took my hair back out of the ponytail. "How long until they get here?"

She squirted gel into her hands. "I don't know. Maybe an hour."

"Do we have a designated driver?"

Maddie spiked her hair. "Dale doesn't drink, and he can take my car."

The image of Stuart walking along the road played in my head. I unbuttoned my shirt one button, so you could see the hint of upper chest. Then the thought of sitting next to Stuart, his thigh touching mine, made me paralyzed, and I buttoned back up.

"Sammie." I looked at Maddie. "Relax."

"That's the worst way to relax someone."

"Your teeth are audibly grinding."

"I do that when I'm concentrating!" I told her, which is true. "Do you not want me to concentrate on the task at hand?"

"You know what?" She opened a drawer from her bedside table and brought out a deck of cards. "We're going to play a game."

I felt my muscles loosen a bit. Games meant winning. I liked winning. "What game?"

Maddie set the deck in front of me on the floor, and handed me the bottle of gin. "It's called Loosen the Fuck Up."

"How do you play?"

Maddie pointed. "Pull the first card."

"It's a queen of hearts."

"Take a drink."

I did. "Now what?"

"Do it again."

"That's it?"

"That's the game."

"This isn't—"

She held up her hands. "Any more talk of the game will defeat the purpose of the game."

Maddie is the only person who I would let interrupt me. I don't know why. Because I always liked listening to her. I rolled my eyes and swigged.

"Is Stacia coming?" I asked.

Maddie flexed her abs in the mirror. "She better."

Stacia is Maddie's "something." Maddie told me she doesn't call Stacia her girlfriend because she doesn't believe in monogamy, but I also think it's because Stacia isn't totally sure she only likes girls. Stacia is tiny with red lips and huge eyes and a breathy voice. She paints the sets for all the plays and, at some point, everyone has been in love with her. Including a teacher, which got him fired.

Maddie, because she's Maddie, has been the only one to get Stacia to want her back.

She put on a sleeveless black T-shirt over her sports bra. I stood up next to her. I was wearing my dad's old button-down, black leggings, and Keds. I stared at my pale lips, my ballooning thighs, my butt, my waist invisible under the sack of a shirt. "I wish I had features traditionally considered attractive."

"According to who?"

"According to . . ." I laughed a little. She was asking for sources.

Maddie pulled the next card from the deck on the floor. "Three of diamonds! Doesn't matter." She tossed it aside and took a drink. We both laughed. You had to give it to her—Loosen the Fuck Up lived up to its name.

"Then again," I started, still thinking about what sources to give her. The tangibly measured, very nontraditional attractive-ness of Maddie fought against what I was saying. So I fished around. ". . . to the average appearance of people who have had another person express attraction to them. Openly. I mean, you could take a poll at Hanover . . ."

"You can go on all day about what's wrong with you or you can just fucking own it and enjoy yourself."

"Easy for you to say," I muttered.

"What was that?"

"I said, easy for you to say. You have the confidence of a bull in a china shop," I said. Maddie furrowed her eyebrows. "But like a really, really well-coordinated bull."

She cackled and took another swig of the bottle, handing it to me. I drew a card. "Ace of spades."

"Cool!" Maddie said, shrugging. I threw it across the room. She continued. "Have you ever considered that I might have confidence because you mostly see me in situations that require confidence?"

This was true. Debate practice. Debate rounds. School plays. High school in general. "I see your point," I said, and lifted the bottle to my lips. I choked down a couple of swigs, feeling the burn.

As I drank, she returned to the mirror to put on eyeliner. "Like, for me, every situation requires a ton of confidence. You know?"

"Sure."

Maddie had shaved her head when she was fourteen. When I met her, she had just gotten suspended for punching a bro who had called her a dyke, and she had joined debate because her mom said she had to diversify her extracurriculars, she couldn't just do theater. Within a week, she was first team. Oh! And she eventually made friends with the guy she punched and convinced him to join Queer Union as an ally. She had dated at least two girls at our school, as well as a Dartmouth girl.

After picking up the deck, Maddie drew a card, swigged, and

handed the deck and bottle to me. "And you, too, are in a battle with outside forces. So be brave."

"Nine of clubs. I don't know, though, Maddie, I think it's different." I swigged, and handed both back to her.

"Well, yeah, I mean, we're up against slightly *different* forces, that's true. You're not gay. But I'm telling you, Sam, you're down on yourself for no reason."

I mean, I wasn't down on myself for just *no reason*. I thought about my pain medication in my purse, which I hadn't taken because I knew I would be drinking. I thought of shaking my hands out while she turned her back, trying to get the numbness out of them.

"But . . ."

She stood up. "I'm done arguing with you. Dale and Stuart and Stacia are on their way, so if you want to leave, you're gonna have to find your own way home."

Maddie went to the stereo, took a drink, and started dancing. She lifted her knees and ground her hips into the air and shook her Mohawk from side to side. It was as if I wasn't even there. My brain started churning. I had avoided these situations for a reason: because it was easy to screw them up. Because there was no right answer, and except for those in stupid romantic teen movies, there were no rules about how they should go, and I had no control over anything that occurred outside of my body.

In fact, I had no control over my body as it is. My body hated me.

Maddie had turned up the music as loud as it could go. My mouth tasted like pine trees.

I started to think of Freud's theory of the Death Drive, the idea that organisms could oppose the life force intentionally—the idea that evolution could work backward—and instead of loving and living, people could want to destroy themselves. But I happen to know a different kind of way that death can work in people's lives.

I know this is dark, Future Sam, but there's something freeing about thinking about death. Like I didn't think I was going to die right then in Maddie's room, and I had no desire to die, but when you realize you're close to death—when it's that real—being scared of it, or being scared of even smaller things like people and parties and Stuart Shah; all of that seemed silly.

I have a bigger, more formidable opponent.

"Okay," I said, and Maddie turned around from where she was shimmying across the room. I took the bottle from her and sipped, followed by a chug of seltzer. "I'm doing this. And guess what else?"

Maddie was punching the air. "What?"

I stood up. "We're going to win Nationals."

"Yeah! Yeah, we are!"

I started moving from side to side with her, my best attempt at a dance.

Then I got a wave of fondness toward Maddie, Future Sammie. A kind of fondness I had only felt before toward my siblings, toward my parents, toward people I trusted. I wasn't going to find my own way home. And I wasn't going to be a deadweight, either. As Maddie had said, we needed each other.

I picked up the cards off the floor and tossed them up in the air. "Do I win?"

Maddie smiled. Her brown eyes lit up underneath her electric hair. "Everybody wins."

ROY, ROY, ROY

After a few more songs, when I was starting to feel light and warm and sort of pretty, I heard them coming up the stairs, laughing. I unbuttoned my top button. The door opened, and there was Stacia, a pale fairy in overalls, there was Maddie, her hair now dry and alight with red, her lean arms pulling Stacia's hand, there was Dale, his freckles pulsing, his vintage shirt tucked into polyester, and there was Stuart.

He wasn't wearing his usual black. He was in gray—gray jeans and a gray sweatshirt. His skin was darker than I remembered, dark brown, and his black hair was the same, shorn short and old-fashioned.

"Hey!" he said right away.

"Hey!" I said. Mimicry, I remember thinking. Just mimic the way everyone is talking and you'll get by.

"Hi, Sammie," Stacia said in her almost-whisper, folding herself on Maddie's floor.

"Samantha," Dale said in a robotic, sort of British voice. "Samantha McCoy, the reigning monarch of Hanover High."

"The monarch? What do you mean?" Then, to make it sound nicer, I let out a "ha-ha."

"The villa-Victorian!" Dale answered, twirling his fingers.

The valedictorian. I swallowed my instinct to correct him, and reminded myself what a joke was, and that people made jokes.

Maddie glanced at me with the trace of a smile and said, "Stu, do you know Sammie?"

"Not really," Stuart said, sitting next to Stacia and extending his hand. "I remember you, but I don't think we ever knew each other."

I remember you, he said. I shook his hand. It was the shape and texture of a human hand but it almost burned me.

"That's right," I said, and when I took my hand away, blood was beating through it.

He was still looking at me. Maddie and Stacia passed around the bottle. Dale went to change the music.

"Yeah," he continued, "you were in Ms. Cigler's class when I was a senior. She read our entire AP class your essay on *Huck Finn*. She was like, look at this sophomore. Y'all better step up your game."

"Huh," I said, and nodded. I vaguely remember Ms. Cigler asking me for permission to share my essay, but I thought it was just for the other sophomore class. The thought of him admiring my work gave me goose bumps. I wanted to ask him about his writing, or how he liked being back in Hanover, but by the time I had picked which question and started to form the words the correct way, Maddie was passing him the bottle.

Stacia began to sway to the music, her dangly earrings swooshing. Maddie gave one of them a little tug.

"Ow!" Stacia said, and laughed. She flicked a spike of Maddie's Mohawk. Maddie raised her eyebrows at me. I uncrossed my arms.

Stuart took in Maddie's room. "Who's playing?" he asked Maddie.

"The Knife," I said before anyone else could answer.

Stuart nodded with a small smile, a smile like the clerks at the Co-Op give to Mom when she tries to ask them about how their day is going during a rush. *Just let me do my job*, it said. When his gaze came back to me, just for a second, I jumped on it.

"You're in New York?" I asked.

"Yes. I love it. Maybe a little too much."

"Me too," I said. "I mean, I'll be there, too, next year."

"Oh?"

"At NYU."

He raised his eyebrows. "Congratulations."

On the end of his words, I couldn't help it, I got intense. "What do you love about New York?"

He tilted his head to the side. "God, what a question. I mean, there's the stuff everyone loves, like the history, the nightlife, whatever. But I have a feeling you want to know about what I, specifically, love about it, and I haven't thought about that in a long time."

"Yes, that's exactly what I want to know," I said, and took a swig. He was matching the intensity. Maybe he didn't like small talk, either.

He looked at the ceiling, thinking. He had a long, smooth neck. Finally, he held up his hand, as if he were cradling his answer in his palm. "I love everything and everyone pressed together. I love being on the elevated part of the Q or the N. The windows of the upper stories of buildings are right there, just feet from you, and you're right there, so close to someone else's life. Or, like, when people fight or kiss on the subway right next to you. I think I just like being close to other people's lives."

"Without having to mess with them," I offered.

He laughed. "Exactly." Making Stuart laugh was like making something burst open, that satisfying feeling when you pop bubble wrap or bubble gum.

Right then, Dale jumped up and clapped his hands. "All right, last shots, you winos. I'm ready to head to Nervig's."

In Maddie's tiny two-door Toyota, as if in a dream, Stuart and I ended up in the back, next to each other. The music blared so we couldn't talk. Our legs didn't touch except on turns, when he put his arm around the back part of my seat, saying, "Sorry."

"It's okay," I said back, and looked out the window, savoring his solidness next to me.

I would enjoy this while I could. His eyes had wandered. But he had remembered me. I hadn't asked him the right questions, the flirting questions. But he remembered me. What Stuart said about New York kept bouncing around in my head: the train, sandwiched between lights and buildings and a huge world full of stories.

At the last stoplight out of Hanover, on the way to Norwich, Dale turned down the music to get directions from Maddie.

Stuart scooted forward to look out the window and asked, "So, where do you live?"

I snapped to attention, like a bunny in a garden, hearing a noise. Danger. But this was a good kind of danger.

"Strafford," I said, and noticed I couldn't turn my head without getting unbearably close to his head.

"And?" he asked as the car eased forward.

"And?" I repeated, hoping he couldn't see the huge grin on my face in the dark.

"What part of Strafford do you love?"

"Ha!" I let out immediately. "Not much."

"Not one thing?"

I suppose I hadn't been asked a question like this in a long time, either. I thought about it, feeling my adrenaline spike, and rolled down the window to catch the air coming off the mountains. It smelled like pine and clouds and like someone nearby was having a fire in their backyard. I loved the scent, but it was more than that, like what the scent was saying—the idea it had smelled like this since the mountains were formed and could still be so fresh. The sensation was hard to communicate, not just to Stuart, but to anyone. I took a deep breath. "This," I said, and gestured toward the night.

"Mm," Stuart answered, closing his eyes as the wind moved through the backseat. The look on his face said he knew exactly what I meant, and the pleasure of being recognized was like fingers tracing my back. "Yes. This is nice," he said.

As we wound our way up Ross Nervig's driveway, we could already hear the bass thumping from the house, past the trees. We parked behind a line of cars and slogged the rest of the way, Dale lighting up a cigarette, Stacia and Maddie linking arms. The house became visible, people perched on the porch railing, in clumps on the lawn, streaming in and out of the giant Colonial on the side of a green slope just like mine. Except ten times bigger. And full of people I didn't know.

I started to get nervous again, and tried to make my breathing steady. "Here we go," I muttered.

Beside me, Stuart heard. "Parties, right?"

"Parties," I echoed, shaking my head, as if I had been to a million parties to the point of shaking my head bemusedly about them.

He put his hand on my back, just for a moment, and I twitched with surprise. "Don't worry, it'll be fun."

Was he flirting? Was this flirting? Or was this just regular human interaction? I was dying to ask Maddie, but she was already jogging up the yard, followed by Stacia, leaping onto the back of a friend of hers, laughing as he twirled her around.

"Stu-ey, Stu-ey, Stu-ey," the legendary Ross Nervig greeted us from the center of the porch, a mountain man with a full orange beard, holding a Solo cup. "How's the city, fucker?"

Stuart joined him. I found a corner and listened, vaguely shaking people's hands as Dale introduced me.

From what I could gather as they talked, Ross was in Stuart's class at Hanover, where he had played rugby until he injured himself senior year. Now he worked for his dad's contracting business, steadily growing a fan base for his drone music popular among Dartmouth hipsters. An Upper Valley resident for life.

Stuart, I found out, was here to finish a collection of short stories, and to occupy his parents' house in Hanover for the summer while they visited family in India.

"Are you seeing someone?" Ross asked Stuart. "Are you still with that playwright with the hairy legs?"

My ears almost physically extended across the porch.

"Not really," he said.

Not really does not mean *no*. It means yes, in a way. Of course he had a girlfriend.

I shook it off. I scanned the crowd for other people I recognized who I could stare at awkwardly. I had done what I came to do, what Maddie had challenged me to do. I had talked to him.

But it still didn't feel like I had won.

I followed Dale inside, glancing back at Stuart briefly, who caught my eye, but I turned back around. *Oh well, oh well*, I kept repeating to myself, and looked around the gigantic wooden living room filled with skinny girls taking photos of themselves and baseball players taking photos of themselves. Is that what people do at parties? Stand around and take photos of themselves to prove that they were at a party? I had my laptop with me in my bag, and briefly considered asking Ross for the Wi-Fi password.

A chair opened up by a bookshelf, but before I could sit, I heard my name through the shrieks and bass.

"SAMMIE MCCOY!"

Coop, good ol' Coop, was pummeling through the bodies with a Solo cup of his own, his dirty blond hair tied up in a sweaty bun.

"SAMMIE MCCOY!" he shouted again, and now people were following his eyes in my direction. "THE WOMAN OF MY DREAMS."

Christ. "A simple hello would suffice," I muttered.

I thought of when we were younger, when he used to freak out every time one of our moms made hot dogs. Every hot dog lunch, without fail, Coop would stand on the top of his chair, pumping his fists, and yell, "Hot dogs! Hot dogs! Hot dogs!" as if he had won the lottery. He was an excitable kid.

He wrapped me in a sour hug. His words were slurring. "Never in my life would I think I would see Samantha Agatha McCoy at a party. Never in my life."

"Well, here I am!" I extracted myself. "And you remember my middle name," I added, but he didn't hear.

"Do you know," he started saying to me, then directing it to the crowd. "Do you know, that I have wanted to get drunk with this girl my whole life?"

"What a coincidence," I said, rolling my eyes.

"My whole life," he said, almost solemnly. "This girl is my childhood friend. We're from the same mountain," he told a disinterested junior with a nose piercing nearby. "My childhood friend!" he repeated, and took me by the shoulders, his navy eyes wide.

"It's good to see you, too, Coop." I smiled.

I noticed Stuart and Ross coming through the front door, and I took a step backward.

Coop kept going. "And the first time we talk in fucking years you tell me you're sick!"

"Whoa," I said, and put a finger to my lips.

"Oh," Coop said, imitating me, finger to his lips. "Okay." I wasn't sure I was imagining it, but his eyes looked almost watery, as if he was about to cry.

"I don't want to tell people quite yet," I said low to him. I was not looking at Stuart, but I knew he was still there, because I was finding out that when someone who you like touches you, you become connected to their body in an echolocation sort of way, and when they get closer, as Stuart was, my body also began to get warmer.

"But you told me," Coop said, way too loudly, a weird pride behind it.

"Yeah, and now I'm wondering why," I said off to the side.

"Don't be like that," he said.

"Coop!" someone yelled. A girl I can only assume was Hot Katie made a beeline toward us. Her long, tan legs fell from tight, acid-washed shorts, and her flat stomach sparkled with drops of sweat or beer or some other liquid under a crop top. I watched Coop's eyes, and everyone else's eyes for that matter, travel her body. I knew she didn't do it on purpose, but girls like her made me feel like garbage. Like, what's even the point with girls like her around.

"Coop." Hot Katie propped herself on his shoulder, and whispered into his ear, giggling. "Come with me," she said, and they went. It was that easy? It was that easy. Oak trees belong with other oak trees.

I could see Stacia and Maddie sharing a chair in the room next to ours, their legs entangled.

I picked up a book called *Anagrams* and started to read. I felt someone's eyes on me and looked up. Stuart. I held up the book like someone would hold up a glass. *Cheers. Parties, right? Ha-ha. It's not that I don't know what to do or say it's just that I've been to so many parties that I'm tired of them and would rather read this book ha-ha so don't worry about me I'll just be here.*

Then he walked toward me. I stared back down at the book, my eyes unmoving, but somehow I knew that he had just sidestepped a chair, had said *excuse me* to a girl who was dancing, and now he was here, next to me. He picked out a book of his own, a hardcover called *The Writing Life*.

"Hey," he said, thumbing through the pages.

"Hey," I said, reading the same sentence over and over again, my skin burning through my clothes.

"Ross's parents have a good book collection."

"Thankfully," I said, and we both laughed a little.

"Giving up this early, huh?"

Instead of answering, I chugged my drink. And that was when I realized why the art of small talk eluded me. When I had a purpose, I could ask and answer questions to break someone down. When I had no purpose, I hit a wall. I was tired of the wall. An idea, or maybe an impetus, or maybe I was just mimicking the Hot Katies of the world; anyway, something grew.

His beautiful eyebrows began to furrow, wondering.

When I want something, I want it. And I wanted Stuart Shah.

I looked at him straight in his deep, black, beautiful eyes and said, "I want you to know that I have always had an enormous crush on you."

And I put the book back on the shelf and left.

WHICH KIND OF TREE AM I— AM I EVEN IN THE FOREST?

And now I'm here, sitting on the hood of Maddie's car, giggling to myself in the dark. I can't believe I actually just said that to Stuart Shah. I feel like what a superhero must feel like. I feel like I can hear everything, see everything, still feel the vibrating air between us and the snap of the book in my hand as I shut it and the edge of his sleeve I brushed as I left. I can't remember when I felt such a rush.

Probably when we found out we had gotten a good enough score to qualify for Nationals. Or, no, maybe when Mrs. Townsend told me that I was in the running to be valedictorian.

Oh god, I was reckless.

I was reckless but I feel like I won. Maddie told me to be brave, and I was.

And funnily enough, Future Sam, when I did it, I thought of you. I thought of you looking back on me in that moment and watching me melt into the background, or go home and feel sorry for myself, and I got angry.

If you are me later, let's say . . . next year, after you've had your first successful term at college, I want you to be fucking cool. And not just cool as in a perfect, happy image of someone having a perfect time, the kind of stuff that I see in the photos people share at parties like this one, not a person defined by the captions you paste on your life. I think people fake that they're having fun a lot of the time in photos, because they want people to think they're having fun. Well, that's not life, is it?

Sometimes life is really terrible. Sometimes life gives you a weird disease.

Sometimes life is really good, but never in a simple sort of way.

And when I look back, I will know I have tried.

But now I'm sort of stranded here on Maddie's car. It's probably been an hour or so.

She texted me: *Where r u??*

I told her, but when I texted her again to ask when we were leaving, my phone died. I don't have Internet. I also didn't get to warn Maddie about what I said to Stuart.

Shit, it's gonna get lonely out here, Future Sam.

Okay, good. I can hear footsteps coming down the driveway. Probably Maddie here to chew me out and tell me to get back inside. *Nooo way*, I'm going to tell her. I said my piece.

I may be socially impaired but I know enough not to go back in there. I am going to pretend like I am typing something on my laptop because I am super busy as to effectively ignore Maddie.

Oh god.

It's not Maddie. It's someone dressed all in gray, looking around at all the cars.

It's Stuart.

OH MY GOD

When he found me on the hood of Maddie's car, Stuart just said, "Hey-y-y," and started laughing, and I started laughing. The echolocation was overwhelming.

"Maddie wanted me to make sure you were okay," he finally said.

"Yes. I'm okay," I said. "Are you okay?"

"Why wouldn't I be?" he said.

Before he finished asking, I blurted, "Because I just dropped, like, an emotional grenade on you. I just took out the clip and threw it and let it explode."

I realized I wasn't looking him in the eyes, just staring a hole straight through his broad gray chest.

"Yeah, you could have at least yelled, *cover!* Or something." He made exploding sounds with his mouth. I giggled, which I try never to do except within the comfort of my own home, which is saying something about Stuart and how he made me feel.

"Yeah," I said. "I should have."

Then we were quiet. And the full weight of what I had done started to sink in, like for instance, the fact that I probably stared at him a lot, not just when we were in high school together, but a lot over this evening, without saying much more than telling him (a) that I was obsessed with him and (b) that we would be in the same city next year.

I said, "Sorry if that was creepy."

Stuart said, "No! No, don't worry about it," and by then, thankfully, we could hear Dale and Maddie and Stacia coming down the driveway after us, so we stopped having to talk.

I purposefully sat in the front, trying to shrug the whole thing off. Trying to forget what I said, believe it or not. I remember thinking, damn, I might just erase the whole night from your memory, Future Sam.

When we got to my house, I called, "This is me!"

As I shut the door, Stuart called from the backseat open window. "Sammie!"

And of course I answered, "What?"

"Come here!" he said.

I turned around, thinking I had forgotten something, probably a half-eaten peanut butter sandwich in a Baggie that fell out from my bag or something.

Then he took my arm—that's right, you read correctly—he took my arm, and turned it over, as if he were administering a shot. He brought a pen out of his pocket, uncapped it with his teeth, and wrote his email. Each curve of each letter of his name was like, I don't know, having sex. I have never had sex, but have you ever had someone write on you? Have you ever had a writer write on you? He might as well have been doing it with his fingertip.

"I'm not a great texter," he said.

It's been a day since the party and I still have the faded letters of Stuart's email address written on my arm in marker. I have his email because he gave it to me, and now he has mine because I emailed him.

Holy. Saint. James. Iago. Joan. Of. Fucking. Arc.

I still can't believe it.

Wait. He's online now. HE EMAILED ME.

Sammie,

Hey, glad you survived. Like I said last night, don't worry about it. We were both in weird party mode. It was actually kind of refreshing. I mean, we don't know each other very well but I will say I always felt this strange connection to you when I was at Hanover. Not a crush per se (ha-ha), because to be honest, I was always too busy acting and writing and doing homework to have much of a crush on anyone. But I remember seeing you in the cafeteria, and when Ms. Cigler read your essay aloud, I really was impressed. Maybe I should have chased after you tonight but it seemed like you wanted to get out of there. I guess I'm just not used to being so upfront with anyone. But I was glad when Maddie asked me to go find you. And I'm glad you told me that.

-Stu

Okay—I wrote back asking if he had a girlfriend. Not going to keep refreshing and checking for a reply. I have plenty of other things to do. I wait for no man. OH WAIT LOOK:

Ha-ha! No, I don't have a girlfriend. If we're going to keep playing the frankness game, I said "not really" to Ross because he always used to give me shit for not having a girlfriend. I had one before, in New York, but things ended last year.

Jesus, you really do just dig into it, don't you? Ha-ha. Um. Why did I give you my email? Because I think you're cute and smart.

-Stu

PS That book you were pretending to read? It was *Anagrams* by Lorrie Moore and when you get the chance (maybe when your schedule clears up) you should read it. It's one of my favorites.

I have just been going back to my email inbox in between doing homework, expecting these emails to disappear, and they never do. Especially this part: Because I think you're cute and smart. Because I think you're cute and smart. Because I think you're cute and smart. ^^^ He said that. Stuart Shah said that!

THOUGHTS

Okay, it's two a.m. but this thought just occurred to me: Maddie is a bigger fan of simplified plans as opposed to plank plans in 1AR (first affirmative rebuttal, in case you forgot that), but I think it's just because she's stressed and wants less to memorize.

Plus, if we go by records alone, we'll probably be facing Hartford Prep, and those fuckers pack planks like they're going out of style. Again, don't worry if you forgot planks—it's just what it sounds like—flat statements of "what we intend to do about the problem" on top of each other in a really specific order. Simplified plans are much easier and more natural to say, but planks are better at preventing you leaving anything out or (ahem) forgetting anything.

So I'm going to tell her, leave researching the planks to me on both the 1AR AND 2AR, and I'll give her cards, she can just do the thing where she acts like each idea is occurring to her as she's saying it.

Okay, you know what, I'm going to email this to Maddie.

Still up at four a.m. I hear a car coming up the mountain—Mom's home from her shift.

Went down to visit Mom before she went to bed, and she was making tea. Her turquoise scrubs clashed with the old red-and-yellow tile on the counters and walls. Coop always used to say our kitchen and dining room looked like a McDonald's. The house was dark except for one light above the kitchen table. While she filled up the kettle, Mom kicked off her white tennis shoes.

When I said "hi," she jumped. I scared the bejesus out of her.

"What are you doing up?" she asked when she recovered and sat down at the chrome table.

I sat across from her. "It's two days before Nationals, Ma, what do you think?"

She shook her head over the steaming cup. "Oh, Sammie. You gotta sleep. You can't push yourself this hard."

"You should talk. You've been working a lot of overtime."

She muttered, "Well, these medical bills aren't going to pay themselves."

She immediately said, "Oh god," and put her hand on my arm.

I knew she was sorry. I forgave her. Her big eyes had dark circles around them.

"So what's the deal with this one? With Nationals," she continued. "It's the big show, right?"

"Yes, ma'am."

"And you're done after this, right?"

I sighed. I hadn't really thought about it that way. "Yeah, I guess I am."

Mom smiled a bit, relaxing. "And does this mean you'll be spending a little more time at home?"

"Depends. Why? I mean, Harrison is going to be fourteen soon, he can babysit just fine. Plus I paid him to do my chores while I'm gone this weekend . . ."

"No, hon. I mean just to be with us. Just to watch a movie or something once in a while." She rubbed my arm. I got goose bumps.

She used this guilt tactic a lot. She would whisper to Bette and Davy while the rest of the family was watching the Patriots play on TV, sending them screaming across the house to coerce me from doing homework. When Puppy needed to be let outside, she would send him into my room until he practically dragged me from my desk. While he ran around me in circles, banging into the screen door with excitement, I would hear her from her spot curled up in the living room, laughing to herself.

I pushed out, "Yeah, sure. Maybe after graduation."

"Mmhmm," Mom said softly.

After a bit of silence, she reached for my face. "Can I—" she started, and after years of her checking for sore throats, for brushed teeth, for hidden hard candy, I opened my mouth automatically.

"Hmm," she said. "How's your tongue?"

I seized up and pulled away. "Fine. Why?"

She looked at me and shrugged, pasting on a smile. "Nothing."

I put my hand to my jaw. "What, was I slurring?"

"No! No," she said quickly. "Are you packed?"

She was trying to change the subject. Tomorrow, Maddie would tell me if I sounded weird. I mean, sure, I'd have to make up an excuse, like perhaps I drank a slushie too fast and my tongue was frozen, but anyway, nothing a few of her theater-kid tongue twisters couldn't fix.

"Yep," I said. I had packed last night. I would probably unpack and repack again, just for the satisfaction.

"Got your prescriptions?"

"Yep."

"Even Zavesca?"

I grunted.

(What is Zavesca, you ask? Future Sam, have I not told you about Zavesca? It's kind of like the grapefruit soda Fresca, except it's not at all like Fresca, because actually it's just a terrible pill! Side effects include: Weight loss! Stomach pain! Gas! Nausea and vomiting! Headache, including migraine! Leg cramps! Dizziness! Weakness! Back pain! Constipation!)

"Doctor's note?"

"Yep."

"Do you want some spending money?"

Now it was my turn to change the subject. "No, no, no, no worries, Mom."

"Are you sure?"

"Yes, we raised enough at the raffle this year to cover everything we'll need."

"Mmhmm," she said again, in only the way Mom can do it. Those "m" sounds. Her mantra. Her strength. If a hurricane started blowing the windows in, Mom would breathe through her nose and say *Mmhmm*. Once, when I was nine, I had slipped right where I was sitting tonight and hit my head on the edge of the counter, cracking my skull. Mom had made it from the yard to the kitchen in minus-five seconds without a word, wrapped my head in a T-shirt, and called 911, all the while rocking me and saying, *Mmhmm, mmhmm, mmhmm*.

I stood up from the table, feeling the scar on my scalp. "You know, Mom, someday I'm going to pay you back. When I'm a successful lawyer, or whatever. I'll pay you back for all the medical bills."

"Oh, honey," Mom said, and came around the table in her stocking feet to hug me. I held her tiny body. Her head only came up to the crook of my neck.

"I'm serious! You can even make a ledger . . ."

"You just get better," she said, muffled by my shirt. "That's all I need. You just get better."

"Okay, I will," I told her.

And I will.

BY ALL ACCOUNTS, HERE'S HOW NATIONALS SHOULD UNFOLD:

SOME PREDICTIONS BY SAMMIE MCCOY

Maddie and I arrive at the Sheraton Boston via Pat's van. We check in, hang up our suits, and camp out with snacks. We put on German techno. We go through fresh copies of every article on the living wage and highlight everything we need with the same color. *With the same color.* That is very important.

As the sun is rising, we roll into the lobby, both figuratively, in the badass word for "arriving," and literally, because we are pulling tubs full of evidence on wheels. We register and find a spot to practice away from all the other teams.

We set up behind the affirmative desk, on a platform, under lights, in the largest conference room. We watch the other team set up with stony looks on our faces.

We shake hands with the judges.

Then the battle starts.

Maddie stands at the podium and offers the affirmative. Maddie presents a plan. She says why this plan will work. As I said, she's damn good at it. The emotions she can pack into eight minutes stating nothing but facts in a particular order—it's a beauty to behold. Think of every motivational speech at the halftime of every sports movie you've ever seen, but at the beginning of the movie, and with less tears, less yelling, and more logic.

The negative rebuts. They state their philosophy. They say why our plan won't work. I listen to their points so closely I can hear their spit sloshing around.

Second affirmative: Here's me. I gather all the holes in their argument, BUT. But. I have to frame them as if our plan anticipated all these holes to begin with. This is where pantsuits come in handy. Not for any utility reason, just to look down on in order to remind yourself that you are a streetwise BAMF who is never surprised by anything.

They point out the disadvantages of this brand-spanking-new plan.

Maddie comes back in, tries to talk about how stupid they are for arguing against our perfect plan (without losing sight of the original plan).

They pick further holes in our argument, and blow up their own balloon of an argument bigger. This is their last hurrah.

I am the final voice. I find the best facts on our side, the worst facts against them, and reaffirm with some poetry. It is my job to pop their balloon-argument once and for all, and to release our balloon-argument up to the sky. I am essentially Robin Williams in *Dead Poets Society*. No, I am Théoden, at the Battle of Helm's Deep, and the round judges are the Riders of Rohan, holding out their questions like spears. I ride past them on a steed of rhetoric, and tap their spears with my sword of facts, leaving them no choice but to follow me.

Sorry, got a little carried away there.

Anyway, voilà, we convince the world that the minimum wage should be raised.

We do it again in a second round.

We do it again a third.

Then, if we can do it one more time, we will win the national championship.

LIFE DURING WARTIME

Last debate practice of our high school careers. We went through some mock rounds versus Alex Conway and Adam Levy, and by the closing statements, Alex was about ready to claw my eyes out. She would have loved to see me go down one last time. Not on your life, Conway. Maddie and I are both made of steel. No, mercury. We're fluid and poisonous.

I'm going through cards like a nun praying on rosary beads, mouthing each phrase.

Maddie is pacing with her jacket over her head, reciting her opening.

Stacia walks past the government classroom, peering inside. Maddie's saying, "But in the United States . . ."

"Maddie!" Stacia calls, leaning on the doorframe.

Maddie pauses and lifts up her jacket. "Hi, Stac," she says.

"Wanna take a break?" Stacia offers.

"Nope, can't," Maddie says. "Sorry, dude."

Stacia shrugs.

Maddie has put her jacket back over her head.

And that, ladies, gentlemen, and Future Sam, is our life during tournament time.

SO IT BEGINS

At the Sheraton after our first round, Maddie is highlighting while I give my eyes a rest. Bass pounds from the speakers. She is hunched over on the floor, next to three stacks two feet high full of economic analyses and the names of obscure bills and percentage signs. Just a few more to go and we'll be ready for bed. We both wear our complimentary white Sheraton robes. Our suits hang in the corner.

A momentary silence as the song ends.

"Deutschland, Deutschland! Again!" she shouts, lifting her pink highlighter.

"Again?"

"Again!"

We've been playing the same track on repeat for the last hour over the portable speakers Maddie brought. It's basically three driving, heavy notes under voices of indiscernible genders screaming in German. It motivates us. Well, it motivates Maddie, and because it motivates Maddie, it motivates me. It's our tradition.

Her mom, who's in the connected room next door, has learned to bring earplugs.

Three years, twenty-plus tournaments. Thirteen first-place titles, four second-place. When everything is highlighted, and when the clock hits nine a.m., there's nothing more we can do. This is it.

Last year we watched the outgoing seniors and I clenched my fists in anticipation, talking about how I wouldn't make the same mistakes, how I would spend the next year honing on slower speech, on evidence organization, what I would wear.

And now it's just hours away. Our reputation, our reasons for getting scholarships, the countless iterations of "sorry, I can't come," now packed into a twin double.

Stuart texted me. *Good luck!*

I said "Thanks!" and turned my phone off.

If I didn't, he might start a conversation with me, and then I wouldn't be able to stop imagining him writing an entire novella on my naked body.

Which would be distracting.

Okay, I had to go splash water on my face in the bathroom and say aloud to my reflection, "Sammie, now is not the time for you to be a lover. Now is the time for you to be a warrior."

* * *

Well, the highlighters are out of ink. Maddie and I chugged a couple of glasses of tap water, tucked into our parallel beds, and turned on some shitty TV.

As we turned off the lamps, Maddie said, "Sammie."

"Yeah?"

"I'm super stressed."

As she said this, I realized I was grinding my teeth. "Me too."

Her voice sounded different than normal, a little higher, a little softer. "It's okay if we don't win, right?"

I sighed. "I don't even want to think about that."

"Me neither," she said quickly. "But I was thinking about what you said the other day, about cutting your losses."

"Yeah?"

"Like, even when we've gotten second or third before, it was like, 'Whatever, that was a fluke. We just need to get to Nationals.' I mean, even you would say stuff like that, and you hate losing."

"It's true." I would say, *Whatever, this doesn't matter. Nationals is what matters.*

"We didn't really decide to cut our losses by coming here, did we?"

I held my breath, staring at the ceiling. "What do you mean?"

"We put all our eggs in one basket."

I was quiet. She continued.

"This year has been weird. I . . ." She blew out a breath. "I feel like I can do a lot of the things I do because I usually go after stuff that *I know I can do.* I can act and run QU and make out with people not just because I want to, but because I know I can. You know? And lately this year, I've actually started to *want* things. And not just things that depend on me being able to be good at them. I want bigger things that have nothing to do with me."

I believed her, though I was surprised. I knew why I wanted this, but never really thought Maddie was as wrapped up in this world as I was. Then I remembered the other day at practice, her jacket over her head. Last week, inviting me to places even though she didn't have to. We were in this together.

"I've noticed that," I said.

"Yeah?"

I swallowed. I hoped this is what she was talking about. I hoped I wasn't going to sound stupid. "You used to make fun of me for being so invested in debate. Even when you were super good at it. But now you're as crazy about it as I am."

She laughed, almost her regular cackle, and I joined in, and there's something about laughing on your back that makes you keep going long after anything is funny. It's like something solid from your back and shoulder and chest is being released in the air to dissolve.

After the laughter faded, it got quiet again. We could hear the elevators whoosh.

"I actually want Stacia," Maddie said quietly, almost as if she were talking to herself. "Not just because . . . whatever."

"I know what you mean," I said after a while. "I *actually* want to win. Not just because I'm competitive. It doesn't even have to do with anyone else. I just want it for me. Does that make sense?"

"It does," Maddie said. "I want it, too."

Soon after that, she fell asleep. I can almost see all the stuff we laughed about hanging in the air, rising, moving elsewhere through the walls, and I think I'll sleep, too.

SUCK IT

FIRST ROUND

Madeline Sinclair and Samantha McCoy,
Hanover High School, Hanover, NH
vs.
Thuto Thipe and Garrett Roswell,
Stuyvesant High School, New York, NY

Hanover High School: 19   Stuyvesant High School: 17

Yep. Staying focused. Victory meal at Legal Sea Foods.

SECOND ROUND

Madeline Sinclair and Samantha McCoy,
Hanover High School, Hanover, NH

vs.

Anthony Tran and Alexander Helmke,
St. Louis Park High School, St. Louis Park, MN

Hanover High School: 18   St. Louis Park High School: 16

Two down. Had a splitting headache last night, so we were worried, but it went away by round time. Would normally be judging Maddie right now for taking a phone call from Stacia outside, but I can't freak out about that. Whatever we're doing, it's working.

In the elevator just now, two eliminated dude debaters reeking of cologne got on, not even seeing me.

"Did you hear about Hanover's pair?" one of them was saying.

"The girl with a Mohawk? And the one with the ass? Yeah, dude."

"They're in the finals."

"My money's on Hartford."

The doors opened.

As the doors closed, I called out, "You're mistaken!" and flipped them off.

Watching *Caddyshack* with the sound off on the hotel TV, gargling with salt water. Trying to keep my mouth limber. I'm on edge but not nervous. I'm feeling blank but not scattered.

Third round's tomorrow at ten a.m. When we win that, we go to the championship round.

UNTITLED

Remember this, Future Sam, because so help me God and Jesus and all the other saints, it will never happen again. This morning I first looked at the clock at exactly 7:56 a.m. Maddie spiked her hair like always and I slicked my curls as tight as they could go back into a bun at the nape of my neck. We went down into the lobby and split a bagel from the continental breakfast. We went outside briefly to pose for a picture in front of the WELCOME DEBATERS sign. I remember there was a maroon Corolla idling in front of the Sheraton, just outside the sliding doors. I remember there was a man in a Carhartt jacket smoking a cigarette. Do you understand what I'm saying? I'm not crazy. My brain still works. It was a poppy seed bagel with plain cream cheese, *I remember that.* And I remember that the carpeted halls smelled like they had just been shampooed, and the sun coming through the big windows in the lobby was so bright, people were shading their eyes with their hands. We rolled our tubs into the Paul Revere Room. The Hartford team was comprised of a sharp-faced Nigerian girl and a chubby white kid, Grace Kuti and

Skyler Temple, respectively. The chairs were filled with eliminated teams and their families, some of them staring us down, some of them laughing and screwing around, relieved to be done. The lights dimmed in the huge hall and they flicked on the hot stage lights, and after the short-haired woman in dress slacks and a linen shirt welcomed everyone, there were about SEVEN SECONDS of applause. The moderator's name was SAL GREGORY. And he had a BALD SPOT and a ROLEX WATCH. I'M CAPITALIZING EVERYTHING TO EMPHASIZE HOW DEEPLY I REMEMBER EVERYTHING. MADDIE CLEARED HER THROAT BEFORE SHE STOOD UP, AND AGAIN AFTER SHE GOT TO THE PODIUM. SHE LOOKED DOWN, AND WHEN SHE LOOKED UP, SHE SAID, "LADIES AND GENTLEMAN, ACCORDING TO A RECENT ANALYSIS FROM THE CENTER FOR ECONOMIC AND POLICY RESEARCH, THIRTY-SEVEN PERCENT OF AMERICANS WHO GAIN THEIR SOLE SOURCE OF INCOME FROM MINIMUM-WAGE JOBS ARE BETWEEN THE AGES OF THIRTY-FIVE AND SIXTY-FOUR. LOW WAGES AREN'T JUST FOR TEENAGERS LOOKING TO EARN SPENDING MONEY. THESE PEOPLE ARE MOTHERS, FATHERS . . ."

I remember I had just finished second affirmative. Maddie had stepped up, given me a pat on the back as we passed each other, and I'd sat down. I remember squinting my eyes against the stage lights, and itching my calf. We were fine. Someone was talking. Everything was going perfectly fine. And somehow, then it wasn't. It wasn't like a moment, or a flash, it just was. It was like waking up, except I had already opened my eyes, and I was trying to remember a dream. Maddie was looking at me, and without knowing what I was doing, I kind of laughed, because it was funny that we were there, in the morning, after I was just waking up. My first thought was, *What is Maddie doing here?*

Then she said, "And my partner will now [something, something]," because it was sort of garbled, and then I thought, *Oh, I'm at practice,* and then I remember squinting at her and wondering if we were at practice, why was it so bright?

I looked across at our opponents and wondered who they were. And I looked out at the crowd, and that's when I realized we were in the middle of Nationals, and I was supposed to be doing something, but I wasn't sure at what point in the round we were, or which round, and I looked down at my cards, and back at Maddie, who was now standing beside me and making the *stand up* motion with her hand.

"Time-out," I said.

The judges gave us thirty seconds.

"What's up?" Maddie whispered. Her voice was clipped with annoyance.

My throat was so dry it hurt. "I don't know where we are. I mean, I do now, but I don't know . . . yeah. I don't know where we are."

"What the fuck? What are you talking about?"

I felt like I was blinking at five miles an hour. My fingertips started to tingle. "Just tell me if we're at 2AR or closings."

"What?"

"2AR or closings? Just tell me!"

"Closings! What is wrong? You look pale. Do you need water?"

"Yes."

Maddie pushed her half-drunk bottle toward me and I drank in deep gulps.

Thirty seconds were up.

I stood. My knees shook, my hands shook, I tried to keep them tight. I knew the major points. The closing was not the problem—it was that I didn't know what our opponents had said over the entire round, or what Maddie had just said, or even what I had just said. I took a deep breath.

I didn't know, so I guessed.

I summarized, vague and bleak and choppy.

I didn't even make it the full four minutes.

When I sat back down and they concluded the round, I didn't look at Maddie.

I didn't look at anyone.

I just went outside the hall, up the elevator to our room, locked the bathroom door, and cried. I've spent the last three hours sobbing so hard that Maddie's mom knocked on the bathroom door, asking if I was choking. I messed everything up really bad. Really, really bad.

I have been dreaming about this day forever.

I turned fifteen, sixteen, and seventeen by blowing out birthday candles, thinking of this room, this hotel, this tournament.

And we lost because I forgot where I was.

THIRD ROUND

Madeline Sinclair and Samantha McCoy,
Hanover High School, Hanover, NH

vs.

Grace Kuti and Skyler Temple,
Hartford Preparatory Academy, Hartford, CT

Hanover High School: 14   Hartford Preparatory Academy: 19

You know, sometimes it's good to be reminded that you're just a weak sack of floppy bones in a polyester pantsuit who talks to herself on a tiny laptop computer in a hotel bathtub.

You are not actually the star debater of the East Coast, you are not "the team to beat," you are not the valedictorian, you are not a Future Anyone, you are not a strong young woman, and in fact, you remind yourself of the same pubescent girl you always were, wearing your huge glasses. You are reminded specifically of that day you were sitting at the kitchen table with a gallon of chocolate milk from the general store in Strafford, reading a fat Terry Goodkind book, drinking glass after glass of milk while you read for hours, until it's time for dinner but you don't want to stop reading, but there's not enough room for everyone to sit down, they say, and they get annoyed, and they send you outside with your lukewarm half gallon of chocolate milk, your one pleasure in the world. And at first you think to yourself, wow, you finished a fantasy novel and drank an entire gallon of chocolate milk in one sitting. Good for you.

And then you realize everyone else is inside, being normal, and even your family can't stand you, and you are completely and utterly alone.

These other losers, the ones who got knocked out, the ones you strode past feeling like a million bucks, they're going to go home and move on to the next thing. They're going to come back next year, or they'll graduate, like Maddie, and they'll look back and say, well, it was just a bad weekend.

I thought that's what I'd be saying, too, just six months ago.

But now I have to worry if this, the shittiest weekend of my life, my ultimate failure, is actually going to be the best weekend I can remember.

What if this is just the beginning of a series of failures?

What if this is all I am?

What if this is it?

FUCK IT

When I heard the door close and Maddie's and Pat's voices fade down the hallway, I came back here, to my bed, and kept the lights off. We leave tomorrow morning.

Maddie had left me alone, except briefly asking me to dinner, so I think I'm in the clear. As in, though my mom had told Pat about NPC before we left for the tournament, Pat had not told Maddie.

As in, to Maddie, the episode earlier was just a breakdown. The thing is—and, Future Sam, I have had some time to think this through while snotting on myself for the entire day—this was not a fluke meant for both Maddie and me. It was part of a bigger fluke. A huge, blank, stinking hand of cards that, if I'm not careful, will last the rest of my life. But that's not Maddie's fault. She deserves to know that none of this, in any way, was meant to happen to her.

And Christ, if humans supposedly know how time works, how can it be possible to blow four years of work in thirty seconds? It's not fair. It's not fucking fair.

SERIOUSLY, FUCK THIS

I wish we were riding home in a limo—not for the glamour, but so Maddie and I could sit on opposite ends. I'm writing this with the screen facing away from Maddie, in the car home.

On the elevator ride down to the pool, I had rehearsed how I would tell her why I forgot everything, and that I was sorry, and if we could do it over again, I would not have even tried to go to the tournament. I would have let Alex Conway have my spot so that Maddie could have won.

I found her in the hot tub, wearing a sports bra and basketball shorts. Other debaters laughed and splashed one another across the room in the pool. I sat next to her and put my feet in the boiling water. My face felt crusted like a salt lick. Her face was red, too, and her hair was flat and slick. She didn't speak.

"Well," I said. "It's over."

She tried to smile at me. "Yeah. We did our best."

I jumped on this. "Actually, no, I didn't."

"Yeah, it's just . . ." Maddie's face scrunched up, trying to keep her cool. "Now is not the best time. Can we not get into this?"

"Let me say one thing. Actually, a couple of things. You were amazing. I messed up." I took a deep breath. "When we were talking the other night, before the tournament began—actually, before the party—I should have told you something really important that I found out about myself recently. Actually—god, I'm saying 'actually' a lot."

"I'm going to pause you for a second," Maddie said, her jaw clenched. "I'm requesting this as a friend. It's nothing to do with you, okay? I let you be with your thoughts. Can you let me be with mine?"

"Yes, but this is something pertaining to why we lost—"

Maddie's voice got louder, echoing around the pool. "I don't care! You don't care. People do things. Let's just not care."

I wasn't sure what she was talking about. I was close to crying again, because I knew what she was saying wasn't true. What about what we had said before we went to sleep that first night? I wanted her to acknowledge that, at least. "But we both wanted . . ."

"You don't get what you want! You don't always get what you want!" She was yelling now.

The debaters at the deep end giggled and looked over at us.

"What are you looking at?" Maddie yelled.

They grew quiet.

She got out of the hot tub and walked out, hitting the glass wall so hard it shook. My stomach felt like it had taken the punch. I stood and noticed a phone lighting up on one of the plastic tables. I picked it up, thinking it had been left behind. It was open to several texts.

Stacia: We need a break

Stacia: We weren't even serious

Me: At least give me a reason. What did I do?

Stacia: Idk while you were away I had time to think

Stacia: It's not anything you did

Stacia: I just need to be on my own

The phone was Maddie's.

Some other key highlights of this four-hour car ride home, so far:

- Me saying I'm sorry about Stacia
- Maddie saying I don't know what I'm talking about
- Maddie's mom telling us not to snap at each other, that we had a stressful few days
- Me saying at least we got that far
- A deer running into the road
- Maddie saying she wishes she was a deer so she could get hit by a car and die
- Me telling her not to take death lightly
- Maddie telling me to stop being so intense for once in my life
- Maddie's mom chastising both of us
- Maddie wishing she had never joined debate in the first place
- We got ice cream

TRUTH BOMBS

As we got about a half mile to my house, I was about to burst out crying again because as you know, when I had tried to tell Maddie about NPC she wouldn't listen, so like any reasonable human being, I tried again.

The car was kind of quiet because Pat had turned down the radio so I could give her directions, and it was sort of peaceful just hearing the air-conditioning and watching the trees go by, SO SUE ME, I THOUGHT IT WAS A NICE MOMENT.

I said, "Maddie, I have a disease that makes me forget things. That's why I blanked during the round."

Maddie was silent, which I thought was a good thing, until I looked back at her from the front seat and she was staring straight ahead.

She said, "What."

Pat sighed and I continued. "I was diagnosed with Niemann-Pick Type C, which is a degenerative brain disease. Me forgetting where I was—that's a symptom of the disease."

I watched her scrunch her eyebrows together in the rearview mirror. "Mom?"

"Yes?"

"Is this true?"

Pause. "Yes."

Maddie made eye contact with me in the mirror. "How long has this been going on?"

"Since winter break." We pulled up to the end of my driveway, and as Pat's car started to kick up gravel on the steep hill, I said, "It's okay, you can stop here. I'll walk up."

"Sammie—Jesus. I'm sorry." Maddie didn't sound sorry. She sounded mad. "Why didn't you say something before?"

I unbuckled my seat belt and lifted my bag. All my papers fell out. Sheets printed with round times, scores, a welcome map of Boston. "I thought you wouldn't want to be partners with me," I muttered, gathering the pile.

Maddie made a sound between disgust and sadness. "What kind of person do you think I am?"

"Not because of you rejecting me as a friend or whatever, just because you might have thought I wouldn't be able to handle it," I said, shoving papers in clumps on the seat.

"That's not the point!" Maddie yelled, then said quieter. "You lied to me!"

Pat reached behind her to touch Maddie's knee. "Girls, why don't you give yourselves some space?"

"Well . . ." Maddie made another sound, breathing air through her nose. "Isn't that convenient."

"What?" I said, almost ripping my bag as I closed the zipper. "What did I do this time?"

"You just drop bombs and leave," she was saying under her breath out the window. "That's the Sammie McCoy way. Just droppin' truth bombs. Who cares what comes after?"

"Thanks, Pat," I said to Maddie's mom, forcing a smile, and slammed the door.

As I walked away I heard Maddie's window roll down. "I'm sorry you're sick but you can't pretend you didn't wait on purpose to tell me right when we got to your house!"

"Maddie," I heard Pat say behind me.

I turned around. "What does it matter when I tell you? I'm telling you! It's my thing! I get to decide!"

"Exactly," Maddie yelled as they reversed. "You control everything!"

"Yeah, right," I said to no one. "Believe me, I wish." She has no idea how wrong she is.

QUASIMODO RETURNS
TO THE BELL TOWER

After fighting with Maddie, all I want to do is burrow into my bed with *The West Wing* and not come out until graduation, but I was going to get a talking-to about what happened. When I walked up the driveway, Mom stopped mowing the lawn in the middle of a row.

I had left her a voice mail last night. She'd called three or four times until I texted her back. I would rather just have a conversation about it, I told her, and I needed to recover from losing Nationals.

"Hey," Mom called across the yard as I stalked toward the front door. "Hey!'

"Give me a minute," I told her, almost running inside.

Now here we were, in person, and I couldn't avoid it. I could feel her energy rocking and swaying like a ship in a storm. Bette and Davy were putting a puzzle together on the floor. Dad was in the kitchen and dropped the dish he was washing when he heard me coming down the hall.

They followed me and stood in my doorway in their day-off

outfits, Mom in ripped jeans and a Mickey Mouse baseball shirt, Dad in a Patriots cap and sweats.

"What happened?" Dad asked.

As I unpacked, I gave them a careful summary, being sure to leave out the curse words and the sobbing. Before I could finish, Mom came across the room and yanked me up into a hug.

"I shouldn't have let you go," she said quietly.

"It wasn't that bad," I said, my heart trying to decide between sadness and anger. "Not going would have been worse."

"But we weren't there, Sammie," she said, pulling back to look at me. Wisps of her hair were coming out, crossing her face, her eyes wet. She looked young, unsure. I didn't like it. My stomach hurt. I didn't like making her look like this.

"Okay." I tried to peel her off slowly. "We've got to be strong. We're going to make a plan—"

"Sammie, just slow down a minute," Dad said, and his voice was higher than normal.

I looked back at them, waiting. "What? What do you want me to do?"

Dad swallowed. "No, I just—nothing. Do you get what I'm saying?"

No. I didn't. Especially when he talked to me in that *poor baby*, Santa-Claus-doesn't-exist voice. I threw a shirt into my closet. "I can't slow down. I can't stop. I can't go back in time and not go to Nationals."

Dad spoke fast, lifting his cap and running his hands through his curly hair. "What if you had been on the street, Sammie? What if you had forgotten where you were and wandered into a dangerous place? What if you had gotten lost?"

"We just need to make sure we can help you!" Mom put on a sweet smile through her tears. She looked and sounded just like Davy, trying to coax a chicken back into the coop. *Here, chicky! Come on, chicky!*

I didn't like this conversation. I don't like hypotheticals, especially considering I had already gotten over it. I already had my crying time about how much it sucked, and now I didn't want those feelings to come back just because my parents wanted to cry about it. No, thank you.

"Sammie? Earth to Sammie?" Dad asked.

I tossed a pair of pants in the closet. Don't know why I even bothered unpacking, I was just putting the same pile of clothes into yet another pile. "You need more information, is what you're saying."

"We need to make sure we're not going to lose you," Dad said.

That stopped me.

Mom crossed her arms and cleared her throat. "This is the first time you'd left and we weren't sure what state you were going to be in when you came back."

Right then she sounded more like Mom and less like a kid, more like the *mmhmms* and the exhaustion and the pushing and pushing she did all day, almost never losing patience.

I think I was beginning to know what they meant. But that didn't mean I agreed with them.

I walked toward Mom and grabbed her hand, and grabbed Dad's hand with my other one, and we sat on the floor in my room. That felt right, that felt calm and stable. We used to sit this way as they read to me, a stack of library books in the middle. Then later, as I read to them, the littler kids draped over their bodies.

"So, what's this plan, Sammie?" Dad picked up a paperback copy of *A Wrinkle in Time*, flipping through it as he spoke. "How are we going to make sure that you're taken care of if *something like this* happens again?"

Much better. This, I could handle. That is, I could handle it if they listened and didn't argue with me and let me do whatever I wanted.

"If the memory loss continues at the same rate, I might have a slight episode every four months. This is assuming that I would have an episode at all. With those odds, I see very little need to panic."

My mom laughed drily. "Ha."

Dad said, "Dr. Clarkington told us—"

"Dr. Clarkington doesn't have enough information about someone my age with this disease."

Dad shook his head. "The fact that you have the capacity to lose your bearings is enough information for me."

Mom agreed. "Once is already too many times."

"Goddamnit." I thought we had gotten past this part. I let go of their hands. "I love you both so much but you can be so *stupid* sometimes."

"Watch it," Mom said.

"The specialist told everything he knew to Dr. Clarkington. What more do you want? Do you want me to leave and go live in Minnesota so I can rot at the Mayo Clinic? "

"Don't get worked up," Dad cautioned.

"Is that what you want?" I couldn't look at their close-to-tears faces so I kept my eyes on the ceiling.

I heard Mom mutter, "That is the last thing you say to Sammie when she's worked up."

"I know everything is scary but *I'm* the one going through it, okay? And I get to decide how to feel about it. Which is very, like, practical. And rational. You should be glad that I'm not depressed, like that girl from"—I brought my gaze back to both of them— "Michigan who found out she had leukemia and got suicidal!"

"Christ, Sammie . . ." Dad said.

Mom looked toward the hallway, making sure Bette and Davy hadn't overheard.

"Read about it in the *Detroit Times*! It's a real thing! I'm happy, I'm focused, and I will do everything to get better. Except for compromise on my goals. Ralph Waldo Emerson once said, once said . . ." I was flustered. "He once said . . ."

"Samantha," my mother said. "Listen to me."

"Okay!" My fists were clenched. She waited. "Okay."

"We can't be around all the time to monitor your health . . ."

I opened my mouth to protest.

". . . and we might not always know what to do anyway," Mom said, holding her hands up. "So you've got to, you've *got to* help us. You've got be smart."

"Are you kidding?"

"Smart doesn't always mean grades and vocabulary and all that, Sammie. We need you to be realistic."

Dad started in, too. "Start preparing for the future."

"What do you think I've been doing for the past eighteen years of my life?"

"No, I don't mean that, I mean a future where . . ." Suddenly, he stopped, and I didn't know why. Mom was looking straight ahead, but I noticed one of her arms was behind him where he sat. Pinching him, probably. She did not want him to go on. Now, *that*. That pushed a button—maybe because they worked so much and were rarely together, I wasn't used to the magnetism of their powers combined. Jupiter and Mars aligned. Those bastards. The two biological sources of all my strength and weakness in one place. They think they're protecting me. But I know them as well as they think they know me.

"Well," I said. I swallowed, and went on. "I am no longer competing in debate, so I will be able to focus my efforts on completing the year without incident."

"Good. And resting," my mom said.

"And maintaining my status as valedictorian."

Dad moved one of my clogs to match it with other, making a pair on the floor. "And visiting the doctor."

"And finding a *new* doctor that we trust in New York City."

Dad nodded. "We'll take it one day at a time."

I nodded with him. "Yes, one day at a time, moving toward next year. I agree."

Mom put her hand on my hand. "Okay," she said. She smiled at me less with her mouth, and more with her eyes. "Yes."

And that was that.

But now I'm here, back at the attic window, and things look

dark. I am not dumb, Future Sam. I am not blind to the tone with which my parents speak to me, and the bright-eyed choo-choo-train innocence with which I respond. *Next year! I'll get better! I'm fine! I can beat this!*

I even speak strategically to you.

Because the truth is that my memory loss was much worse than I had described it here. Before I remembered who Maddie was, I was inches away from drooling and taking her hand on the debate platform like a little kid lost at a playground, asking her to take me home to Mommy and Daddy.

I don't know how long I was quiet up there, blinking and looking around, before I called "time-out." It felt like hours.

No matter what plans I make, no matter how much I help my parents, I feel like my body is failing me, and I don't know how to stop it.

SPEAKING OF PITS OF DESPAIR, DON'T SPEAK

I just went to get a glass of water (thanks for the reminder to hydrate, Zavesca!), and I could hear them talking downstairs.

"There's no way," Dad was saying.

"But what's the point of telling her that?" Mom whispered back. "You know what that would do."

"I'm on her side! We're both on her side! I want her to go and live and be happy. But how are we supposed to ignore fuckin' science, Gia?"

"Stop cursing."

"I'm serious!" Dad's voice was almost raised now.

Mom made a shushing noise. "She's doing great right now. I don't think anything will get worse for a long time. She gets to just . . . be herself. I refuse to treat her any differently."

"This isn't cancer, G. The thought of her . . . forgetting to do things, or forgetting where she is, or forgetting who we are."

"I know."

Long silence. A couple of sniffs. I wondered if they could hear me listening. I held my breath.

"She only has a few weeks until school is over," Mom finally said. "I say we let things take their course."

"You're right," Dad said.

"Really?"

"Yeah. We take all the safety precautions, but we don't, you know, force her into a cocoon. The specialist said it was better that she doesn't get depressed."

"Exactly."

I hate that word. To hear it was just like it sounded, like two giant hands pressing down on me from above and below. I'm not *depressed*. I may be *pressed*, sure. I've got a limited timeline and lots to do, and sometimes the pressure is a lot, and sometimes it feels like I'm just pushing myself onward for the sake of pushing myself, but I am not *depressed*.

Dad continued. "But we'll just agree together that, no, she is just not in a place to go to New York next year."

"Agreed," Mom said.

I let out my breath. Red flashed in the dark, and I realized I had my eyes squeezed shut.

"Thank you," I could hear Mom say.

"For what?"

"For being on my team."

Then I could hear them kissing. Ew.

I almost went downstairs to argue, but then I stopped. I remembered a key phrase. Dad said, she IS not in a place to go to New York next year. *Is*. Of course they would say that right after an episode. They're only thinking of the *present*. You and I know,

Future Sam, that the present is merely a road to something else. Whatever's ahead.

The other good thing to come out of this is that they're not going to try to take me out of school again, at least that's what it sounds like. So, this is bargaining, Future Sam.

This is where they give you an inch, and inch by inch, you take a mile.

I mean, sure, they'll say, *Sammie can finish out the school year, but can she keep her grades up?*

I mean, sure, Sammie can keep her grades up, but can she be valedictorian?

I mean, sure, Sammie can be valedictorian, but can she make it through a semester at NYU?

And so on. So I'll just show them I can do those things. I can do them all. And then they won't be able to stop me from going to college, not when I've proved to them I can do it.

They'll see.

TASK FORCE

In order to become less *pressed*, and to achieve my goals episode-free, I have assembled an NPC task force of my favorite feminist icons, each in charge of inspiring me in a different way. I cut out pictures of them and arranged them on my wall, and wrote quotes in marker in little speech bubbles. Good thing no one ever comes into my room because this is the cheesiest thing since the invention of cheese (5500 B.C., in what is now Kujawy, Poland).

The NPC Task Force includes:

ELIZABETH WARREN

Purpose: researching as much about the disease as possible and making sure health providers are straight-talking to my parents, and not taking advantage of us for insurance money.

BEYONCÉ

Purpose: reminding me that I'm flawless, and that I'm an independent woman. Or rather, girl. Even if Stuart rejects me, I will love myself.

(Still haven't heard from him about when exactly he wants to get coffee. Whatever. Independent girl.)

MALALA YOUSAFZAI

Purpose: helping me remember to be less selfish, and that young women can do a lot. I always think about what I'll do when I'm older, but she was like, no, I will do good for the world now, even though I'm only a teenager.

SERENA WILLIAMS

Purpose: learning something new (tennis), which is supposedly good for people with memory loss. Taking better care of my body and not being afraid to be a "jock." I'll probably need new muscles if my old ones grow weaker.

NANCY CLARKINGTON

Well, this woman is literally my doctor so I have to trust her expertise and listen to everything she says. I asked her for her cell phone number so I could text her questions anytime, day or night, just in case. Is that weird?

No matter what happens, I can't have an episode like I did at Nationals, at least not until my grades are in and my status as valedictorian remains intact.

If I'm going to deal with all this stuff, I'll need to be more than just inspired, I will need to be even *more* strategic. I will need different methods than what worked before. I need to put my best self forward, and hope I don't run out of it too soon.

YES, YES, YES

Stuart Shah: Hang Wednesday?

NO ONE CARES AS MUCH AS WE DO

A few days later, the sun is soaking through the walls and the daffodils are out and the birds are singing and inside my stomach it feels like horses are running, which I assume is just the biological thing that happens when your chemicals combine with someone else's. Stuart had asked me to meet him outside on the benches after school, because apparently he lives near there, and he figured we could walk into town.

I was wearing my favorite outfit besides my debate pantsuit, a dress my mom bought for me for church two years ago, a light blue cotton thing with a V neck, and I had let my hair go without the dryer this morning so it hung loose and curly near my shoulders. I didn't know if I looked hot, but after an imaginary conversation with Maddie, I decided I didn't care. I remembered her looking at herself in the mirror and saying, *According to whom?*

I had just finished my calculus homework, and Stuart walked up right as I closed the textbook. He was wearing his usual black and sunglasses. He walked quickly.

"Sammie!" he said. "Hi!"

I stood, shoving my work into my bag. "Hey."

When he was close enough to touch, he stopped. He took off his sunglasses, and I could tell he was looking at my dress. I followed his eyes, hoping I hadn't spilled something on it. When we met each other's gaze again, he seemed nervous.

"It's been a while," he said.

"A week," I said.

He smiled. I smiled back.

"What do you want to do?" he asked.

"Walk somewhere?"

"Yeah."

And then we couldn't shut up. We walked close, arms touching sometimes, first along the footpaths, then in town, Stuart waving occasionally to people he knew. He asked questions one after the other, like a nice reporter. *What schools did you face? Where did you stay? Had you been to Boston before?*

When I told him about the loss (leaving out some possibly pertinent details), I could see him wince. He put his hand briefly around my shoulders and squeezed, which sent a confusing combination to my gut: a punch that would happen whenever I thought about the loss, along with a fluttering that happened whenever any part of Stuart's body got within six inches of my body.

"That sounds terrible," he said, and told me about how on the last night of his run of *Hamlet*, he forgot an entire soliloquy. "On the last night! I'd done it a thousand times!"

"I didn't hear about that," I said, trying to remember if I actually hadn't.

"Yeah, because no one noticed."

"No?" I asked.

"Nope! And even if they did, they wouldn't have cared."

"You just went on with the show?"

"Yep, and no one was the wiser. But I'll remember it forever. Because I failed."

"Yeah. I'll remember the debate tournament forever, too." *I think*, I remember adding silently.

Stuart and I moved out of the way for two Dartmouth students skateboarding down the sidewalk. "Maybe we depend too much on other people for what we think of as success," Stuart offered. "Like, maybe we share too much. Maybe that's why good things lose their good feeling because we give it all away."

"As in, success can't just be when people notice you."

"Right. That's the funny thing about caring about stuff as much as we do," he said. "We have to get used to the idea that no one cares as much as us, because guess what, they don't. Succeed, fail, whatever, no one is going to give you a pat on the back for spending all hours of the day studying, or researching, or giving up everything to write. So we've got to just do it for ourselves."

By the time his speech was over, Stuart was standing in the middle of the sidewalk. He could never seem to walk and talk at the same time, especially if he was passionate about the subject. It was cute.

Then I realized he was contradicting himself. "But you did get a pat on the back!" I said. "You're published!"

He stopped walking again, and this time he was more serious. "But what if I hadn't been published?"

"You . . ." I swallowed. "Yeah, all you would have to fall back on is whatever you liked about what you did."

"Exactly. And I would probably be working twice as hard now," he muttered.

"I know what you mean," I replied. I thought of Mom and Dad, and that awful phrase, *recognize your limitations*. Maybe what he was saying went the other way, too. All the limitations Mom and Dad were talking about were just the limitations put on me by *other people*. I was going for *my own* goals.

We continued walking, quiet. Heavy stuff, I guess.

I had gone in trying to keep it *super casual*, Future Sam. Like rel-a-a-a-xed. No big deal. But that wasn't me. And I wanted to melt with relief to discover that it wasn't him, either.

He broke the silence with, "What are you reading?" and of course, the flow was back, because I'm reading a book about this amazing alternative to capitalism called "heterodox economics," which basically says that economics as we know it is tied to . . . oh, wait. Sorry. Anyway.

We stopped for iced coffee and sat on the grass on the Dartmouth campus. I saw the spring-clad bodies everywhere and thought of that SAT word, *languid*.

"So how do you get around New York?" I asked.

"If I have time, I just walk everywhere. The subway is only faster if you have to go between boroughs."

"Really? That doesn't seem physically possible."

He put up his hands in surrender. "Okay, that's not always true. I just like walking."

"But you're able to get everywhere on time?"

"I don't have a very, uh, strict schedule."

"You just write all day?"

He squinted, almost as if it were painful that I asked. "I try. I also work as a barback a couple nights a week at this place downtown. Basically it's just wearing all black and listening to rich people's conversations, so it's ideal. It's what I would do anyway," he said, and laughed.

Stuart did an impression of a snobby woman ordering a cocktail. "And make *sure* the lime juice comes from a locally sourced *lime tree*, I don't care if limes don't grow here."

"And the ice is from a glacial *stream* . . ." I added.

"And the glass from a Swedish *glassblower* . . ."

We laughed so hard I snorted.

I was feeling the echolocation again, the waves of energy coming off his body as he leaned on the earth while I remained upright, conscious of the shaving nicks on my bare legs.

His nose, straight except for one bump near the end, where he must have broken it.

He has a freckle on his collarbone.

He gave me a sip of his iced coffee and I just did it, I just put my mouth on the straw, and he didn't care.

I am learning:

There is no secret language, Future Sam, that you have to speak in order to talk to someone you like. You just talk to them. Bonus points if they can speak intelligently about life and work and the best coffee shops in Manhattan.

I had imagined Stuart moving down the sidewalks of New York with his long strides, passing everyone, head down, thinking of settings and dialogue and characters, but here he was now, very different. Softer. More relaxed.

And maybe there might be a softer version of myself, too.

You don't have to be a robot, Future Sam. What you're doing doesn't have to be going *toward* something. Sometimes you can stop, or at least pause. Sometimes you can just be.

Anyway, eventually Stuart had to leave to work at the Canoe Club, where he was picking up a couple of bartending shifts while he was back in Hanover.

We stood up.

He looked at me for a long time with those wet black eyes, and bent slowly toward my face. Oh my god, he was getting very close. Radioactive burns imminent. I gasped.

He stepped back quickly. "Sorry. Can I kiss you on the cheek?" he asked.

"Is that standard?" I asked, and immediately blushed.

"Standard for what?" he asked.

"A standard good-bye for what we . . . for what just happened?" Remember how you had *just decided* that you don't have to be a robot?

He didn't answer right away. Now he was nervous. He played with the hair on the back of his head, looking around. "What just happened?"

"I mean, what we did today. Hanging out."

"Uh . . ." Stuart tried to hold in a smile. He shrugged, looking off into the distance, then looked at me. "We don't have to categorize it."

"Let's categorize it," I said quickly, and waited. Stuart opened his mouth, puzzling, and I felt guilty, briefly, for pushing him, but then I didn't. A kiss without context or meaning is the kiss equivalent of small talk. And what would happen if he *didn't* want to categorize it, and just ran away forever and didn't talk to me? I'd go back to my work, to my little room above the attic, pining for him from afar. Big deal. I'm used to it. What else is new? "Sorry," I continued. "I just have too much up in the air right now to fuck around."

"You do not . . ." he said, laughing, shaking his head. "You do not fuck around."

He put on his sunglasses against the setting sun, and the lenses lit up with two blazing spheres. He took one of my hands with both his hands and said, "I want to kiss you on the cheek because I think we had a nice date."

Date. *Date.* I nodded in agreement.

He bent again and pressed his lips on my cheek, barely an inch from my own lips—one-one thousand, two-one thousand, three—and let go.

UUGGHHGHGHGHGHGGGGHHHHHH

Then the other shoe drops. When I got home, an email from Mrs. Townsend dinged on my phone:

Sammie,

I was sorry to hear about your debate loss. Don't sweat it, kid! Hope you are healthy and rested. I also wanted you to know: Though they are not aware of specifics, I have informed your teachers of extenuating circumstances, and I have asked them to come directly to me with any issues or concerns.

I know you've got a heavy load these days, so I wanted to make you aware of the following assignments you may have missed over Nationals week:

AP Chem

- Chapter 14–15 Review
- Chapter 16 Review
- Chapter 14–16 PreTest

Ceramics

- bowl with glaze

As we approach the end of the year, especially finals, please let me know how I can help. TAKE YOUR TIME.

And come visit me. I miss you.

—Mrs. T

How did I miss those due dates? They were written down on my calendar, on this very computer, on the same desktop as this very document. Green for biology, blue for AP Lit, orange for AP Euro, brown for ceramics, and yellow for chemistry. It's right fucking there! I'm looking at them so hard they're burning a hole in my retina!

This is freaky. I do not like this.

I followed the path of each color through the days left on the calendar—just a few weeks—and double recorded each assignment and test coming up, once on my computer, once in my planner.

After I was finished, I noticed a new color, bright purple, an hour every day on the week leading up to graduation. On the day I graduate, it takes up the entire calendar.

It reads *Valedictorian speech.*

I flashback to my parents' whispers, *Agreed,* and wondered how many inches I had taken in the long mile toward making them believe. Was I really fooling anyone? I picture blinking against the lights as I come through the Sheraton blackness, Maddie looking at me, angry, and the fear so cutting I want to cry.

I could blow the whole thing in a second, and if I do, NYU is gone.

Shit.

ALTERNATIVE RESOURCES, PHASE ONE

So I was in the corner of the ceramics studio, skipping lunch, scraping and kneading the hell out of wet clay, sweating with the effort. My chemistry homework was open on a stool next to me. I was pausing every few seconds to write the answers, then going back to molding this godforsaken bowl, which at this point looks more like the alcoholic cousin of a bowl, loopy and friendly and just not functional at all, like my dad's cousin Tim, who at family gatherings always asks me when I'm going to put my brain to good use and go on *Jeopardy!* and win him some money; reason #5,666 why I need to keep said brain intact and get the hell out of here.

Anyway, in walked Coop, shutting the door behind him. He pulled out a Baggie and a pack of Zig Zag rolling papers from his back pocket.

"Sammie?"

I turned off the wheel. "Yeah, what are you doing?"

"Hey," he said, not answering, and he giggled and walked over. In addition to the pocket for weed paraphernalia, Coop's Carhartts had another back pocket for a folded-up notebook, and in the side pocket, a row of mechanical pencils.

"Nice storage facility," I said, pointing at his pants with a muddy finger.

He sat across from me, pulling a stool between his legs, and began to work, hunched over like a craftsman, delicately pinching and sprinkling little green stubs. A strand of his hair fell in his eyes and he blew it back, brow furrowed. "Yeah," he muttered. "Backpacks get too hot this time of year."

"Were you really just coming in here to roll a J?"

"It's my lunch routine," he said, licking the edge of the paper with a shrug. "Then I saw you. So. What are you doing?"

"Catching up."

"Oh, from Nationals, huh."

"How did you know?"

"You told me that night at church. Plus, everyone was talking about it. I mean, not that you lost, but everyone was like, whoa, we went to Nationals in debate? People get excited about that stuff. I was bragging, like, 'I know that girl.'"

I laughed. Coop rolled the impeccable little cylinder between his fingertips.

"But now I'm screwed." I pointed to my chem homework, also muddy. "Not screwed, but. You remember . . ." I paused, wondering if we should get into this again. But Coop hadn't told anyone after I had asked him to keep it quiet at the party. Which was nice. "You know how part of the disease is memory loss?"

"Yeah," Coop said. "How is that going? Are you okay?"

"I forgot all these assignments. I *never* forget assignments. Never. And now I'm scared I will forget stuff during a test, or forget my speech at graduation, or . . ."

Coop smiled a lazy smile, and put the joint behind his ear. "So you're worried you're going to be normal."

I gave him a little punch. "No . . ."

"Those are all the things I worry about, all the time."

I considered that for a minute, and glanced at the joint. "Yeah, but you could just, I don't know, stop smoking so much?"

He looked up at the ceiling, pretending to think, and back at me, shrugging. "But if the valedictorian is worrying about the same shit, then what's the point?"

Then I had an idea. "Can I ask you something?"

Coop leaned on the stool with his forearms and looked at me like there was nothing else in the world he'd rather do than answer my question. "Shoot, Samantha."

"How do you get by in school without flunking?"

"Hmm," he said, drumming his fingertips on his biceps.

"I mean, how do you make sure you pass even when you're, like . . ." I glanced at the joint again. "Mentally altered?"

"Well, first of all, I don't just 'get by.' I get okay grades."

"I know."

"How do you know?" he asked, and it had been a while since I saw Coop's surprised face. Probably since we were kids.

"I always look for the names of people I know on the honor roll."

"Oh." Coop started in again. Granted, he probably was high, but he was also going deep. "Well, I don't 'do' a lot of 'work.'"

He held up quotation symbols. "I learn what needs to be learned, which is mostly how to effectively communicate that I have learned something, without actually learning it. Do you follow?"

"I do." I watched this side of Coop with fascination—it was far from the stoner, "I don't give a crap" person I had assumed he had turned into since we stopped being friends.

"For example," he continued. "With your memory thing. I don't memorize things. That takes too much time. Instead, I set up opportunities for . . . alternative resources. Like phones, or makeup tests, or other kind souls who happen to be near me."

As he spoke, I thought of the colors on my calendar bleeding together, all the dates, all the assignments, all the moments that I might look away from my paper and look back to see nothing but numbers or words that meant nothing to me, having no one to reach out to and call "time-out," flubbing test after test until they let me graduate out of pity.

Coop was still leaning forward, watching me formulate. "What is that look on your face?" he asked.

"Can you show me this stuff?"

"What stuff?"

"All these alternative resources you have."

He tilted his head. "Are you asking me how to cheat?"

I sighed. I didn't want to say *yes*, but as Mom always says, "Call a spade a spade." I have tried doing it the old way, Future Sam, the honest way, where I work hard, and study, and memorize, and look where that got me. Plus, it's just two weeks out of four years. The morality scale is still tipped in my favor, right?

"Yes."

Coop smiled and winked, and sure, at that moment, I could see why girls wanted him to be the foundation to their human pyramid.

"Okay," he said, sliding each tool back into its rightful pocket. "Come over whenever."

A SCENE FROM PROVINCIAL LIFE: IN WHICH MOM SWITCHES TEAMS (FOR NOW)

Mom is doling out spaghetti in heaping bowls while I take notes on José Saramago's *Blindness* for AP Lit and try not to think about how Maddie was *still* giving me the silent treatment at school. Dad's on his way home from work. Harrison is taking his computer time. Bette is under the table, cutting out construction paper shapes for god knows what. Davy is also under the table, playing a game she likes to call "Little Mermaid," where she wears one of Mom's bras, collects all the forks, and doesn't talk, only gestures at things with wide eyes unless you pour water into her mouth.

Davy tugs on my jeans, pointing at her bowl of spaghetti, then at Mom near the stove, and then at me.

"What?" I ask. "That's your spaghetti."

She points at mine, which is covered in sauce, and shakes her head.

"Oh, no sauce?"

She nods fervently.

"Mom," I say. "Davy wants to make sure you don't put sauce on her spaghetti."

"I don't play Little Mermaid," Mom says, sitting down to dig in. "Not after the toilet incident."

Once, Davy had been so committed to Little Mermaid, she wouldn't tell Harrison where the toothpaste was, so he splashed her with water from the toilet. Davy looked at me with pleading eyes.

I took a little from my glass of water and poured it on her head. Davy gasped.

"No sauce, please!" Davy said, giggling, wiping the drips from her eyes.

"Can I have a fork from your collection?" I asked.

She took one from the floor. I wiped it on my jeans. Clean enough.

Bette's voice rose from under the table. "Who's Stuart?"

I ducked down. She was cross-legged, holding my phone, as casual as could be.

"Give me that." I reached out.

Bette giggled, shaking the phone. "Stuart says . . ." she started, staring at the screen. "How about you come to the Canoe . . ."

"Who's Stuart?" Mom asked.

"Give me it!" I yelled.

"You don't have to raise your voice," Mom said.

"Fine . . ." Bette said, and tossed the phone on the ground.

I shoved the phone in my pocket. We ate in silence for a while. I thought they had forgotten until Harrison yelled from the other room.

"Who's Stuart?"

Stuart: How about you come to the Canoe Club while I work tomorrow night? It's a Tuesday so it'll be slow. You could sit at the bar and do your hw. Keep me company.

Me: Yeah!

Later, I ask Mom and Dad while they're reading in the living room, Mom's feet propped on Dad's lap.

"Can I go to the Canoe Club tomorrow night?"

Mom turns her head to look at me. "Will there be a trained first responder in the building?"

I consider this. Technically, most people who work at restaurants are, like, legally required to be first responders.

"Yes," I said.

"Who?"

I'm terrible at lying. God, I'm awful. Whenever I try to lie, my tongue dries up. I'm like a messed-up version of Pinocchio. I hope you get over this, Future Sam. I am not unaware that lying is part of the legal profession. I just always hoped that it never had to come to that.

"Whoever the manager of the Canoe Club is," I say.

"Who is that?" Dad counters.

"I don't know, but whoever it is, that person is legally required to be a first responder." Then I add, "I think," very quietly, because my tongue was starting to get dry again.

"I don't think so," Dad says, looking back at his Stan Grumman novel.

"What, you think I'm going to have a *seizure* in the middle of the *Canoe Club*? Come on."

"Yes," Dad says without glancing up from his book. "That's the risk."

Not my best, I'll admit it. I regain composure.

"Sammie . . ." Mom sighs. "Don't you want to concentrate on school?"

"Yes, but I also don't want to be a robot who has one week of high school left and will graduate having never gone on one date."

This time, both parents turn their heads. Mom is smiling. Dad is not.

Everything else out of my mouth sounds like I'm trying to sell a curling iron on late-night TV. "I'm just doing homework while my friend works! He said it's slow on a Tuesday! I was going to walk over there after school! You can pick me up right after!"

"Okay," Mom says, and starts nudging Dad with her elbow.

"Really?"

"Yeah!"

"Gia . . ." Dad says to my mom quietly.

I clear my throat. Of course, I had saved a little tidbit as the clincher. "In the event of an emergency, the medical center is closer to the Canoe Club than it is to this house."

"True!" Mom says, elbowing Dad again.

"Ow!" Dad looks at me. "Fine."

COME ON

On the drive to school today I passed three fishermen walking next to 89 through the scrub in their Carhartt overalls, carrying their red bait coolers, waders slung over their shoulders. They were on their way to the Connecticut, probably, and when I crossed over the bridge outside of Hanover, I had an urge to pull over and take off my shoes. I didn't, because I had to finish some calc, but I realized I hadn't waded in the creek by our house since the summer when I was eight or nine.

Anyway, I was sort of floaty through the halls at school, wondering about life and Stuart and how fishing actually works when I noticed Maddie sitting on the floor next to her locker with a few people and the same sort of easy feeling came over me, so I walked up to her and said hello, as if I had done it every day, or as if we hadn't fought the last time we saw each other.

They were in the middle of laughing, and Maddie nodded, smiling.

"Hey," she said back, friendly enough.

Super casual. Re-l-a-a-a-x.

"Guess wha-a-a-at?" I said, holding my hands out.

"What?" she asked, glancing at the people around her.

"Stuart and I are going on a date!"

"Cool," she said in a monotone, and smiled with her lips closed.

I don't know what I expected, I guess some form of recognition, maybe something that sounded like it included an exclamation mark, considering she was there and mostly responsible for the first time Stuart and I actually spoke.

"Yeah . . ." I said. "It is!"

Maddie pulled out her phone, which, as we know, means *this conversation is over.* But I wasn't ready for it to be over. Things were finally looking up for me. I wanted her to be there to see that. I wanted to share it with her.

I bent nearer. "So, like, can we talk?"

Maddie was still scrolling through pictures.

"I feel like your mom was right," I started. My mouth was feeling Zavesca dry. "That we needed some space, and I just wanted to apologize."

No response. Her thumb moved faster. Maybe I wasn't getting my point across.

"I'm trying to say I'm sorry for not telling you about . . ." I looked at her friends, who were also scrolling. "You know."

"Damn, girl," Maddie said suddenly, putting her arms to her knees. "Can you not read social cues?"

I stood straight. I remember making a noise that I hated, like a child who is told they can't have dessert. "I can . . ." I started, then stopped, and kind of just stood there, staring.

Maddie stood and pulled me aside a few feet away. I could tell that she was still mad at me, but it was just a relief she was even responding.

"I'll say it for you directly into your face. You hurt me by not telling me."

I tried on a smile. "And I'm sorry! We're on the same page! That's what I'm trying to say!"

"Sammie, I'm not done."

"Okay," I said. She could keep going forever, as long as we were friends again. I breathed a sigh of relief (prematurely, as it turned out).

"I don't know how to handle you being sick."

I sucked the air back in, letting it sink through me with her words. But they didn't land anywhere that made sense. "What do you mean?"

Maddie put her hands into a prayer position. Her nails were painted deep purple. "Suddenly we're friends, right when you get sick? You never wanted to hang out with me before, outside of debate. But now it's like, you need someone to bring all your woes and sadness and realizations about life to, and I'm the most convenient instafriend."

"That's not—"

"I'm just saying . . . I made a huge effort to be real friends, and you can't even tell me the truth of what's going on in your life? No, you're too obsessed with your own stuff, too busy with the Sammie show."

I threw up my hands. "The Sammie show?" Me? The person

who could barely peel herself off the wall at a party? The person who talked to a computer instead of people? What the hell was she talking about?

"I mean, you aren't always like that, Sammie," Maddie said, closing her eyes briefly. She opened them again. "I was exaggerating. But I avoided you because I was afraid you would use me as, like, emotional support, whenever it was convenient for you, without giving any back. And of course I could never question you, because you're sick and you should have what you want . . ."

"I would never do that," I said quietly.

"People do it without realizing it," she replied. "It's not their fault."

I just looked at her, waiting. Now I was afraid to talk, for fear I was dumping something on her.

Maddie put her hands on the side of her face and sighed, looking at me. "Does what I'm saying make sense? I don't know. Maybe I'm putting too much of my own shit into this."

I swallowed and said the smallest thing I could think of. "I'm really confused."

"Me too," she said, and the bell rang for first period.

JUST A TUESDAY,
LIKE ANY OTHER TUESDAY

I AM FREAKING OUT. Stuart texted again, telling me he gets off work at six p.m., so I would be heading there after school toward the end of his shift and hanging out with him for three hours at the very least. AT THE VERY LEAST.

Okay, I text him.

"What time will you be coming in?" he asks.

If I respond within five minutes, is that too eager?

What if I'm trying to do to Stuart what Maddie said I was doing to her?

But I wasn't doing that to her. I swear to you and all the saints, Future Sam, that I was never trying to use Maddie.

I can't tell Stuart about NPC. Who knows how he'll react. If he freaks like Maddie, then I'd be down to no one.

Is ten minutes too long, like I'm not interested, more of a friend thing?

I go with eight minutes, because he had taken the initiative to text me first, but I realize I pretty much forced him into saying it was a date the last time we hung out. So, right in between. Statistically sound.

Oh my god, I only have one nice outfit, which I already used. My glasses are smudged. I'm wearing clogs, cutoffs, and a huge sweatshirt that says DAN & WHIT'S SURPLUS because Puppy threw up all over the clean laundry this morning and my only other option was a shirt my dad bought me as a joke that says GOT CHOCOLATE MILK?, which, of course, has a chocolate milk stain by the collar because, yes, I do "got chocolate milk," thank you very much.

This is an outfit that says, "I am just a normal, ambitious, laid-back young woman who does not have a debilitating disease." Right?

It is not traditionally feminine, but if Elizabeth Warren worried about what she wore, she wouldn't have time to condemn corrupt banking practices. Oh god, he said, "See you in a bit." Okay, I will see him in a bit. I will see him in a bit for the second date of my entire life and perhaps the last because watch me forget my own name. Watch me enter the Canoe Club and everyone I know is there, like an intervention. And the entire NPC Clubhouse (as I have taken to calling them after receiving two newsletters) is there with their wheelchairs and tropical shirts to say, *Surprise! We paid your crush to pretend to like you so that you wouldn't feel more socially alienated than you already are! But you're one of us now! You're a shooting star!*

Maybe I should be nicer to people.

Maybe I should have worn the chocolate milk shirt.

Oh god. Screw him. I mean, *it*. Sorry. I meant "screw it." Freudian slip.

HUMANS HAVE BEEN DOING THIS FOR CENTURIES: A LESSON IN ANATOMY

The Canoe Club used to be a place I had only walked past, that my parents had only gone to on anniversaries, that Dartmouth students take their grandparents to when they're in town. But now it feels like mine forever.

The sidewalk in front of it is mine forever.

The turn we took to Stuart's house is mine.

His driveway is mine.

I'll start from the beginning.

When I walked in, Stuart was wiping down the lacquered wooden bar with a white rag in front of rows and rows of bottles that stood in the interior of a giant, hollow canoe hung on the wall. He was wearing a black button-down shirt with the sleeves rolled up. When he noticed me, he came around the bar and gave me a hug. I remember how long he held me, and the way my fingertips felt on the muscles near his spine. I had never been this close to another human, in that way, at least. Never contemplated someone else's bones.

I set my backpack on the leather seat next to me, one seat over from a middle-aged woman who was reading a book, drinking a pint of dark beer under the green-shaded hanging lights, the only other customer at the bar.

"How was your day?" Stuart asked.

"Fine," I said, trying not to let my teeth chatter with nerves, or maybe it was just cold—why did every place have to keep the AC set to freezing? I watched his hands, twisting a glass under a streaming tap of water, and shaking it dry, adding it to a stack. "How was yours?"

"Just doing this," he said, glancing at me, shaking dry another glass. "And trying to write."

"Are you on a deadline?" I asked, catching his eyes again as he began to slice up one of a long row of limes and toss the wedges into plastic bins.

"Always," he said, giving me a little smile, which filled me with relief for some reason. "What are you working on? Finals?"

"Almost," I said. "Preparing."

"Must be hard when the weather's this nice," he said.

"It doesn't make much difference to me," I said, pretending to play with my coaster.

"No more parties?"

"Ha! No. Ross's was my first and last." *Remember*, I told myself. *You don't have to be a robot.* "Probably."

Stuart finished, wiping his hands on his apron. "What about graduation? I went so crazy the night before mine, I almost overslept. I had to run to the stadium with nothing on under my robe but my boxers because I didn't have time to get dressed!"

"Well." I swallowed. "That's definitely not an option—I have to wear more than underwear under my robe—"

We both blushed. Stuart looked at my sweatshirt.

"—because I'm giving a speech," I finished.

"That's right," he said, shaking his head slowly.

"What?" I asked, looking at him.

"Nothing," he said, and kept his black eyes on mine. "That's so *cool.*"

Those words coming out of his mouth, out of his body under his clothes, he might as well have written them on my skin again.

The middle-aged woman cleared her throat. "Could I bother you for another, Stu?"

"Oh! Yes. Of course." As he refilled the woman's glass, Stuart said, "What a day for you to come in, Sammie, because this is also— well, this is Mariana Oliva."

"Hello," I said, and we shook hands across the seats. The woman had gray streaks in her long brown hair, and laugh lines on her copper-colored skin.

Stuart gestured toward her as she took a sip. "She's one of my idols."

"Oh, do you teach at Dartmouth?"

"No, I live in Mexico City," Mariana said. "I'm just here to do a little reading later this week."

Stuart kept looking back and forth between me and the writer. "Her book *Under the Bridge* is probably one of my favorites of all time."

"Thank you," Mariana said, lifting her glass to Stuart. "You're kind."

Stuart and Mariana got deep into a conversation about first-person narration versus third person, and I felt like what I guess sports fans must feel like when they watch their favorite team play, but the sport they played would change every few minutes, and the ball would change, and the arena.

Mariana and Stuart had something to say about everything under the sun.

On Shakespeare: "He was not one man. A group of sexually confused friends, trying to one up one another."

On small dogs: "Little rats. Little neurotic rats."

On the moon landing: "I believe it happened. Then again, I also believe in astrology, so take that with a grain of salt."

On novels as a dying art: "Novels reflect a country's consciousness. If we say they are dying, then we admit failure. It depends on if you're ready to do that."

"I'm not," Stuart said.

"Me neither," she said, and they shook hands.

They included me, and I spoke up when I could, but mostly I listened. "What do you think, Sammie?" Stuart would ask.

And eventually I just had to tell them that most of the time, I didn't know. "I'm sort of a sponge," I said, and could feel my mouth get dry. "I have a few strong opinions, but they might change. I just want to find out everything I can."

Mariana reached over and took my hand. "That's wise," she said, and squeezed. "Very wise for a girl your age."

I could sense Stuart smiling at me, and we looked at each other, his eyes running up and down my face.

Mariana continued, sipping her beer. "I would love to be your age again. I would have spent so much less time chasing men, so much more time absorbing."

Stuart coughed a little, and I could feel my cheeks getting hot.

"Oh!" Mariana laughed, looking between us. "I'm sorry. No, love is a beautiful thing. Don't ever avoid it. And I regret nothing. But my work is my love now." She turned to me. "What do you want to study?"

"Economics and public policy. Then law school," I said, and sat up straighter.

"Good. But don't put yourself in a box. Study everything."

"Like what?" I said, and I almost wanted to bring out my notepad, to write everything down.

Soon the three of us got into talking about politics, and then living wage conditions, which as you know I have a fair amount to say about, and when the three of us looked up, Stuart's manager had his hand on Stuart's back, telling him his shift was over.

Stuart counted his drawer and cleaned up the bar.

Mariana said good-bye to me with a kiss on both cheeks and told Stuart she'd see him at the reading.

Finally, he came out of the bathroom in just a T-shirt, his button-down shirt slung over his shoulder, wearing his sunglasses.

"Ready?" he said.

"Yes," I said. My hands were twitchy and my stride was strong and my thoughts were chatty as we walked out into the setting sun, and that is how I hope I will remember Stuart forever, as he was last night, his skin almost orange in the sunset, the rays again reflected in his lenses.

I hope the rest of my life is like this, I remember thinking. *Just hanging out with famous writers, having conversations about books and politics.*

"I want to be a writer like Mariana," he said after some silence.

The sun had gone behind the trees then. We paused in the middle of a tiny side street, his street.

"I bet you will be," I said.

"Yeah, that's not . . . whatever. I lose focus. I have trouble . . . finishing things. I just want to be a writer who writes all the time, who writes these full, rich, deep stories. Not little flashes in the pan."

"You'll get there," I told him, and touched his arm in what I hoped was an encouraging way.

"I better," he said. Up until this point, he'd been hopeful—longing, yes, but hopeful. Now he sounded tense.

"What do you mean?"

He held up his hands. "I gave up everything to do this. I didn't go to college. I can live at my parents' place now, sure, but not for long. I have to succeed. Like, what we were talking about last time we hung out. My own definition of success. I just want to finish."

We kept walking until we reached an old cream-yellow house with white trim.

"Yeah." I touched the place between my ribs, near my sternum. "It's like, here. This constant pressure coming from inside, not outside."

"I can sense that in you," Stuart said. "You've got this drive. It's so nice to be around."

"It's nice to be around you, too," I said, quiet and soft. So unlike myself. Because it was the kind of thing I'd never said before. And that would have been enough for me, for him to say he liked my ambition.

"So, what are you doing right now?" Stuart glanced behind him at his parents' house, folding his sunglasses in his hand. "You want to come inside?"

"I want to," I said. I looked at my phone. My mom had texted me, asking if she should pick me up at the Canoe Club on her way home from work. "But I can't. I'm sorry. I want to . . ."

"Of course," he said, and got closer to me, looking at me with his black eyes kind of sleepy.

He put his hands on my waist, pressing through my sweatshirt. "Is this okay?" he asked.

"Yeah, but I've never . . ." I didn't know how to phrase it. So I just said it. "I don't really know how to do this."

Stuart smiled. "Do you want to try?"

In answer, I lifted my lips to his, where they stayed, and his lips moved a little, soft at first, and then more solid, unlike any touch I'd ever had. I felt his tongue, so I opened my mouth a little. *Humans have been doing this for centuries*, I remember thinking, and then not thinking at all, because his mouth was warm and wet and tasted like limes.

Then it was like someone dumped warm water on me, slowly, and it made me want to hold him tighter. I brushed my hands down his arms, then up again, across his shoulders, to his face.

I wanted to keep going.

My phone buzzed in my pocket. I let go. He let go.

"Bye," I said, and tried to keep my mouth closed because my breaths were coming heavy.

"Bye," he said, and closed his mouth, too, like he wanted to say something else but couldn't.

I walked back to the Canoe Club, got in the car with Mom, and pretended like everything was normal.

But I can't stop thinking about it. I didn't know I wanted such a feeling until it happened. I just made out with Stuart Shah. *I just made out with Stuart Shah.*

I feel I am a different person than I was twelve hours ago, like my hard, cracked skin is falling off to a new layer of pink raw skin, like I am making the transformation. Like Mrs. Whatsit in *A Wrinkle in Time,* when she left Earth through different dimensions, for a purple-gray planet with two moons. She was a bundle of rags and boots on Earth, and on the new planet, she became a brilliant creature with a powerful body and wings, almost beyond description. I'm still wearing my clogs and sweatshirt, still smelling the night on it, but I look different. I am different.

I know how love works, Future Sam, I read about it in *National Geographic.* It's a firing of neurons and a release of dopamine, what neuroscientists call "attachment chemicals," and this combined with the evolutionary imperative to reproduce creates a conditioned pattern of behavior. You seek out your love object for the same reason you seek out another piece of candy: because you want those sweet feelings again.

But no one ever told me how easy it would be, how good it would be. I mean, they did, they tried, Shakespeare tried, the Beatles tried, but I still didn't know it would be like *this.*

COOPER LIND'S GUIDE TO
ALTERNATIVE RESOURCES

Went over to Coop's backyard to get his "guide to alternative resources," which was mostly just an old legal pad from middle school full of doodles of Garfield doing slam dunks, occasionally interspersed with ideas, but there was good stuff in there. We sat on the fence between our properties like we used to. I wrote more notes and Coop pitched a football at a nearby tree, trying to hit the center.

Okay, and if this is the official record, let it be known I will only be using these *as necessary*. Necessary is defined as *only at risk of failure*. Failing grades on finals could bring Bs and Cs in overall grades, which could threaten my valedictory status. Otherwise, I will be shooting straight all the way to the end.

(List edited heavily to exclude seducing people in my classes and having them give me all the answers)
- "the printer smudged this, can't read it," while teacher is looking at the paper, glance at neighbor's test; especially effective for math tests. [USE FOR CALC FINAL]

- go to the bathroom immediately before and as soon as people start turning in their tests, as to avoid suspicion, but when there, check phone for refreshers. [USE FOR AP LIT QUIZZES, esp. multiple-choice section]
- evade test dates in order to take the actual exams in "alternative situations," aka alone after school, when textbook can be accessed. [AP EURO]

After I copied everything down worth using, I said that phrase to myself, *Well, I have everything worth using,* and what Maddie said the other day popped into my head, so I said, "Coop, I'm not using you, am I?"

"Like . . . wait, what?"

"Like taking too much from you and not giving back."

"No! No," he said quickly, running to get the football from in front of the tree.

When he came back, he said, "Trust me, I've been used before, and this is not using. You asked for what you wanted directly, and I said yes."

"Who used you?"

Coop shrugged. "Girls."

I hopped off the fence. "Yeah, right."

He threw the ball again. "They flirt with me to get into parties, get booze, drugs, new friends. It's the way it goes."

"It's not just that."

"Sometimes it's not."

I held up the pad. "They flirt with you for your Garfield drawings."

Coop snorted. "You used to draw those Lord of the Rings characters that looked like turds. I'm surprised you don't have a boyfriend by now with those skills."

I smiled, staring at my hands, thinking of Stuart's lips on mine.

"What the hell is that look?" Coop was staring at me, eyes wide.

"I don't have a look."

His voice got lower. "You have a boyfriend?"

"No . . ."

"Who is it?"

"No one."

Coop ran to get the ball. As he ran back, faster this time, he asked, "Who is it not?"

It was hard to resist telling him. It was also hard to keep out a tone of *see, I'm not a loser, ha-ha.* "It's *not* Stuart Shah."

"Oh," Coop said, and looked away. "Cool."

That time the football sailed beyond the tree, and the next one, too.

As he ran, he yelled over his shoulder, "See you."

"I wasn't—" I began, but I remembered he used to do that a lot, when he wanted to be alone. He'd always say good-bye before you'd ever thought about leaving.

LOOK, TEXTS FROM STUART SHAH

Holy shit, this is crazy. I accidentally shampooed my hair three times yesterday, just thinking about him and, yeah. Doing what we did again.

Stuart: Mariana's reading tonight at the Dartmouth library and she asked me to read with her!!!

Me: OMG. Congratulations!

Stuart: It's at 5. Come?

Me: If I can finish the Blindness essay due tomorrow, yes.

Stuart: Well, what are you doing still texting me? Write write write!

Me: hahaha

Stuart: See you at 5. ;)

Me: God willing

Stuart: I didn't know you were religious.

Me: I'm sorry, I meant dog willing.

Stuart: GO WRITE SO I CAN SEE YOU!

BLUE RASPBERRY

I finished my essay at 4:45, and all the way to the library, I did that awkward thing between walking and jogging that people do when they cross the street in front of traffic. When I got there, the library was packed, rows of chairs in the lobby filled up with people spilling into the shelves, and Mariana stood behind a microphone, already reading.

Stuart was in the front row, his head bent, staring intently at the floor, listening.

Finally, Mariana looked at Stuart, and I followed her eyes. In profile, his long lashes curved toward his nose and his lips were open.

"As any of you know who have seen me read before," Mariana began, "I love to make two works converse with each other. For the last two sections, I want to bring up a young writer who sent some work to me the other night. I don't think he expected me to read it . . ." The crowd chuckled. "But after keeping my beer glass full, it was the least I could do." They laughed again. "And I was very impressed. So we'll read short sections in conversation."

When Stuart cleared his throat and looked down at his printed page, I wanted to know everything about him I couldn't see.

What brand of toothpaste did he use?

Did Stuart dream often?

Were the dreams vivid?

What was his favorite flavor of Jolly Rancher?

His work was good. Everyone could tell it was good, because no one was fidgeting.

I wanted to tell everyone around me, *I know him. I kissed him*, and when he began to read, my eyes were glued to him. But he didn't look at me. Maybe he didn't see me. Maybe the warmth I felt was made up, or a fever, and he didn't actually want me to come.

The reading concluded. I clapped as hard as I could, and everyone stood up around me.

Future Sam, I had started to lie awake at night, thinking about our conversations, smiling to myself at things Stuart has said, and thinking about that opening-a-can-of-soda feeling that happens whenever I make him laugh. But ever since talking with Maddie, I wondered if I didn't just put too much weight on the hours that we spent lying in the Dartmouth grass, throwing ideas up into the sky, taking the words out of each other's mouths.

Stuart moved behind the table where Mariana was set up to sign books, craning his neck. He was looking for someone. Maybe me, maybe not.

Maybe he was biding his time until he could say something like Maddie said, something like, *I can't be the person to whom you bring all your woes and realizations about life*, and he had just decided to kiss me in the meantime.

A long lined formed. I moved between the bookshelves.

But I didn't want to bring all my woes to him. That's the opposite of what I wanted to do. I wanted to listen to him, and sure, occasionally talk—okay, maybe talk a lot—but I wanted him to like what I said. I wanted to talk about ideas and books and things smart people talk about, things that people like Stuart talk about.

Two Dartmouth students moved in line near my passage between shelves, saying, ". . . and Stuart Shah, wow. I read his piece in *The Threepenny Review*, too. Prodigy . . ."

I was pretty sure I didn't belong there. I was pretty sure someone who was banking her future on cheating on high school finals and the likelihood of a ten-minute graduation speech changing her fate wasn't supposed to be there, next to Stuart Shah, and all the people who admired him.

I heard his voice nearby, and a crowd of people laughing.

I retreated to the Philosophy section and tried to slow down my heart rate by breathing slow and staring at the floor, like Dr. Clarkington taught me. This was awful. *Caring about someone is awful*, I was thinking. *I should be locked back in the bell tower, where I can't throw any emotional grenades*, and suddenly I saw brown shoes.

"There you are," I heard Stuart say, and the words were so quiet it felt as if they were meant only for me.

Hands took mine from where fists had formed on my waist, and Stuart bent to put his lips on my cheek. I couldn't look at him.

"Stuart." I stepped out toward the floor. "You did a good job."

"Thank you," he said. Then, "Are you all right?"

"I just want to say . . ." I began, and took a step backward, meeting his eyes. "It's okay if you don't like me as much as I like you. You can just tell me."

"I mean . . ." he started, and tilted his head. "You never said how much you liked me."

I took in what I hoped would be the last in a string of deep breaths. "Can I tell you?"

He smiled a slow smile. "Yes, I would like that."

"I'm sorry if this is weird. God. I've got the social skills of . . . of a Neanderthal."

He laughed, his black eyes flashing at me and then upward, tossing his head back, which sent a wave of looseness through my whole body, on the whole Philosophy section, the whole library. The books got a little brighter. I laughed with him.

"I like you a lot," I said.

"I like you a lot, too," he said. "If you can't tell."

"I can't," I said, shaking my head. "I can't read social cues very well. I was just told that recently."

Then he kissed me deeply, and that was the perfect thing to do, because it felt good, yes, but also because I understood it fully, and to be honest, it was maybe the first time those two had gone together.

ALTERNATIVE RESOURCES, PHASE TWO

Lying in the nurse's office, watching the clock. I "threw up" my breakfast in the classroom trash can with the help of a sip of a smoothie I held in my mouth for ten minutes. The school wanted to call my parents, but I told them it was an expected side effect of Zavesca, and began to list all of them until the nurse was disgusted, and she dropped it. All the rest of my classmates are taking their AP Euro final. When the final's over, I'll "recover" and take the test in the library later today, where no one will watch me consult my notes if (and ONLY IF) I need them.

I probably could have done it, but I didn't want to take any chances on drawing a blank, especially with my mind swinging back and forth from Stuart to school to Stuart again.

After the reading, we had found a spot on the Dartmouth campus to kiss and talk and kiss some more. He tried to run his fingers through my hair and couldn't, because my curls are so thick and tangled. We laughed and he kissed my neck, which sent horses through my stomach again—not just horses, Shadowfax, the Lord of all horses—and I put my hand under his shirt and, actually, never mind, it's too weird to be typing about this in the nurse's office.

Almost over.

Every time Mrs. Dooley, the nurse, looks at me I try to look forlorn and take a little sip of water.

And who walks in but Cooper himself, employing his own method. I wave at him but he's putting a finger to his lips, pointing at the nurse, and sitting down beside me with a big, fake-sick sigh.

I'm pretending to type something important on this Word document.

How's it going, Coop?

"fainted" in my comp sci final

This system is nuts. My heart is beating so fast.

it's working though am i right

I can't believe it's working.

welcome to the last four years of my life

LOL

you're sitting right beside me, you don't have to type LOL, you can just laugh

I'm afraid if I laugh they'll think I'm not sick.

whatever you do, don't laugh right now

GODDAMMIT now I'm laughing

hahahahha :)

BIKINI BOTTOM

Watching *SpongeBob* with the family on Saturday night, because it's Davy's turn to pick what movie we watch. I pretended to complain with Harrison and Bette, but as you know, I secretly think this show is hilarious. And to be honest, Squidward reminds me a lot of myself.

I texted Maddie, by the way. I told her I was sorry again and asked if she wanted to meet up. She just texted back, "It's cool," and ignored the second part. She's probably really busy. Every time I see her at school, she is leaving with a group of screaming, happy people on their way somewhere. I wonder if she heard about me and Stuart being, like, a real thing. Then again, I don't know if Stuart is telling anyone about us, or, if he is, what he's saying.

This makes me wonder.

Me: You working?
Stuart: Yeeessss what's up?
Me: Am I your girlfriend?
Stuart: The title of your memoir will be "Sammie McCoy: Cutting to the Chase"

Me: Seriously, though, am I?

Stuart: Let's talk about it in person. Later tonight when I get off?

I look over at Mom and Dad, Davy sprawled on their laps, Bette between Mom's knees as she brushes her hair. I remember how sad Mom's eyes were when she asked me to spend more time with them. I remember my NPC Task Force, and how I am trying to be less selfish.

Me: I can't, I'm with my family tonight.

Stuart: Ah, ok. Tomorrow?

Me: Okay. But if you were to give a short answer now, what would it be?

I watch the screen. Stuart is typing. Shit. Maybe I pushed him too far. Why can't I just be casual and cool and whatever? Because I'm not casual and cool and whatever, that's why. And I have been waiting on him for two years. I don't want to waste another minute. I put my phone under a throw pillow and decide to never check it again.

Squidward gets a bucket of water dumped on his head at the Krusty Krab.

SpongeBob tries to get the bucket off, and ends up pulling so hard he lodges it on Patrick's head.

I check my phone.

Stuart: Short answer? Yes.

THE CLOCK HANGS IN THE JUNGLE

My tongue was heavy yesterday, Future Sam. Numb, like I had just gotten a dose of Novocain from the dentist. I noticed it when I was brushing my teeth. It was like having a huge piece of meat in my mouth that I couldn't chew or spit out. A shot of fear ran through me, and I started to cry.

I was just going to stay in bed and let it pass, grateful it was a Sunday and I didn't have to talk, but the goddamn NPC Task Force of Feminist Icons practically winked over on the wall above my desk. I recalled that I had promised myself that, in the spirit of Elizabeth Warren, I would find out everything I could about the disease, and approach it with nothing but straight talk. Even if straight talk was impossible because I had a steak for a tongue.

So I took the day off from school today, and Mom was going to go in late for her shift at the medical center so that she could bring me to Dr. Clarkington's office.

"Did you talk to her on the phone?" I asked Mom.

"Yes."

"There's medicine for this, right?" My heart hadn't stopped beating hard since it happened, thinking about having to cancel my speech. Or worse, pushing through it, leaving my classmates with the impression that I had guzzled a slushie before graduation and couldn't get rid of my brain-freeze.

"Yes, there's medicine for it."

"Do I sound like a dog who suddenly started talking?"

Mom laughed. "No, you don't sound like a dog who suddenly started talking."

"That's how I feel."

"I'm sorry, honey," Mom said. "You sound much better this morning. And hey, I'm glad you told me. You can always tell me when you're feeling bad."

"What about when I'm feeling good?" I asked, thinking of Stuart's text Saturday night.

"That, too."

We sat in silence for a bit, watching a toddler bang two blocks together on the floor. Stuart and I emailed back and forth all day yesterday, about our romantic pasts (or rather his past), about our impressions of boyfriends and girlfriends and what we thought they were supposed to do, about our fears.

"Hey, Mom."

"Mm?"

"Guess what."

"What."

"I have a boyfriend."

She turned to look at me, eyes wide. "The same guy you went to the Canoe Club with?"

"Stuart Shah."

Mom gasped, a sly smile growing on her face, though I could tell she was fighting with her is-this-a-good-idea instincts. "You have had *such* a crush on him forever!"

I smiled with her. "How did you know that?"

"Honey, you made us go to *Hamlet* three times. You couldn't take your eyes off him."

"Oh, yeah." I laughed, thinking of my poor family three years ago, suffering through Alex Conway putting on a fake British accent as Ophelia. Maddie was fantastic as Hamlet's mother. You would have never known she was only fifteen. "Time is passing so quickly."

Mom put her hand on my knee and squeezed. "Tell me about it."

"So, in that case . . ." I began, trying to swallow so I could speak as clearly as possible. "I would like to, you know, be able to spend time with him without you worrying . . ."

Mom made her sound. "Mmhmm. Hm."

"Mom?"

"I'm thinking," she said. Then, "Does he know?"

She meant about NPC. "No. But he will."

"Okay."

"I'll be so careful," I offered.

"Mmhmm." Mom laid her head back and closed her eyes. She had been up way too late the night before, helping Harrison finish a science project.

"He's a good person."

"I'm sure he is," Mom said, eyes still closed. "I'm going to worry about you either way, Sammie. Just be careful. Don't go anywhere without telling me, or without thinking about the possible medical repercussions." She smiled to herself. "Guard your heart, too. This is your first real romance. Don't jump in too quickly. Then again, you probably don't have to worry about that. You have never been much of an impulsive one. Too much of a planner."

I thought about the night of Ross Nervig's party, of speaking my mind to Stuart without planning to, and grabbing him suddenly and kissing him. Maybe there was a part of me Mom didn't know. There was a part of me I didn't know myself.

"I don't know, Mom. Now that I'm about to graduate, I plan on being more spontaneous."

Mom opened her eyes and burst out laughing.

I said, "Got spontaneity on the calendar for next Tuesday."

She doubled over again, letting out a snort. I joined her and we laughed until the nurse called my name.

TWO, FOUR, SIX, EIGHT, WHO'S GONNA HELP 'EM GRADUATE?

SAMANTHA!

SAMANTHA!

SAMANTHA!

THREE, FIVE, SEVEN, NINE, AND SHE WON'T FORGET THE LINE!

ANXIETY!

ANXIETY!

ANXIETY!

I did it, though. I wrote the speech, and transferred it to notecards. I'd prefer to memorize it without any resource, but, you know. At least I'm not going to read it off a paper like some kind of amateur. I went with an "overcoming your obstacles" theme. I'm digging it. Some highlights, for posterity (as in, at least someone should be able to experience this if I have a repeat blank-out on the stage this coming weekend and have to be carried off like an invalid):

"I think it's easy to group all the factors that get in your way into one big wall: money, race, sexuality, relationships, health, time. These are the forces we supposedly have no control over, that conspire against us. But we'll never get over them if we look at them that way. As we grow older, we have the opportunity to learn where exactly these obstacles find their root.

"If we keep learning about the history of our obstacles, we will have the opportunity to dig the poison out of the world. We will have purpose. Whether the obstacles are individual, like a disease, or bigger than that, like a societal injustice, once we clear one, we have room for hope.

"Optimism does not have to be blind."

Et cetera.

I just wrote the speech that I would like to hear, you know? After listening to Dr. Clarkington tell me that I might start declining more rapidly, I kind of, just . . . I don't know. I wanted to write about optimism. I wanted to write the speech I need.

Because honestly, who's to say that I won't improve?

We can't eliminate that as a possibility.

I could get way better instead of getting worse. Is it likely? No. Is it possible? Absolutely. I mean, just getting this disease in the first place was against all odds. One in one hundred fifty thousand. Was that likely? No. I have a hot boyfriend who is a published writer. Was that likely? No.

Not much is likely. Anything is possible.

PDA

I'm at dinner with Stuart (well, technically I'm in the bathroom on my phone—I couldn't wait to record this). Over Vietnamese food, we got into a disagreement about whether the formation of capitalism was an inevitable part of human nature.

When it got so heated that I banged on the table, lifting the hot sauces a centimeter out of their brackets, Stuart said, "Sorry. I didn't mean to argue."

He looked actually worried, as if I would storm out or something, and took my hand across the table. "You're really torn up about this," he continued. "We should stop."

He looked so cute. He was wearing a blinding-white button-down that brought out the best brown in his skin and the lights in his eyes.

I leaned across the table and whispered, "Are you kidding?" I hadn't argued like that since before Nationals. I could feel my cheeks full of blood and heat, and my head was still climbing all over his position, scrambling to spar with a worthy opponent. "This is the most romantic thing we could possibly do."

"Really?"

"I want to . . ." I looked around. The place was full to capacity with chattering families. "I want to make out with you in the middle of this restaurant."

Stuart leaned back in his chair and raised his eyebrows. "Then do it," he said, daring me.

So I did.

I mean only for a few seconds. But I did it.

LAST FINAL, LAST DAY OF SCHOOL

I drew a blank.

It was not as huge as Nationals, but all of a sudden, in the middle of an equation, I forgot what I was doing. And again, Future Sam, it was so strange because, yes, I was confused and upset, but there was also this sort of loopy happiness that made no sense, like I had just woken up from a long nap. And again, I almost laughed or smiled or something at the absurdity of it. Like, huh, what did I come in here for? What was I doing? Was I multiplying something? Huh, well, la-di-da.

As the fog cleared, I retraced my steps. I went back to the beginning of the problem and tried it again. But I couldn't keep track of where among the numbers I went astray. I couldn't reroute without erasing everything and starting completely over, and I didn't have time for that. I was panicking.

So I cheated. I thought of which of Coop's methods would work, and I really, really cheated. I made sure no one was watching, I licked my thumb, and I moved it across the ink of the next problem until the numbers were unrecognizable.

While Mrs. Hoss looked closer at my paper, I zeroed in on Felicia Thompson's desk in the front row. As I walked back to my spot with a new test, I chanted her answers quietly to myself. *A, A, B, D, C, C, A . . .*

Over lunch I felt so guilty, I completed an entire practice test, just to prove I could have done it if it hadn't been for NPC. (I aced it. But still.)

On the last hour of high school, while everyone in the senior hallway was ripping papers and books out of their lockers with vicious glee, I caught up with Coop and told him.

"Aw, baby's first guilt trip," he said, and put his hand on top of my head, ruffling my hair. "It's over! Who cares? You would have killed it, right? You didn't do anything wrong. Sometimes it's just about timing."

"Sure," I said. For Coop it was.

Coop stopped in the middle of the hall, next to me. "What are you doing now?"

"Walking," I said without thinking, because I was thinking about a million other things.

"People are coming over to my house to grill hot dogs."

"That sounds fun!" I said, and waved good-bye.

Later I realized he might have been inviting me. Oh well. Me and social cues.

As we walked out of Hanover's doors for the last time as high schoolers, I wasn't reminiscing, I wasn't crying, I wasn't celebrating. I was praying. *God, Jesus, Mary, and all the saints,* I said over and over. *Please, please, please let graduation day be the right timing.*

BUT WHAT IF IT'S NOT

It's three a.m. and I just woke up in a cold sweat from a nightmare where I got onstage to give my speech, but a bear started moving through the crowd, and no one was scared of it except for me, and it came barreling through and everyone stepped aside for it even though it was heading straight for me, slowly, and right before it went up on its hind legs to maul me, I woke up. And I realized: Coop's methods may work for tests and class time, but they don't work for speeches. I'll be up there with nowhere to escape, and no way to avoid it.

UNTITLED, IN A GOOD WAY

This morning I was up again at sunrise. I recited my speech in a long, hot shower. It's a beautiful spring day, practically summer. Mom and I had picked out a dress from one of the boutique sale racks earlier this week, simple white with thick lace, and Mom took in the waist and let out the shoulders so it fits just right. She also bought some stuff to make my curls less frizzy, which I worked through my wet tangles, and I even brushed on some of her mascara.

Soon Grandma and Grandpa (just the ones from Dad's side—Nana can't make the trip from Canada) will meet us for lunch before the ceremony. Stuart asked if he could take me out before all the craziness and family stuff began, and Mom said yes, since today was a special occasion.

We went to the 4 Aces Diner in Lebanon and sat in a booth. Because I was so nervous and my stomach couldn't take solid food, and hell, because today was the first day of the rest of my life, I ordered an Oreo milk shake for breakfast. Stuart burst out laughing and ordered one for himself, too.

"You look adorable," he said as we sucked on our straws.

"I feel like I'm going to start puking into this glass in two seconds."

"Good puke or bad puke?"

"Both."

"You probably wouldn't be the first person to lose it over a milk shake here. They are so good."

"I can barely taste it."

Stuart dug in with a spoon. "That's a tragedy."

"We'll have to come back here after this whole thing's over," I said.

"Two milk shakes in one day? Living fast and loose."

I laughed. "No, I mean later this summer."

Then we were both quiet for a minute. Even though we talked about our futures constantly—Stuart finishing his collection of short stories, me going to NYU—we never really talked about what *our* future looked like, or whether there was even an *our* future in the first place. I had moved so fast to make things clear between us, I didn't really think about why.

Maybe it had a lot to do with the fact that I thought it was almost too good to be true. That I wanted to get as much out of him as I could before he moved back into a world where there were thousands of girls just as smart as me and just as encouraging and ten times more pretty, and there he would move on.

I wondered if he was thinking the same thing.

"Stuart . . ." I began.

"Yeah?" he asked, still digging into the glass with his spoon.

"Look at me," I said.

Looking puzzled, he stopped and took my hand across the table. I loved when he did that. I always had the urge to look around to see if anyone was looking at us when we held hands, a sort of silly, vain little thought that they might look at us and think, *Aw. That couple is in love.*

But my words caught in my throat. Maybe now wasn't the time to have this conversation, on the brink of one of the biggest moments of my life thus far. And anyway, we had never said "love." I've said it here, but I realize I have a very small understanding. A very true understanding, but a pretty small one.

I took a breath and said, "I should have gotten peanut butter cup."

"Ha!" he said, shaking his head, and resumed eating. "Oh! You know what?"

"What?"

"This just reminded me—there's this ice cream parlor in Brooklyn, I can't remember what it's called, but they have *the best* milk shakes. Like maybe even better than here. I'll have to take you there."

I swallowed another gulp. "Take me there?" My heart started beating hard. Even harder than it already was, which was very hard.

"Yeah, this fall," he said, and gradually, my pulse slowed. Relief melted from the top of my head to my toes. This fall. As in, we would be together then. Together enough to go to an ice cream parlor. Suddenly, I got very hungry.

"Thatta girl," he said, watching me dig in with my own spoon.

I swallowed a mouthful of milk shake, and didn't try to hide my smile.

"What?" he asked, smiling with me.

"Nothing," I said. "Just happy."

I HAD TO WIPE THE SWEAT OFF
MY PALMS ON MY DRESS
SO I COULD TYPE

I'm hiding from everyone in the girls' locker room. My graduation gown keeps dragging on the floor so it's hanging on the hook on the door.

After Mom and Dad and the kids dropped me at the gym entrance to park the car, I thought I had forgot everything until I pushed out the first words to myself in a whisper, "Oliver Goldsmith once said . . ." and the rest would come. I kept repeating it, *Oliver Goldsmith once said, Oliver Goldsmith once said*, as if every time I said it I had been drowning and came up for air.

As all the teachers and administrators grouped together at the front, I saw Mrs. Townsend, her black poof of hair rising above the others.

"Hey, Mrs. T," I said, and she turned around.

"Sammie," she said slowly with a soft smile, and pulled me into a hug. She smelled like so many different products mixed together, lotion and shampoo and perfume, but in a good way, in a way that fit.

"Thank you for everything," I said, and choked back the tears I had been holding in all day.

"You're going to be great," Mrs. T said.

Then I couldn't help it, the tears came for real, because of how many times she had said that to me over the last four years, before my first week in AP classes, before my first tournament, before the beginning of my senior year, before the disease came along and tried to mess up everything, and after. I knew this would probably be the last time she'd ever say something like that. Before she moved on to say her good-byes to someone else, I touched her arm.

She turned back to me.

"Will you introduce me out there? I mean, the speech?"

"Oh!" she said, considering.

"I know Principal Rothchild is supposed to do it, but it would mean a lot . . . you know . . . because you're the only one who knows how big . . ." I swallowed back more tears. "How big a deal it is for me to do this."

Mrs. T smiled again, determined. She nodded. "Of course I will," she said. "I'll go chat with Mr. R."

Now the gym is standing room only, and everyone's voices are swirling around in one big roar.

I should probably go. They are lining us up out there by last name. I'll be between William Madison and Lynn Nguyen. Everyone is taking photos of themselves, and here I am, typing on a toilet. If I fail, let it be known that I was here, in a bathroom stall, going over the speech one more time. I tried.

It's funny that I'm thinking about Coop again, but I can't get what he said the other day in the hallway out of my head: "Sometimes it's just about timing."

Speak of the devil, someone just peeked his head in here and yelled, "Samantha Agatha McCoy! You better get your butt out here!"

Yeah, that had to be Coop.

Here goes nothing.

YOU CAN TAKE IT FROM HERE

For a minute, everything about Nationals seemed to repeat itself in a terrifying display of one-upmanship. *Nationals: The Sequel. Nationals 2: The Return of Dementia.* Rows and rows of fluorescent gym lights replaced the stage lights, and the audience multiplied from a few disinterested high schoolers and their families into a country of faces, my classmates into huddled blue boulders, punctuated by the flashes of hundreds of cameras, all silent and waiting.

I was in the wings.

Mrs. Townsend walked across the stage, her heels echoing, and took her place behind the podium, a scholarly maroon ribbon now around her shoulders.

"Ladies, gentlemen, families, graduating class," she said, and she paused for the screams and whoops of the seniors. "Your valedictorian, Samantha McCoy."

I walked—no, skated—no, floated. To steady myself, I put my elbows on the podium, and clasped my hands.

To the blurs that were everyone's important people, I called out,

"Oliver Goldsmith once said, 'The greatest glory in living lies not in never falling, but in rising every time we fall.'"

Then my brain turned off, but in a different way than it had done before. It turned off any other words or feelings or thoughts besides the ones coming out of my mouth. It was as if it knew that this was not the place to question, and told me, *Okay, we're here now. I'll take it from here.*

As I spoke, instead of thinking, I saw. I saw many random things, Future Sam. Stuart's eyes under dark lashes across the table from me at the restaurant, looking at his milk shake and laughing, and Mrs. Townsend's relaxed face as she typed at her computer, and the blue glow of the aquarium in the doctor's office on Davy's face as she watched the betta swim.

Ten minutes later, I was saying, "So when it all gets to be too much, it's all right that you might ask yourself where you have fallen, why you have fallen, and to tell yourself that you will never fall the same way again. That's how our education, both in life and at school, will serve us. But the work isn't over. Use the knowledge that you will rise for the purpose of joy, and goddamnit—" The crowd laughed.

I hadn't planned that part, but it just came out. I looked back at the teachers, some of them tittering, some of them shaking their heads.

"Goddamnit," I continued, unable to contain a laugh myself. "Get back up."

My classmates' faces came into focus. "Thank you," I said, and they cheered.

But the real reward was after. Like, right now. Well, not right now.
Right now I'm in the car. But right after the ceremony.

Okay, you know how sad and pissed I was about how unfair it
is that thirty seconds could change four years of work? It turns out I
spoke too soon, because it works the other way, too.

When we cheered for the last time as high schoolers together,
and our caps floated down, it was like the senior class at Hanover
had been this Jenga tower of blocks that immediately fell.

Lynn Nguyen turned to me and hugged me as if we'd known
each other all our lives, and we both high-fived Will Madison, and
people who I only knew by name and the backs of their heads came
up to me, telling me "good job," but that's not the best part: The best
part was that suddenly I remembered what was great about them,
too, as if I'd been soaking it up all this time without realizing it, and
I wanted to tell them everything, and know everything about them.
But not, like, their deepest desires or how they felt about income
inequality, but just how they *were*. What they were *up to*.

"Lynn, will you be sticking around the Upper Valley? I heard you
were going for an internship at that magazine."

"Elena, your solo was amazing. Where did you get those tennis
shoes with the heels? I didn't even know tennis shoes could have
heels!"

"Will, are you going to play soccer at the University of Vermont
next year?"

Future Sam, I was *small-talking*.

And pretty soon we were all making plans to hang out at Ross
Nervig's tonight (not that I was invited, specifically, but they didn't

exclude me—I mean, they said I should come, but anyway), and I actually want to go.

Not to mention, Maddie will be there. She had woven through a couple of rows of chairs, and when she got close enough to me to say something, she didn't speak at all, she just hugged me, and I hugged her back, hard.

"I'm sorry," I said into her exposed ear, the buzzed part of her hair dyed a deep maroon to match Hanover's colors. Along with the rest of the members of the Queer Union, her robe was draped in cords of every color of the rainbow.

"Sorry for what?" she said back, and we let go.

"If I used you."

She smiled a sad smile, "I'm sorry, too. I was going through some shit."

"There was some truth to it, I think."

"But now . . ." She gestured around to the buzz of happy people in the bright gym. "It's actually no big deal now. We're graduated. High school is no longer a big deal. Especially for you."

"You're so right!" I said, and let out a *ha* sound, because a knot had come undone inside me. It was a knot that held a lot together, so it was necessary for a time, but she was right. High school was no longer a big deal.

"But you know what I will still be sorry about?" I said, gulping.

"What?" Maddie said, making a little frown, poking fun.

"I am sorry we weren't better friends earlier."

"Well!" she said, tossing her cap and catching it. "We've got plenty of time now!"

"Maddie!" Stacia called Maddie's name from over by her parents. Pat was with them, too. I didn't know if Maddie and Stacia were back together, but like everything else, it didn't seem to matter. Maddie seemed happy.

"Gotta go," she said.

I caught her sleeve. "I'll see you at Ross Nervig's tonight?"

As she walked backward in Stacia's direction, Maddie's mouth fell open, then closed. "Sammie McCoy wants to party." She pretended to zip it shut. "Not going to ruin this. Not going to say a word. But yes. I'll see you tonight."

When the crowd had thinned somewhat, Mom and Dad and Grandma and Grandpa found me, followed by Harrison and Bette and Davy, all tucked in and brushed and buckled into their church clothes.

"We're so proud of you," Mom said as she hugged me, one of her clutching hugs that verges on the brink of too tight but never quite gets there.

"So proud," Dad repeated, and joined in.

Bette and Davy took my waist from either side with their skinny arms, smelling like the popcorn they were giving out in the lobby, while Harrison touched Bette's head and said, "This is me hugging you," which was good enough.

Grandma and Grandpa took their turn, their white heads the same exact height. Grandma handed me a thick envelope tucked in a copy of *Caddie Woodlawn*, my favorite book, which I would ask her to read to me as a little girl, which set me off crying again.

Above all their heads, I saw Stuart standing several feet away, looking like he'd stepped off the cover of *GQ* (in my opinion), my favorite white button-down glowing under a thin black tie.

We made eye contact and smiled so huge and excited, I swear the way my heart jumped it was like the first time I had seen him all over again, except this time I was the opposite of paralyzed, I was resisting the urge to run and jump into his arms. He looked away for a moment, and I tried to wipe the trail of mascara that was probably running down my cheeks on the back of my hand.

When I looked back up, he was making a "one minute" motion—it appeared Dale and his parents wanted to speak to him on the other side of the gym. I gave him a thumbs-up, and turned back to my family with the sweetest smile I could muster.

"Hey, Mom and Dad, can I go to a party tonight?"

"Nice one, Sammie, get us when we're in a good mood," Dad said, putting Harrison in a playful headlock.

"But seriously! Please?"

"Mmm," Mom said. "You can have friends over to our place, if you'd like!"

"But . . ."

"I don't think so, honey," Dad said.

"Oh, Mark, let her go," Grandma said, putting her hand on my back and giving me a small smile. "She deserves to celebrate."

"Ha!" Dad said. "Like you would have let me go to a graduation party."

"No, but your dad did," Grandma said, tossing a look at her husband.

"It's true, I did," Grandpa said, and winked at me.

Mom sighed. "You're going to make my hair turn gray," she said, looking at me. Then to Grandpa, "No offense."

"Is your friend with the Mohawk going?" Dad asked. "The one who can do CPR?"

"Maddie? Yeah!" That was almost a yes. I had to resist clapping my hands with excitement. Maddie was still across the gym. "Maddie!" I shouted.

"What?" she shouted back.

"We're hanging out tonight, right?" I gave her a pointed look.

"Yep!" she shouted. "Definitely!"

I told them that I would meet Stuart or Maddie in the parking lot, that we would go together. After tons of photos and kisses good-bye, and one last "be smart" from Mom and Dad, everyone left.

So now I'm sitting here in the parking lot, in the car, which Mom and Dad are letting me take as long as I get home by midnight.

What happened at Nationals was just a mistake. Bad timing. And even if it happens again while I'm at NYU, I can explain my condition. *It only happens rarely*, I can tell them. I will never be as bad as the worst-case scenario.

I'm writing to you right now, even when I could be celebrating, because I have realized the common factor every time I've succeeded—writing to you, Future Sam. It must be working. Something, at least, is working. To make up for all the nights spent at home, in the library, bossing people around, all the nights spent memorizing—I want to celebrate tonight, and I want tonight to last for a long time.

The only problem: Stuart already left to let me be with my family, and is now twenty minutes away. Maddie left, too. I told Stuart no big deal, go with Dale, and that he could meet me there. SO. I'm sure my parents wouldn't mind if I went by myself. Coop texted me the address. It's just one drive, after all, and my mind is stronger than ever.

I am so embarrassed. I'm sort of lost. I can't quite remember why. So I'm reading this back and of course I remember that I'm going to this party at Ross Nervig's and that Coop texted me the address, but I'm looking at the address and I can't remember how to get there. So I'm just going to put it in the GPS, duh, but then I forgot what street I was literally on! So, yeah. I pulled over until this passes.

It's graduation. Duh. I looked at what I wrote earlier. BUT now I'm just like WHERE AM I GOING AGAIN.

So, this is not a good sign.

I should proabbly call my mom but she would murder me, so I'm just going to let this pass.

Okay, I read earlier that I'm going to graduation, I know that, because I read it TWICE NOW because this is so embarrassing.

I mean, not graduation, to the party AFTER graduation.

hi is this okay its very dark and at least this is light and bright i shut off the car don't worry

im okay i think im just not there yet but my hands are kind of shaky

future sam okay I am feeling a little better but i can't rememebr where i was going! i took a little walk by the car. there were other cars heading somewhere and i almost flagged one of them down but they didn't see me, their headlights are too bright and they look very bad and have mean eyes

i was driving to school I was coming from school

OK. Okay. This is stupid.

Boy I am lost. This looks familiar, this looks like my street.

once i read a story about a giant a friendly giant in london who blew dreams into peoples bedrooms in little bubbles and the girl saw him but he caught her and put her on his shoulder and took her to giant country

the friendly giant is a good one it was a whole chapter book why was i talking about giants oh yeah

coop and i used to build houses out of pine needesl and play giants stomping on the houses did i ever tell you that the dark feles like the shadow of a giant down the road coming toward me and stomping on the mean cars

Did I call Coop? I'm not doing so well. I'm doing so well. I'm going
to call COop again befre this get s worse

 uh oh feeling weird agani FEELING WEIRD WEIRD WRIED
WIERD I'm just going to sit for while until If eel better

 write about things you know

 when you're scared you can write about things you know

RUNNING

I'm Frankenstein's monster, lying in the cleanest room I've ever seen.
I just woke up to a card from Bette lying on the table next to my
hospital bed with just a big, blank circle that she drew, it says "get
better"

Flowers from the Townsends

Flowers from Maddie

Flowers from Stuart

But the card made me cry because it continually reminds me of
what I forgot

I got lost on the route around the mountain, past town

It reminds me of the maps we used to draw

When she and Harry and Coop and me (Davy was too small)
would spend the day circling through Strafford, first running
down the mountain, then running to the creek, then running into
Strafford, saying hello to Fast Eddy where he sits outside the general
store—Fast Eddy, the self-appointed policeman who also acts as
the mailman—and then into the general store for Cherry Vanilla Dr

Pepper, then running back to the creek for lunch, then running back up the mountain to the backyard to play giants, then dinner

Once we drew a map of our world and plotted our route, and of course it was very simple

It was just a circle, and it was enough

PLEASE

Coop found me on the side of the road and took me home. I've been in and out of the hospital for a week. There are new updates every time I go in there, all of it reducing Mom and Dad into dark-eyed sacks of fabric next to my hospital bed, all of it bad. I have:

jaundice-like symptoms

an enlarged liver

an enlarged spleen

All of this contributes to the grand prize: I am also in the process of "mild retardation"! That's why I saw giants on the side of the road and typed like an infant.

I haven't written much to you until now because I don't really want to remember any of this, Future Sam, and *you*, as I had initially conceived *you*, don't exist anymore. Stock up on palm tree shirts. Resign to swollen lips, yellowing skin, droopy eyes. You will have a useless high school diploma and a gimp leg. You will drool a lot.

I can't imagine what I look like now. All my bodily functions in one bed already grosses me out, but thankfully I haven't seen anyone else.

I told Stuart my parents had changed their mind the night of graduation and made me stay home, where my phone had died. Then, when I found out I would be practically living at the hospital, I told him I was sick, a bad case of strep, and he shouldn't see me because I am contagious. I wish Stuart would come find me anyway, find me sleeping and kiss me awake, like a Disney movie or something, and never leave my side. Then again, my mouth would taste like hospital Jell-O and dry rot from sleeping with my mouth open and barely getting to brush my teeth, so maybe that's a bad idea. And it will never happen anyway.

We are waiting to find out whether or not I can at least go to college, at least first semester, before all this shit goes down.

Their initial answer was no, but I was like, please, please, this won't last forever, just let me go, put me in classes for dumb people, just let me get out. The one thing I can still have, please. Please please please please please.

They got me on some kind of sleep medicine–type stuff because I am awake in the middle of the night and I am pretty sure I'm not supposed to be awake

I'm pretty sure there is something standing in the corner of the hospital room. Not sure if it's a nurse or not because it's too dark, but my beeping is still going, which means I'm still alive, and I can type, which means my brain is still connected to my hands, but there are daggers in my throat every time I swallow, and I can feel a deep brown bruise throbbing where the IV is pumping food in, or blood out, I'm not sure at this point

I remember someone sticking a long cold needle in my butt cheek

This blanket is so itchy but when I take it off it feels like ice in the air, way too cold

I can't bite down all the way, I don't know what's in there

My eyeballs ache

I tried to do some reading on the Internet but this thing isn't hooked up to the Wi-Fi and I have honestly been sitting here awake for perhaps hours just trying to figure out what that white thing in the corner is

It doesn't disappear so it's not those floaty things across your vision

It doesn't move so it's not a human being

It's too big to be a curtain or coat rack

All I can do here is wait for the sun, which I have no idea of knowing how close or far away I am from the setting or rising because someone fucked with my computer battery and the time is just blinking 12, 12, 12

So I wonder if I am supposed to remember when I went to sleep

Maybe they didn't give me anything at all

Maybe I just don't know

Kill me now.

Here's a shock: According to my doctors, a person with mild retardation can't go to college, can't live in a city away from their parents, and eventually will barely be able to think for themselves. It doesn't matter if I still have the ability to communicate and walk and think right now, because apparently, in addition to being doctors, they are fucking SOOTHSAYERS and they know these things. So they have decided to break my dreams and render my life completely meaningless.

I was like, "How do you know? The episodes could still be really rare!" WHICH IS ACCURATE ACCORDING TO PROBABILITY AND LOGIC. THREE BREAKDOWNS OVER FIVE MONTHS DOES NOT EQUAL IMMINENT DANGER. THAT IS LITERALLY A TWO PERCENT RATE ON ANY GIVEN DAY.

The sickening fucking look Dr. Clarkington had, like she was simultaneously crying and letting out a fart, when she said, "I'm sorry, Sammie. There's nothing we can do." I almost punched her in the face.

If there's nothing you can do, then why are you fucking with me, huh? There's plenty of things I CAN STILL DO. LIKE GO TO COLLEGE. Great, now I'm crying.

Now they're telling me none of it will ever happen. If my mom's chant is *mmhmm, mmhmm*, then my new chant is *this will never happen*.

I love to-do lists! How about lists of things I will never do! How about it! I can list everything I've ever wanted for myself, and after it the phrase, "This will never happen."

NYU: this will never happen.

Stuart Shah: this will never happen.

Harvard Law: this will never happen.

The UN: this will never happen.

Everything is over, and I will die.

die die die die die die die die die die die die die die die die die die
die die die die die die die die die die die die die die die die die die
die die die die die die die die die die die die die die die die die die
die die die die die die die die die die die die die die die die die die
die die die die die die die die die die die die die die die die die die
die die die die die die die die die die die die die die die die die die
die die die die die die die die die die die die die die die die die die
die die die die die die die die die die die die die die die die die die
die die die die die die die die die die die die die die die die die die
die die die die die die die die die die die die die die die die die die

die die die die die die die die die die die die die die die die die
die die die die die die die die die die die die die die die die die
die die die die die die die die die die die die die die die die die
die die die die die die die die die die die die die die die die die
die die die die die die die die die die die die die die die die die
die die die die die die die die die die die die die die die die die
die die die die die die die die die die die die die die die die die
die die die die die die die die die die die die die die die die die
die die die die die die die die die die die die die die die die die
die die die die die die die die die die die die die die die die die
die die die die die die die die die die die die die die die die die
die die die die die die die die die die die die die die die die die
die die die die die die die die die die die die die die die die die
die die die die die die die die die die die die die die die die die
die die die die die die die die die die die die die die die die die
die die die die die die die die die die die die die die die die die
die die die die die die die die die die die die die die die die die
die die die die die die die die die die die die die die die die die
die die die die die die die die die die die die die die die die die
die die die die die die die die die die die die die die die die die
die die die die die die die die die die die die die die die die die
die die die die die die die die die die die die die die die die die
die die die die die die die die die die die die die die die die die
die die die die die die die die die die die die die die die die die
die die die die die die die die die die die die die die die die die

die die die die die die die die die die die die die die die die die
die die die die die die die die die die die die die die die die die
die die die die die die die die die die die die die die die die die
die die die die die die die die die die die die die die die die die
die die die die die die die die die die die die die die die die die
die die die die die die die die die die die die die die die die die
die die die die die die die die die die die die die die die die die
die die die die die die die die die die die die die die die die die
die die die die die die die die die die die die die die die die die
die die die die die die die die die die die die die die die die die
die die die die die die die die die die die die die die die die die
die die die die die die die die die die die die die die die die die
die die die die die die die die die die die die die die die die die
die die die die die die die die die die die die die die die

I DIDN'T DIE

Bette and Davy are building a fort of cushions around me as I write, which makes sense. I barely move from the floor anymore, so I am an ideal load-bearing structure.

Here's what I see: my feet spread out under a blue fuzzy blanket, the kitchen/dining room table covered in the remains of two peanut butter sandwiches. On the sill of the window above the sink, a line of orange pill bottles with white lids.

Small circular white pills for pain.

Oval blue pills for vertical gaze palsy.

Red pill-shaped pills for numbness.

Prozac for depression.

Et cetera.

The last one on the list, I haven't taken yet. But I'm about at that point.

"Play with us, play with us, play with us," Davy is chanting, the fort abandoned as she and Bette run around the couch. I look around for Harrison, hoping he can distract them, but remember he's at camp.

"I can't," I tell them. Too busy watching a terrible, terrible show about people who compete to find valuable goods in storage lockers.

"Why?" Bette asks.

"I can't move," I say.

"That's not true," Bette says. "You get up to go to the bathroom and get food! I saw you just now!"

She was right. I can move. I just don't want to. Move to go where? Outside? To the border of our property?

The only comforts I have are two fictions: the fiction of whatever is on TV, and the fiction of texting Stuart, who now thinks my strep has turned into mono. (It turns out it's easier to lie when you're typing, and because of medicinal side effects, your tongue is dry anyway.)

And neither comfort requires movement. So.

Speaking of Stuart, where is my phone?

Uggghhh.

I keep it next to me so I don't have this problem. Seriously, I'm not having a memory lapse. I didn't move it.

Then I hear Bette and Davy giggling under the kitchen table.

Oh god.

"See? You can move!" Bette shouted with a triumphant smile on her face when I stormed over and snatched it back. They both ran outside.

Whew, they didn't text or call Stuart.

They texted Coop. They must have found his name as the only one they recognize. Coop sometimes gives them "helicopter rides" at church.

I yanked open the sliding doors and screamed at them. "DON'T DO THAT!"

Bette called from somewhere in the tree line, still laughing. "HE TEXTED YOU FIRST! I JUST TYPED 'OK'!"

Oh, so he did.

Coop: Hey gurl just wanted to check and see how you're doing. Can I drop by? Also Mom made you guys a ton of food so I'm gonna bring that.

Me: Ok

So I guess Coop's coming over. I need to put a password on my phone.

WHAT HAPPENED

I was outside for the first time in a week and a half on one of our plastic lawn chairs, realizing that Vermont had turned into summer while I was indoors. The sky was heavy with potential rain clouds, but the daffodils had made way for lilies of the valley and purple clover, the tomatoes in Mom's garden were streaking red, and there were a couple of hummingbirds at the feeder.

Bette and Davy were watching them, crouched in the bushes near the house, trying not to make a sound.

As Coop approached from down the mountain, holding two bags in either hand, I held a finger to my lips and pointed to the colorful blurs.

I may be a useless sack of shit but all of us McCoys like watching the birds. Especially hummingbirds. I used to know so many facts about hummingbirds.

Coop set the bags down slowly and put on a silly I'm-a-spy walk.

Bette and Davy giggled, blowing their cover, and the birds jetted away.

"Way to go," I said as he picked up the bags again.

"I did my best," he said, shrugging. As he got closer, my instincts fired and I checked for a joint behind his ear. Coop would forget something like that, especially in the summer. There wasn't one.

"I'll put these in the kitchen?" he asked. I waved him on.

I heard him banging around in there through the crack he left in the sliding doors, opening and closing the fridge. "Did you guys move the cups?"

"Yeah," I called. "They're in the other cabinet now."

It was strange to let Cooper Lind go inside our house as I knew him now, always surrounded by this crew of people shorter than him, hanging on him, a huge, doped-up smile on his face.

But then again, we would never see each other in the hallways like that anymore, around all the people.

And there were the ratios I always relied on: Coop had a ratio, too. Fourteen years to four years. Four years he spent in a cloud of parties and weed, fourteen years he spent in this house. He was still seventy percent of the kid who knew where the cups were.

I guess it wasn't that strange, if you think about it that way.

So he came back out with a glass of water, pulled up the other lawn chair from where it was turned over near the gutter spout, and sat down. I braced myself for the questions that were no longer relevant to me.

Are you really that sick?

Will you be able to go to college?

What are you going to do now?

When he didn't say anything, I cut the sound of the breeze and the birds and the bugs, so we could get it over with.

"Thanks for coming to get me that night," I said.

"No need."

I gave him a look.

"You already thanked me a million times," Coop said.

"I did?"

"Yeah." He was squinting against the sun, which had just made an appearance. "Do you remember what happened?"

I can gather from what I wrote, but that was mostly nonsense. I shook my head.

He began to tell me, but as he spoke, shame and fear began to snake in my gut and wrap my head, throbbing at the beginning of a headache.

I asked him to stop.

I went inside, got my laptop, and handed it to him. I told him I would rather read it later. I didn't tell him why.

I would rather he write it because written words seemed more malleable and distant than words coming out of his mouth. He was the only person who really saw the moment, and the only person, at this point, who had seen me get that bad. Because of him, I would be here, stuck, deteriorating for the rest of my life.

Then again, if Coop hadn't seen my calls, if he hadn't left the party, I might not have a life left to deteriorate. At this point I'm not sure which is worse, but I won't get into that.

And there was another reason: this way, if I didn't like what had happened in the written words, I could delete them from my memory book. That seemed more satisfying than forgetting things he said out loud somehow.

He scrolled up and down on this document before I said, "Hold on! Just . . . don't read any of it. Just start a new page and write it." He looked at me, brows furrowed. "Please," I added.

"Are you writing a journal or something?"

"Something like that."

well i started at nervig's at about 7 o'clock, but he was already too drunk to drive to get the kegs so i went back to norwich to pick them up. when i got back it was about 8 o'clock and people had started to arrive. i had to help carry and set up two kegs on my own so again, i was not drunk, and at about 9 i saw i had missed your first call. i called you back but you didn't answer. then you called me again about 15 minutes later and i picked up. you weren't talking directly into the speaker so i couldn't understand you but you kept saying, is this coop, is this coop, and i kept saying yes, yes, and eventually you got on the phone and made sense. you said you were lost, and i said, didn't i text you the address? and you were like yes, but you couldn't remember where you were. your voice was very shaky and you did not sound happy. so i asked you if you wanted me to come get you, and you said, yes, please, and then you sounded like your normal self again. you were like, coop, i'm fine. i'm just lost. i'll figure it out, and hung up.

but that didn't seem right to me, so i called you back, and you didn't answer. i called again and again, and at that point i was kind of debating whether or not to just let it go, to be honest. sorry if that's hard to hear but this is kind of a therapeutic thing for me, too. to write this down. i can understand why you do this. it was really hard to see you like that, and kind of hard to relive it now, but it's good.

anyway, i was debating, because katie kept trying to pull me back to the party, even though she and i aren't technically together, we just hook up. all your friends were there, too. i asked maddie if she had heard from you, and she said no, and i thought about asking that stuart guy i see you with, but i didn't feel like it, and it looked like he was checking his phone all the time anyway, and if you had called him, then he would be leaving.

but he didn't leave, and when you called me again and all i could hear were sounds of cars passing by, i left right away.

you were just a half mile from the party. i found you crying in the driver's seat. i thought you were just drunk or something so i laughed at you and i feel bad for that.

i'm sorry.

i got you to take the passenger seat and figured i would drive you home.

then i realized something else was very wrong, because sometimes you called me cooper, sometimes you called me sir, and sometimes you would remember you were supposed to go to a party, and sometimes you would ask me how i was, and say that you hadn't seen me in a while.

i took you home and as we walked up to your house, you sort of came to and asked me what I was doing there. and i told you, and you thanked me over and over and gave me a hug, which was nice of you. :)

we woke up your parents and they took you to the hospital and that's pretty much it.

now you're sitting next to me texting someone. probably stuart, i'm guessing. i hope that guy knows what he's in for.

^^^ What's that supposed to mean??

why are we still typing

Because I want to curse you out, you asshole, and Davy's sitting right there.

it was supposed to mean that you're not the average girl sammie, it was supposed to be a compliment

Oh, because I'm like ailing or whatever. Like someone can't have normal feelings for me because my liver's enlarged and shit.

i mean, it's a fair assessment

No, that's true, Coop, but you can at least humor me while I have the first real relationship in my entire life and probably the last. So why can't you just be nice?

oh like you guys are serious huh

Yeah, I think I could be in love with him.

word

That's all you have to say?

yeah i'm not going to get into it

Why?

i just said i'm not going to get into it

You don't like him or something?

he's sort of a prick yeah

What??? No he's not.

someone who has three houses but pretends to be this humble literary dude, it's exhausting, like just be real dude

You're grasping at straws.

lol that's such an outdated term

You just don't know him.

i'm not about to either

Fine.

fine. he's probably romanticizing you as a sick person, too, just saying

I haven't told him.

oh? huh

Why do you have that stupid smile on your face?

idk why are you afraid of telling someone you supposedly could be in love with or whatever something so important about yourself?

COOPER WAS KIND OF RIGHT

He was being an asshole about Stuart, but he was right. If I really want Stuart to like me for who I am, he had to know what who I am actually looked like. He needed to know about NPC. So that's why, a couple of days later when I found out that Davy and Bette would start a crafting camp, and that Coop's mom would be the one checking in on me that day, I texted Coop for a favor.

Me: Can you tell your mom that she doesn't need to come today and give me a ride into Hanover for a few hours?

Coop: yeah why

Me: To meet with someone really quick

Coop: cool, i'm actually going into town at 1, i'll swing by, what do you want to do?

Me: Oh, I'm just going to chill w/ Stuart

Coop: Oh word.

Me: Can you also drive me home at 4? Or will you be gone by then?

Coop: so demanding

Me: I'm sick :(

Me: I'll make you treats!

Coop: ya well ur lucky thats when i was going to come back to strafford anyway

We didn't talk much on the ride over, just about what kind of brownies would be his preference (no, I told him, I would not put weed in the butter), and where we'd meet later.

Coop dropped me off at the bottom of Stuart's driveway, and there he was, echoing warm waves back and forth: my boyfriend. He lifted me up to face level and we kissed like it had been two years since we'd seen each other, not two weeks. I had forgotten that he had a scent, a mix of that outdoor sweat and a clean detergent smell.

"You're better," he muttered into my neck. "I'm so glad you're better."

"Not all the way," I said, and tensed a little, but that went away when he took my hand and we walked together toward his house.

As we walked, Stuart jerked his head back toward the street and asked, "Who gave you a ride?"

"Oh, just Cooper Lind," I said.

Stuart opened his white-painted door. "Oh, yeah. I've seen him around. What's his deal?"

The nerves in his voice were puzzling at first, and then as he faced me in his big open foyer, his long, thin arms across his chest, I realized: He was jealous.

"Oh! Oh, no, Stuart—Coop's just my dumbshit neighbor."

This seemed to relax him a bit, and the smile returned to his black eyes. I reached out and stroked his shoulders, touching the freckle on his collarbone. He put his hands around my waist, Stuart's nose touching my nose.

"Yeah, just your friendly neighborhood pothead. He used to play baseball at Hanover until they kicked him off the team for being too high all the time. He told everyone he quit," I said, and laughed to mask the guilt that instantly grabbed my stomach.

I'm pretty sure I wasn't supposed to tell anyone that. Actually, I'm positive I wasn't supposed to tell anyone that. But desperate times call for desperate measures.

Stuart laughed with me. He tilted his chin to kiss me, and by the time I was done kissing him back, we had both forgotten what we'd been talking about.

We walked through his house slowly, Stuart telling me stories behind all the objects: the handwoven rug his parents had waited a year to acquire while it was being knotted by artisans in India, the room full of instruments we could only be in for just a second to make sure the temperature stayed correct, the rack of spices his mother used to make her own chai. I giggled at school photos of Stuart through the years, one with braces, one without, one with long hair, the rest without. And the books, a whole room made of walls full of books.

A section for fiction.

A section for poetry.

A section for biographies, for philosophy, for essays.

After sandwiches, we walked toward the Dartmouth campus. I was nervous at every turn that I'd forget something, forget what I was talking about, forget where I was. I tried not to be distracted, but under everything I said, I was asking in my head, *What if I fuck up?*

"What do you want to do?" Stuart asked.

I shrugged. "How's your writing going?" I asked.

"This is so pretentious of me, but I'd actually prefer not to talk about it. If I talk about it too much, it . . . loses its luster. Takes a different form. Or something."

"I don't mind," I told him. At least one of us had work they were excited about. "I completely understand," I said, trying to put on a smile.

We ducked into the lobby of the Dartmouth performance hall. The last time we were near here, we were making out on the field behind it. Our footsteps echoed on the shining, checkered tile. I'd never been inside.

"What time is it?" Stuart asked.

"It's two thirty," I said. I had been checking my phone every chance I got, in case Mom came home and found me gone, or in case Coop was heading back early.

Through the row of closed, arched wooden doors, the sounds of an orchestra floated out, muffled.

Stuart knocked on the box office door.

Suddenly, a balding man opened the door. When he saw Stuart, he smiled a little.

"Glen, can we pop inside for a second?"

"Eh." Glen glanced toward the doors. "Fine. Go through the side door, though."

I mouthed *what? You know him?* as Glen led us down the hallway.

Stuart whispered, "My parents are on the board."

I raised my eyebrows and resisted whispering back, *fancy.*

We entered the performance hall without anyone looking up. The orchestra was in plainclothes, practicing. It was unearthly beautiful. We found seats near the back, in the dark.

"So your parents . . ." I began.

"They give as much as they can to keep this going—these are tough times for orchestras."

"I can imagine," I said, watching the violinists chop the air in sync with their bows.

"My parents used to be musicians themselves. They always tell me they were never that great, and they met because they were both third chairs." Stuart laughed a little. "They realized at the same time that they weren't going to go anywhere. It's sort of bittersweet for them, but they loved music all their lives—Sorry. I'm talking too much."

"No, no," I said, taking his hand. "I didn't know your parents were musicians." I closed my eyes. "It sounds like a fairy tale."

"This sounds like childhood," Stuart whispered, leaning close to me.

I thought of his house full of books and music, of every day being like this. I sighed. "I can't help wishing I had a childhood like yours."

"What do you mean?"

I almost said *rich*, but it was not about the money. "Where books and music and philosophy brought me closer to my parents, not further away."

I thought of the one bookshelf we had at home, in the living room next to the TV, a mix of Dad's mystery novels, Mom's garbage magazines, and mostly kids' books that Mom and Dad had read to us over the years. All my own books I just stacked on the floor in my room.

And I'd never heard a professional orchestra before. It wasn't as if an orchestra wasn't something my parents would like, I'm sure they would, but it was so far off their radar, it might as well have not existed. The closest they got to a musical ritual was playing Johnny Cash while they sorted the bills. I smiled to myself at the image.

Stuart whispered, "Trust me, it's not all it's cracked up to be. I wish I was closer to my parents, too. I mean, they support me in whatever I do, but I feel like they know too much about books, and music, and writers. They know way more than me about good writing." He let out a little defeated laugh. "Like, how are you supposed to impress people like that?"

I was surprised. "I imagined you all sitting around at happy family dinners, drinking wine and talking about Kierkegaard."

"Ha! More like sitting around an empty table, in an empty house, because everyone's in different cities."

That's right, I remembered. Stuart's family owned houses here, in New York, and in India. The orchestra started over.

Stuart put his arm around me. "My favorite parts are actually parts like these, when the orchestra messes up, when they're out of tune, when they play the same note over and over."

I turned to face him. "Why?"

"I don't like too much perfection. It scares me."

"It doesn't scare me," I said immediately.

"Why?" Stuart echoed.

I thought of all my plans, now ruined, and pushed down the sadness that was coming up in my throat. I would tell him soon. "Because I know it doesn't exist."

The orchestra swelled. Stuart looked at me. "This is pretty close," he said, and our mouths met long and slow. I didn't know how to respond to that, because soon, I would be so far from perfect, I'd be unrecognizable.

Stuart has his own world to juggle, and a book to write, and he doesn't need another person to add to all the questions he has about his life, let alone a person who might slowly lose herself before he even gets a chance to know her better. I was too tired to tell him right then everything that was inside me.

After Coop dropped me off at home, I wrote Stuart an email telling him about NPC. And that I will not be in New York next year. And that it's probably for the best that we don't see each other. I wish we had gotten to be in New York together, at least. It's hard for me to even type that. I want him to stay with me until the end of the summer but I will try to be brave and try not to picture him riding the Q and N trains he loves so much with his arms wrapped around another girl, hurtling through the city.

I'll also say this: I don't know much about boyfriends and dating, and now I won't know much about love. But as last dates go, Future Sam, I'd say that one was pretty great.

THREE NEW MESSAGES

My god, Sammie, why didn't you tell me? I mean that's my initial reaction, but I understand you probably had your reasons. But regarding you and I: Are you kidding? Of course this doesn't change anything. I want to help you through this. I want to be there for you. I don't want to just run away. When can we meet?

I think your phone's off, by the way, because it's just going to voice mail. But seriously, I'd love to come over and talk about this.

Well, I just spent the whole night researching Niemann-Pick. This is so wild, and I can't imagine you going through this alone. I would like to help you in any way I can. Obviously, yes, my life is up in the air right now, but I can't think of just letting you go. Call me when you're ready.

So on one hand I'm dancing around my room in my underwear screaming HALLELUJAH at the top of my lungs. I just want to fucking

ENJOY this because not everything has to make sense. On the other hand, Stuart has known me for two months and is pledging himself to me when he could be enjoying his summer diseased-girlfriend-free, and it doesn't make a lot of sense.

Either way, he is coming over.

GRATITUDE

A couple of hours later, I slid open the door and Stuart wrapped his arms around me, clutching my back as if I would float away.

"Hi," he said into my hair.

"Hi," I repeated, and when we let go, I took in his wet eyes, still with traces of sleep in them. It looked like he didn't get a lot of it. "Thank you for being so wonderful," I told him, and as I said it, a bang sounded from down the hall. My family was stirring.

With Stuart and my parents in the same room—a room, mind you, covered in peanut butter–crusted plates and pillows from everyone's various beds and crumb-filled blankets—I felt like a little girl again, looking back and forth from one person to the other, trying to follow a conversation that I didn't quite understand.

Stuart looked around at our wide, low-ceilinged room, the McDonald's colors in the kitchen, the chrome table, the bookshelf in front of him lined with garbage magazines and kids' books. I wondered exactly what Coop wondered the other day: if Stuart knew what he was in for.

"So how long have you and Sammie known each other?" Mom asked after she had settled on the couch in her scrubs, next to my dad. Harrison had stayed in his room, and Dad sent Bette and Davy outside to play with Puppy. All of us held cups of green tea.

"A few years, kind of," Stuart said, looking at me. "But we've been seeing each other for just a few months."

"You understand that Sammie is in a compromised position, healthwise," Dad said, giving Stuart an unblinking stare.

Stuart nodded.

My chest was tight. I pressed my hands into my cup, and took a scalding sip.

Stuart hadn't wanted to sneak out and talk, like I had wanted to. He was the one who wanted to speak to my parents. There was a little part of me wondering, why couldn't he just talk to me? Like, why do we have to bring the adults into this right away? As usual, the McCoys always have to make things so intense. I tried to give Stuart an out.

"Well," I said. "Now that we've all made each other's acquaintance, Mom, Dad, I know you have to get going to work."

I looked at Stuart, searching his face for signs of panic. But his hands were still calm, clasped lightly around his cup, and his gaze still steady. It appeared I was panicking for both of us.

"Before you go, Mr. and Mrs. McCoy, I can't imagine what you're all going through," Stuart said, setting his cup on the carpet so he could put his hand on my back. "When Sammie told me, I . . ." He took a deep breath, thinking, breaking his exterior a bit.

Mom smiled encouragingly. He really did care. I couldn't help but melt a little, too.

"I researched what's at stake, and I don't want her . . ." Then he turned to me, probably aware of the way I tensed under his hand, that he was talking about me as if I wasn't in the room. "Like I told you, I don't want you to have to go through all this alone."

"We don't, either," Mom said, her voice catching in her throat. "And we plan on taking off more work if things get worse, as Sammie knows."

"But for now, it's tough," my dad muttered. "With the other kids and all that."

I sat as frozen as I felt. I was very confused, but I wasn't sure why.

Stuart was saying, "I may have to go back to New York at some point, but I'll stay for as long as I can, and help out with the little kids while your parents are at work."

"No, no need to go that far," I said, but my parents' sigh of relief was audible.

It wasn't as if I didn't know all this already, but I felt I was being discussed as a concept, rather than as a person. A concept everyone in this room deeply cared about, but a nonperson all the same. A generator of consequences.

By the end of the conversation, Dad was taking Stuart outside, hand on his back, so he could show him where we kept the chicken feed. They emerged from the shed, my dad holding a brand-new fifty-pound bag hoisted over his shoulder, pointing with his other hand at the chicken coop.

Hey, it's movie night and it's my turn to choose but Bette keeps saying it's her turn which is just NOT TRUE so fine we're watching Toy Story 3

grandma took me and harry and bette to that one when it came out i think it was my brithday

it was my birthday and we got cupcakes from lou's and i remember we went to the movie and even thogu harry and bette liked it i did not

mom keeps saying what are you writing

non of your buiesness

We're watching Toy Story 3? It's my turn to choose.

They keep saying it's beette's turn but it's not it's either mine or harry's that's not how it goes

they started the movie

grandma took me and bette and harry to toy story 3 last year on my birthday and we bought cupcakes at lou's and snuck them into the theeter in gramma's purse

WHOA there's this little girl here

She's very cute

they tell me to put away this computer and watch the movie but

i don't want to i don't like toy story 3

who's this little girl

i asked her who she was and she started to cry i'm sorry

they're telling me to pt this away

oh i know her

i think she is one of bette's friends from preschool

she's crying

no thanks id rather type

no thanks id rather type

i dont know that little girl

HOW IT WAS SUPPOSED TO GO

Last night I fell prey to one of the standard symptoms of dementia: reverting to the age I was when our movie night tradition first began, or maybe before that. Short-term memory gone, diving deep in the subconscious, I was a kid again. A kid who had not yet met her youngest sister, Davienne.

Poor, sweet baby Davy. When I snapped out of it, and Mom and Dad told me what happened, I held her and rocked her and told her that of course I remembered her, of course, of course. It was just that I was feeling sick, and my brain wasn't working right.

She understood after a while. To make it up to her, I let her put stickers all over me.

Movie night started when I was eleven, Mom was pregnant with Davy. It was the first year we got a TV. Mom and Dad have always held the belief that staring at screens was bad for kids. That's why I had to save up all my own birthday and Christmas money to buy this laptop, and why my parents still only carry flip phones. (Grandma and Grandpa bought me a smartphone last spring because they knew I used it to look things up for debate.) Anyway, it's pretty understandable why they gave in. Three kids and a soon-to-be infant, two full-time jobs, and no options for a babysitter in a five-hundred-person town.

The ones I remember:

WALL-E: Harrison's choice. First movie night ever. Dad accidentally burned the pizza but Mom ate it anyway. In fact, Mom was hugely pregnant and ate the whole thing herself. Mom and Dad were asleep by the end of the movie so Harrison and I started the DVD over from the beginning. When they woke up at midnight, they were astounded at how long the movie was. To this day they still think *WALL-E* is four hours long, with no dialogue, just robots beeping at each other, and will never let us watch it.

STAR WARS EP. 1: A few years later, I'm pretty sure Davy was two or three. It was Dad's turn to pick, and he was excited to "encounter contemporary efforts at the classic science fiction franchise." When Jar Jar Binks started talking, he grumbled, "What is this racist bullshit?" and all of us pretended like we didn't hear him at first, but then Mom started laughing, and Davy yelled, "Bullshit!" Harry laughed so hard he cried.

MY NEIGHBOR TOTORO: Bette's choice. She was around six. Coop came over for this one, because he loved Hayao Miyazaki, the filmmaker. He taught everyone how to pronounce the director's name. The freakiest, most beautiful cartoon I had ever seen, full of colors and creatures, and it wasn't all happy-go-lucky. It was about death and friendship and dark magic. Pretty sure this was when Bette discovered she might be from another planet. Every day for a month after she saw it, she wore Totoro ears she made out of construction paper, and stretched all her shirts out by putting pillows under them, chanting, "Totoro! Totoro!" One day I came home from school and found Coop in the front yard with her, prancing around, his shirt also stuffed with pillows.

THE PRINCESS AND THE FROG: My choice. (Well, Davy's choice. At this point, I had discovered no one wanted to watch the political documentaries I liked.) We actually didn't end up watching the whole movie, because Davy insisted on watching the song "Almost There" over and over, which annoyed Bette and Harrison so much that they hid the DVD one night after Davy fell asleep. Even now, as she's doing something like coloring or filling out a worksheet from school, she'll sing, over and over to herself, "People come from everywhere because I'm almost there, people come from everywhere because I'm almost there, people come from everywhere because I'm almost there . . ." I asked her once if she wanted to learn the rest of the song, or at least the right lyrics. "Nope!" she said.

PRIDE AND PREJUDICE: Mom's choice. It was just me and her, because Dad had taken the kids up to Grandma and Grandpa's house in New Hampshire. We had just found out I had Niemann-Pick, and we didn't know what it meant, really, or how long I would be seeing the geneticist. We snuggled on the couch and ate my favorite snack in the world that we almost never got, dark chocolate almonds. We laughed the most at Mrs. Bennet, how obsessed she was with marrying off her daughters like they were cattle, how nervous and nagging and silly the character was.

When it was over, and Elizabeth and Mr. Darcy had finally kissed and gotten married, I told her, "I'm glad you're my mom. Not someone like that."

Mom had wrapped her arms around me and held my head to her chest. "I'm glad you're my daughter," she said.

"Even if I'm sick?" I asked.

"Especially because you're sick," she had said, the vibrations of her voice soaking into my cheek. "I don't think anyone less strong would be able to handle it."

"Thanks, Mom," I said, and burrowed deeper.

"My first baby," she had said, and kissed the top of my head.

I remember it so well.

If nights like last night are going to happen again, it makes me glad I'm recording all this. Movie night isn't just staring at a screen, it is also laughing, and crying, and fighting, and snuggling.

And I'm glad I'm writing the good and the bad. I'm glad I didn't delete anything. What about all the moments that surround the good things? If you can only remember your aspirations, you will have no idea how you got from point A to point B.

That's the reason why I'm writing to you, I guess, as opposed to just taking a bunch of pictures. A picture can only go so deep. What about the before and the after? What about everything that didn't fit in the frame?

What about everything?

Life is not just a series of triumphs.

I wonder how many movie nights I missed for studying, or debate, or just complaining. I don't want to miss any more.

LUCID DREAMING

Days look like this: Mom creaks open my door and I open my eyes and it takes me a second for everything to come into focus, a sort of heavy wet cloth draping my vision because if I don't take a pill before I fall asleep, I wake up with shooting pains, so I sleep well, almost too well. But then Mom leans over me to open the curtains, smelling like tea tree oil like she always has, and like basil, always like basil in the summer, because she picks thick clumps of it from our yard to put in her omelets and on the sandwiches she takes to work.

I stand at my dresser with a cup of yogurt (because I'm not supposed to have an empty stomach) and swallow eleven pills.

Dad comes in—Dad's smell is Mitchum deodorant, like an old-fashioned mint smell—and gives me a kiss on the cheek.

Smells make things more clear than anything. So after the smells hit me, everything begins to make sense.

Harry gets picked up by one friend or another to go to camp or to go play video games.

Bette and Davy sometimes go to the Linds', sometimes they stay and Mrs. Lind comes over with lunch, sometimes Coop comes over with lunch (but never stays or says anything, maybe because Stuart is there and last time we really talked, he said all those mean things), sometimes a random on-call nurse comes over when no one can come, who mostly just sits in our living room and plays on her phone. Sometimes Mom takes me into town with her, and I stay in the waiting room until her shift is over, reading or watching Lord of the Rings on my laptop.

Sometimes I go with Stuart to the reading room at one of the bigger libraries on Dartmouth's campus, which Mom and Dad let me do because it's close enough to Mom's work at the Dartmouth Medical Center. Stuart and I like to share a big leather chair on the balcony while he reads what he's reading and I read what I'm reading.

Once I told him how I used to try to read all the same books he read in high school because I had such a huge crush on him.

He told me he loved that idea, the idea that he and I were trying to go to the same fictional places at once, and asked what if both of us tried to dream of the same place so we could meet while we're sleeping? Then, that night, Stuart called me and we tried to do exactly that.

"Okay, where should we go?" he asked.

I could feel the medicine tugging me to sleep. "How about the mountains?" I said.

"Which one?"

"On top of my mountain," I said.

"What does it look like?"

And I don't remember what came next, but Stuart told me I described it in detail, the rocky path that is barely a path and the red scrub grass that grows in the cracks and the layer of clouds that sits on the peaks. He went that night, he said, and I was there. I wish I could have been there.

On the days we sit together and I don't feel like reading, I look at books of photography or read old, trippy comics or just stare out the enormous arched window at the people on the lawn.

Sometimes I cry and that is okay.

At first I was embarrassed to do that in front of Stuart, but he told me he cries, too, sometimes for no good reason.

As he reads, Stuart moves his thumb across my hand. These are good days.

CAPTAIN STICKMAN

Maddie came to get me the other day in her two-door Toyota, kicking up dust on the mountain and honking to get Puppy to move out of the way so he didn't get run over. It was late June in the Juniest way, hot and bright, bees everywhere, sticky sugar spilling from the hummingbird feeder. It was Saturday and Maddie gave Harry and Bette and Davy high fives, all in a row, and waved to Mom where she was weeding in the garden and took me off the mountain.

We pulled up to her house, where Maddie's relatives, or more like various versions of Maddie at different ages and with different hair, were sipping lemonade under a banner that said CONGRATULATIONS MADELINE. To be among people who weren't my family, even strangers, I could have sung just like Davy, "People come from everywhere because I'm almost there."

The free air. Nobody asked me questions. I just sat on the porch swing and ate chocolate chip cookies, and occasionally Maddie would swing by and we'd exchange a joke, or she'd tell me a story about how she's been Facebook stalking her new roommate at Emory, a lizard enthusiast.

When she started in on what classes she was taking, I had to bite my tongue. College shit. I couldn't handle college shit.

I nodded along for Maddie's sake, but every mention of higher education was still like someone pinching me and twisting. Mariana Oliva's words rose up behind me, a ghost: *Study everything.* It's not like I still harbored dreams that I could do it. I couldn't do it, I knew I couldn't do it.

But damn. All the hope I had felt, flaunting itself like a peacock in the letters we received from the NYU registrar, every logo, every mention.

After her aunt so-and-so called Maddie away, I noticed Coop and that guy Maddie had punched all those years ago refilling their lemonade cups.

When Coop spotted me, I waved, and he came over and sat down on the swing. We didn't say anything for a while. I remembered I had forgotten to make him brownies for giving me a ride.

"*Qué pasa*, Sammie?" He bumped his cup on mine. One of the last classes we had taken together was Spanish 1, our first year of high school. He used to greet me like that every class period.

"*Nada, zanahoria.*"

Coop turned to me, confused. "Did you just say, 'nothing, carrot'?"

I laughed. "I couldn't remember what *asshole* was."

"Are you still mad at me for digging into that Stuart guy?"

"You can just call him Stuart."

Coop rolled his eyes. "Are you still mad at me for digging into Stuart?"

"Well, maybe I was, but you were right." I took a deep breath. "I told him."

"And?" Coop raised his eyebrows, his voice bracing for another blow.

"Stuart's sticking around." I swallowed. "I mean, for the time being. He even comes over and helps out around the house. That's why my parents haven't asked your mom to check in for a while."

"Wow."

"I mean, not all the time," I said. "He still has to write a lot. And he works at the Canoe Club."

Coop nodded, shrugged, didn't say anything for a second. "Good," he finally said.

We smiled, but there was a little sadness to his—I'm not sure why.

Anyway, the fight was over, like rapid fire, because we knew it was over. It was just like letting him into the kitchen after all those years. We could have been fighting about who got to lick the cake-batter spoon.

Over in the yard, Maddie screamed with delight. Coop and I glanced in her direction.

Pat and Maddie's aunt had just presented Maddie with one of her graduation presents: a navy blue hooded sweatshirt, embroidered with EMORY UNIVERSITY.

I tried not to be jealous, I tried to be happy, but I must have winced. I couldn't help thinking, *That could have been me, too.*

"*Qué pasa?*" Coop asked again, studying my face.

I nodded toward Maddie, hoping he would get it.

He did.

"I'm about to head home," Coop said. "Do you want a ride?"

"Oh, I think Maddie was going to drop me off later . . ."

Coop glanced at Maddie. "You really want to wait that out?"

Maddie was ripping the sleeves off the Emory sweatshirt, because she hates sleeves. When she was done, Maddie's aunt took the sleeves and waved them around over her head. Maddie put on her hood and pretended to throw a few jabs at her aunt. Her aunt slapped her with a sleeve and they chased each other around the yard.

"Yeah, it looks like it's going to be a long night." I looked at Coop, and we laughed.

I put the present I had brought for Maddie on her dining room table—a set of brand-new Remington Virtually Indestructible hair clippers I found online—and we slipped out the back door.

Coop and I hopped in his Blazer.

"When are you supposed to be home?" he asked as he turned the ignition.

"Not for another couple hours," I said. We still had about an hour of sunlight left, those shadowy hours where it was still warm in the light, cool in the dark. Just a couple more hours of freedom. I put on my seat belt.

Coop glanced at me as we pulled out onto the highway. "Want to go to the Potholes?"

I considered it. But going to the swimming hole with Coop probably meant going to the Potholes with everyone. Plus, he'd probably want to "relax," and I wasn't going to take any more risks with mentally compromised people operating vehicles. "Nah," I said. "I can't party anymore. Too many cookies." Coop let out a laugh. "I'm wasted," I added in a fake-drunk voice, which made him laugh more.

"Well, I meant just stop by. Chill. For old times' sake."

The air smelled so good, so clean, and almost wet. I wasn't lying when I told Stuart it was my favorite part of living here.

"Okay," I said, and Coop slowed down to turn the Blazer around. "Can I invite Stuart?"

Coop didn't answer right away.

"You'd like him if you got to know him," I said, flicking him in the shoulder.

"Sure," Coop said, and smiled at me with his lips closed.

By the time we exited off Highway 89 and parked near the banks, Stuart had texted that he couldn't come, he was working, but he'd call me later.

"Well, looks like it's just you and me, Coop," I told him.

I leaned on him as we climbed from rock to rock, until we were in the middle of the little falls, watching the streams split and meet again along the boulders. We talked about when we were kids before phones and social media, when we knew what boredom felt like. This was before either of our parents could afford summer camp, and basically used us as glorified babysitters. We got so bored, we did some weird shit. I mean, all kid stuff, but kind of messed up all the same.

We were cracking up, reminiscing about the time we told Bette she was actually a ghost, when Coop asked me, "When did we stop being friends?"

"Hm." I took a deep breath. "Besides the day you got kicked off the baseball team?" I saw his eyes that day, what had sunk inside him.

"Oh, yeah," Coop said quickly. "Yeah," he repeated. "Thanks for . . ." He paused, clearing his throat. "Thanks for not telling anyone."

I swallowed. Something told me, *Not now.* "I would never . . . yeah. I never told anyone at school," I half lied.

"But I mean before that." He was right. That was only the last straw on the camel's back.

"I think it was a gradual thing, but I remember one time . . ." I said. Cooper turned to face me, his arms perched on his knees, listening. "Freshman year. Even before you got . . . you left the team. I remember you were supposed to come over and help me watch the kids, and you never showed. Then you never said sorry. You didn't answer my calls for, like, a month. And I was, like, screw it."

"Huh." Coop looked down at his hands, picking at invisible dirt.

"And you had moved your seat in Spanish so you could sit next to Sara Gilmore. So it was weird to try to talk to you at school."

Coop shrugged his shoulders, twisting his mouth a little, searching for what to say. I waited for the excuses I figured he would make, how he got busy, or how I was kind of a know-it-all (I was). But he could have at least said something.

"I was a little asshole," Cooper said.

"You were." I nodded, and found myself giggling a bit out of triumph. "Sorry, it's just nice to hear you admit that."

He opened his mouth as if he was going to say something, and then closed it. He stood up and leapt to another rock. He put his hands on his hips, and then raised a fist to the sky.

"Do you remember this?" he called.

I did. When Coop made that gesture as a kid, he had automatically transformed into CAPTAIN STICKMAN! Captain Stickman was a friend to all humans and animals. His special power was, well, that he had a stick. But! The stick could be used as a sword, a walking stick, a flag to claim territory, or a wand that could turn anything into anything.

"CAPTAIN STICKMAN!" I yelled, laughing. "But you're missing your stick!"

I reached over the rock and searched for a piece of driftwood in the water. All I could find was a beer can. I tossed it at Coop; it fell egregiously short.

Coop got on his belly and fished it out. "CAPTAIN STICKMAN!" he yelled, his voice echoing off the falls.

I joined in with a fake announcer voice, as I had done when we were kids. "A FRIEND TO ALL HUMANS AND ANIMALS!"

"A FRIEND TO ALL HUMANS AND ANIMALS, INCLUDING SAMMIE MCCOY!" he yelled.

I smiled at him. He smashed the beer can between his hands.

"IS THIS INDEED CORRECT?" he asked, pointing at me with the smashed can. "I AM SORRY FOR BEING AN ASSHOLE. ARE WE FRIENDS AGAIN?"

"Yes," I said. "Of course." I didn't really know what that meant, especially now. Minus shooting the shit at the Potholes, I didn't really know what Coop and I would do together. Still, he looked more like my friend than ever, out of breath, and hair all over his face, excited for no reason.

"YOU MUST YELL IT TO MAKE IT SO," he said.

I cupped my hands around my mouth. "CAPTAIN STICKMAN IS A FRIEND TO ALL HUMANS AND ANIMALS, INCLUDING SAMMIE MCCOY."

Captain Stickman once again raised his fist to the sky, and then leapt back to my rock, turning back into Coop.

We got into the Blazer. We talked about the time Captain Stickman had gotten too ambitious about his ability to land on his feet after jumping from a tree, and broke his leg. Then, because crutches were an ideal sticklike tool, Captain Stickman again overstepped his abilities and broke the other leg. We were cracking up by the time we pulled into my driveway.

"Hang on," Coop said when I unbuckled. He kept his eyes on my house as he said, "There was a time for me, too."

"For what?" I asked.

"That I thought we weren't friends anymore. I mean, it was kind of my fault. But. Do you know what I'm talking about?" He looked at me, clutching the steering wheel.

I thought back. "That time I corrected you in Spanish in front of everyone?"

"No, before that."

I thought of middle school. "When I didn't believe you that you were allergic to bees?"

Coop laughed a little. "Nope."

"Tell me."

"When . . ." he started, and cleared his throat. "The summer after eighth grade, when I called you. And I asked you to go to Molly's to eat dinner with me. On, like, a Friday night. And I told you I would pay for it with my allowance. And you said . . . Are you remembering this?"

"Oh!" I remembered. Kind of. I remember he was acting weird on the phone, and a couple of weeks after that he avoided me, but then the whole thing kind of blew over. "I thought you were just scheming something, like a prank or something. And I thought you were mad because I didn't want to come."

"I wasn't mad, Sammie." Coop looked back at my house. "But my feelings were hurt." He cleared his throat again. "My widdle feewings. Eighth-grade feelings," he added. "Ha-ha."

"Oh!" I said again, and got out, leaning on the open door. I thought I knew what Coop was saying, but I wasn't sure, so I said, "Well, damn, Coop. I'm sorry."

He shook his head, laughing it off. "It's fine. I was just remembering that. Trip down memory lane."

Mom had opened our front door, waiting.

"See you soon?" I asked, because we were both uncomfortable.

"See you soon," he answered.

OOOOOOHHHHHH

Oh. Coop had been asking me on a date! Oh my god, that's adorable. If only you could have seen what Coop was like then. The kid wore a different color sweat suit every day of the week. Like, he was that guy. The guy who wears sweat suits. As we all were. I mean, but Coop grew out of it ha ha ha and I did not. But anyway, I had no idea. I'll tease him for it later.

Or maybe I won't tease him. I don't like the idea of making him embarrassed. I don't like seeing him, you know, hurt.

But between you and me, that is so funny. I didn't know he could have ever had those kinds of feelings for me. Probably because I was the only person with a vagina that talked to him on a regular basis. As *National Geographic* tells us, those kinds of feelings develop when you put two heterosexual people who aren't related to each other in the same room, and Coop and I were in the same room a lot.

Then he went into the same room with a lot of other vaginas and got over it.

Is it weird to put *Cooper Lind* and *vagina* in the same sentence?

But yeah, even if I had noticed then, I don't think I could have gone on a date with Cooper Lind. I was too busy smashing my face into pillows and reading about Druid Wars.

God, I am remembering the whole thing now. How strange I thought it was that he would call me and ask me to go to Molly's, rather than just coming over and opening the fridge and putting two hot dogs in the microwave, like he normally did.

MRS. TOWNSEND: THE SEQUEL

Mrs. Townsend appeared from out of nowhere from behind the fish tank at Dr. Clarkington's office today, this time in a blue sundress, and at first I thought I was imagining her. But no, it was the real Mrs. Townsend, with her every-good-clean-smell, her hair now woven into long black braids. When we hugged, a belly emerged.

"Baby Mrs. T?" I almost screamed, because I have the tact of a fired circus clown.

"Baby Mrs. T," she said, laughing. "His name will be Solomon."

"After *Song of Solomon?*"

"The Toni Morrison book, not the Bible."

"Good."

"I promise you, he won't turn into a snobby New York kid. So help me god I will make sure that he eats gluten like the rest of the world."

"Why would he be a snobby New York kid?"

"Greg and I are headed to Manhattan. He's getting his PhD at Hunter."

Everyone I like goes to New York. I decided to be okay with that. "And what are you gonna do?"

Mrs. T looked around her in fake panic. "Oh no, I won't have a Sammie to mentor. What will I do?"

"Yeah, who—who—who's going to send you emails at three in the morning asking for a letter of reference?" I finally got out. I had started not to get so embarrassed about my choppy speech. You just kind of have to plow through it.

Mrs. Townsend leaned her elbow on the betta tank, tapping at the swimming forms. "I'll tell you what I'm going to do, I'm going to have this baby, then I'm going to work in the Admissions department. And then I'm going to raise this baby, and then I'm going to retire. That is, unless, the climate changes as drastically as they say it will in the next twenty years. In that case, Greg and I are going to move back to the top of the Green Mountains, and we're going to raise orange trees."

"Orange trees in New England?"

"You're going to want to get above sea level, believe me."

"Can I come?"

Mrs. T took me by both shoulders. "If you have a useful skill, yes."

"I can drink an entire gallon of chocolate milk in one sitting."

"You're in," she said, and we laughed.

TEXTS FROM STUART SHAH, NPC EDITION

You have to hand it to him, the man is a natural writer. Though he asks the same question every morning, I have never received the same text from Stuart twice.

> *Stuart:* how are you feeling today?
>
> *Stuart:* feeling chipper this morning?
>
> *Stuart:* good day today?
>
> *Stuart:* how's my baby?
>
> *Stuart:* is today a good day?
>
> *Stuart:* how's the health?
>
> *Stuart:* feeling dapper?
>
> *Stuart:* is the sun treating you well this morning?
>
> *Stuart:* need anything from me this morning?
>
> *Stuart:* how's it shakin'?
>
> *Stuart:* how's the baby girl?
>
> *Stuart:* what's good this morning lady?
>
> *Stuart:* how's life on this rainy day?

Stuart: how's sammie?

Stuart: how's my girl?

Stuart: ok?

Stuart: ca va?

Stuart: doing well?

THAT MONSTER WOMAN THEY KEEP IN THE ATTIC IN THAT ONE BOOK

Today is not a great day brain-wise. My hands are not good at typing. My mouth is doing the twist. And it was not fun to be a person today. But I have this idea.

I have to do this to make it okay that the other day I forgot the word for *stove* and that I woke up in the middle of the night and thought I needed to get ready for school. Like the other day I could have sworn I saw Grandma and Grandpa in the yard. I didn't tell you because there's not a whole lot more to say and it's not great for me to think about those times. They're just strange. Like I answered Stuart's daily check-in with "never been better" because when I tell him the truth he gets very sad and comes over and strokes my hair.

And most of the time it's good. Like don't worry I'll always tell you when it's good. Or when things are bad enough that you should know. You should also know that I haven't deleted anything from here. I'm pretty sure I told you that. Because I like reading back and that makes it more exciting. But as I said I'm not feeling the best today.

I always told you how I thought I would end up, so I'm going to tell you how I think my brother and sisters will end up, too. They've got much more . . . I don't know . . . time. They've got a lot more ahead of them.

Also, I am not going to use the Internet to look things up anymore when I forget the word, because this is my book and Google is not my brain and this book is supposed to be a part of my brain. You know what I mean? I want this book to have MY WORDS even if they are the wrong words.

So here it goes. We'll start with Harry.

THE MCCOY SIBLINGS: AN UNOFFICIAL BIOGRAPHY

CHAPTER 1: HARRISON

Harrison George McCoy was born on a dark day in December, but many would say his cries rang like the bells of Christmas. Actually, no one said that, but he was born around Christmas. As a child, Harrison was obsessed with old coins. Whenever Mom visited her mom in Canada, she brought back Canadian coins, and coins from France, and sometimes coins from England and coins from Spain. Stuart also brought him coins from India the other day and I can't remember what they're called but that was so nice of Stuart.

Anyway, where was I? One important day however Harrison

went over to his friend Blake's house and discovered the exciting never-ending world of video games. At first I was not happy about this, having been a child of my parents, who do not like screens. But after watching the way his face lights up when he plays them and how if you ask him one question about Minecraft he will talk more to you than he will ever talk about his own life, I changed my mind.

All this to say Harrison McCoy found his calling with the movement of digital blocks onto other blocks. With this knowledge Harrison will excel in geometry and physics. He will make it through high school with many friends who also have his interests. Oh, like a video game club! Harrison McCoy will join a video game club in let's say ninth grade.

Soon this video game club became less of a club and more like a collection. No, collective! They mushed their ideas about video games together and created their own video game. Called Geoblock ← not bad, huh? I should tell him about this idea.

As they got older all their different personalities came together in a perfect balanced way, and they started a company to sell their game. Harrison will be the major video game maker. The boss. And because of his quietness yet also his passion for Geoblock he will be a great leader. The business will succeed beyond his wildest dreams.

One of the members of the collective will be a woman or man that Harrison will always disagree with but respect a lot, because their arguments always find a good answer. After they have taken care of all their business stuff and are full human beings, they will realize they can be perfect life partners as well. They will adopt a puppy and name it Puppy, after the original Puppy. And they will live long after that as a happy family.

(NOT) THE END

HOT, STILL, AMERICAN INDEPENDENCE DAY

Just like every year, they blocked off all the streets in Hanover and people walked around without much clothing, getting sunburned, drinking out of bottles of water or bottles of beer. It was a good day for me, brain-wise and body-wise and otherwise-wise, so while Mom and Dad and the kids went to ride on the rides, I met up with Stuart.

"My little American," he said, rubbing my shoulders when I found him on the main road. I kissed him. He tasted bitter and sweet. "Having some beers?"

"Yeah, I just . . ." He rubbed his face with his hand. "Sometimes I just need a break."

"Good! Yes! You should relax." He had come over almost every day this week, helping to do the dishes, taking Puppy for long walks, driving Bette and Davy to camp.

"How's the writing?" I asked.

"Blah," he said. "America!" he shouted instead, and put his arm around my shoulders.

I laughed. "Fair enough!"

I told him about the biographies. He told me about a regular who had come into the Canoe Club that reminded him of a short story. When we arrived at his house, I could hear people's voices, but couldn't see them. I tried to look up, but my eyeballs don't really do that these days, so I just listened.

"Stu-ey's back!" I heard Ross Nervig shout.

"Are they on the roof?" I asked Stuart.

"Yep!"

Inside the garage I squeezed my hands in and out of fists, and craned my neck to look upward so my eyeballs didn't have to.

"Oh!" Stuart said. "We don't have to go up there. I'll tell them to come down here."

"You don't have to do that," I said.

"No, baby," he said, putting his hands on my cheeks. "They should come down here. I'm so stupid. I will not let you strain yourself."

"It's fine," I told him, and added *I don't like the language, "I will not let you . . ."* to a long list of things that I had not said to Stuart. The list included the following:

Please don't call me "baby."

Please don't remind me to take my medication. If I forget, I would rather my family did that.

Please don't stroke my hair and become sad, because that makes me sad.

I didn't like this part of myself, this part that censored, and Stuart did everything out of love, and he did so much. He would never hold it above my head, but I would. Every time I repeated myself, every time I forgot where I had put my phone, every time I couldn't take Puppy for a walk, it hung above my head.

But I could still do most things. Most everything. Just not all the time. See, Stu?

I swallowed. I thought of myself just a couple of months ago, flitting around like no big deal, thinking I was going to live on my own in New York.

But it's not that you don't fall, it's that you get back up, right? Right. Stuart waited while I psyched myself up, a little encouraging smile on his face.

"Are you sure?" he asked.

"I want to do this."

I gripped the rungs like I was hanging off a cliff. Stuart asked if I wanted help, his hands floating around my calves. I said no, and though I had to wait a moment after each step, I pushed off strong. I made it up both ladders, and by the time I sat down on the flat, warm tar, I was breathing and happy like I had won a marathon. I realized I would do it all over again just for that feeling, like I was back in the world and the world was good. Even if it made me tired.

Stuart went to a cooler that sat in the center and cracked opened a beer.

"My friend Sammie!" Coop was lounging next to a girl in an American flag bikini. He was wearing his favorite THAT GOOD GOOD tank top. I looked around a circle of people I was probably supposed to know, their heads in red, white, and blue bandannas and plumes of cigarette smoke, and goddamn, it was great to see Coop. It's hard to describe the feeling of relief I had, Future Sam, really knowing someone else up there on the roof. He was just so, I don't know, nonblurry. Then I realized the last time I had felt that out-in-the-world feeling was at the Potholes, with Coop. So it made sense.

"Hey, Coop," I said, still taking deep breaths. I pointed to the opening in the roof. "I made it up both ladders."

"Well, cheers to you!" he said, tilting his head, holding up a beer. He swigged it and set down the empty bottle.

"Yes, cheers to you!" Stuart called from the cooler, and turned back to Ross Nervig, who had pulled him into a discussion about poetry.

"Anyone want a water?" Coop asked, getting up. "I'm going to switch to water."

"I'll have a water," I said.

Coop brought me a sweating bottle and sat back down next to Hot Katie. Hot Katie who he was supposedly not dating.

After a minute, I noticed a dark shape land on her leg. She screamed and stood. Coop turned from the girl he was talking to on his other side.

"Get away from him!" I screamed at Katie.

"What?" she shouted, taken aback, still whacking the air.

"Please move!" I motioned her away from Coop.

Coop realized what was happening and scrambled to the other side of the roof.

"He's allergic to bees," I said, quieter.

"Is it gone?" Coop asked me.

"It's gone," I told him.

Thanks, he mouthed.

For the next hour or so I tried out my newfound small-talking on a few people, trying to remember things about them.

At every quiet moment, I quizzed myself: Becca is in Washington, DC, Lynn decided against taking that internship after all, Jeff is working at Ross Nervig's dad's contracting business. Becca: DC, Lynn: no internship, Jeff: Nervig's dad.

Soon I was feeling bleary. I had taken my pain meds after I came up the ladder, and the sleepiness crept in.

When Stuart swooped down to kiss me, I whispered, "Hey."

"Hey," he said. His eyes were sleepy, too, but for a different reason.

"I think I gotta go," I said.

"No," he said, frowning.

"My—what's the thing, with the gas—my tank is low," I said.

"Okay, well, just wait one second and we'll go home."

"You *are* home!"

Stuart talked warm and soft in my ear. "You can stay here. I'll bring you some water."

I lifted my hand to his shirt and pulled him closer. "No. You stay with your friends. You relax. I mean it."

"How about I just kiss you?" he said, and planted his lips on mine, sloppy and salty until I had to laugh.

"Stu-ey, now!" Ross was yelling, pointing at the sky, a book in his hands like a Viking conqueror with his ax.

The fireworks had started.

"One second, baby, I promised Ross I would read this Ginsberg," he said, slurring a bit, and scrambled over to his friend. I laughed again to myself. Coop was looking at me. I shrugged and smiled.

"Everyone! I wanna read this," Stuart yelled as the golden strips of light popped behind him. He looked at the book. He looked at the book, and lines from "America" rumbled out of his gut with great intensity. Verses about hopelessness, about giving it one's all but still having nothing.

Stuart was silhouetted by the colors, all eyes on him. His arms flailed wildly as he read, and Ross stood beside him nodding, clapping his hands at parts he liked. I wondered what he was working on, if he would read his own work like this someday, as if he felt every word. Stuart was majestic. Stuart was drunk.

I thought about five summers ago, the first and only time I got drunk like that. Coop at that party in April, telling me that he had wanted to "get drunk with me his whole life," but actually we had, once.

The summer before freshman year, before the whole "date" incident, he and some of his baseball player buddies had stolen someone's parents' whiskey, and Coop convinced me to try it if he mixed it with Cherry Vanilla Dr Pepper. This was, of course, before I knew I wanted to get out of the Upper Valley, before I discovered debate, before I wanted NYU, before I wanted Stuart.

It had been fun at first, and I gulped it down like I was drinking a soda.

Coop and I kept pushing each other and giggling. He had taken my glasses and ran around with them, and I chased him and hopped on his back. Then he had given me a piggyback ride into the trees, where I slid off him, and after I swayed for a second, I began to vomit.

Coop had held my hair as I puked and kept saying, "Oh no, oh no."

I had started laughing, even as I was wiping puke from my mouth, and said, "I'm never doing this again!"

"You're never going to puke again?" Coop had asked, and by then we were both laughing. It was such stupid, happy laughing.

I remembered him bending beside me, not afraid to be next to me when something so gross was happening. I remembered the feeling of his hand on my back, holding my curls in a bunch.

I watched the girl in the American flag bikini pass Coop a joint, but he waved it off.

He looked back at me, almost like he was remembering the same thing, but he couldn't have been. Anyway, we looked at each other. I don't really know what either of us was thinking, but we looked at each other for a long time.

Today, Stuart was closer to the way he was on the day he read at the library, when I realized I loved, or was starting to love, him. It's been a while since I've seen him like that, actually. He's happier when he's doing what he wants to do, not just what he feels he needs to do. We all would be better doing that, I think.

I asked Coop for a ride home. Ever since he brought me home from Maddie's graduation party, Mom and Dad had started to let Coop hang out and give me rides and stuff, which is nice. Takes the pressure off them to have him just across the mountain, I guess, and he's home more often than his mother. Plus, the nurse gets expensive.

Mom invited him in to have pie, and we ended up eating it in my room because Bette was having kind of a tantrum about pie, and anyway, Coop saw the NPC Task Force pictures on my wall and asked me about them.

After I died from embarrassment and then rose again, I was like, "Oh god, that was kinda dumb. Back when I thought I could, like, make NPC disappear. When I thought I could still do all the things I had set out for myself."

"Well, why forget about them?" Coop asked. "No time like now. They're not going to matter less just because they aren't part of some grand scheme. You just have to . . . adjust the plan."

"Adjust the plan to what?"

"I guess I mean get rid of 'the plan' altogether. Do them because they're good things to do. Do them just for the sake of doing them."

SO I DID

Today, as a tribute to Beyoncé and independent women everywhere, I called Maddie and congratulated her again.

"Can I say something cheesy?" I asked her.

"I'm never opposed to cheese," Maddie said solemnly, and we laughed.

"Seriously, though."

"Seriously," she said. "Cheese."

"Ahem, ahem. All strong women are allies, and if I can't run the world, you should, and you should know I'm behind you."

Maddie was quiet for a bit. "That means a lot, Sammie. Really."

"Well, you mean a lot to me."

"You, too. Your opinion always means a lot to me."

"Will I see you before you go?" I asked.

"I'm already down the coast with my aunts. But I'll be back before school starts. We'll see each other again soon."

"I hope so," I said, and when we hung up, I remembered how I had compared our debate tactics to blowing up a balloon. And maybe this is the NPC talking but something inside me had swelled up, but thankfully didn't pop.

THE MCCOY SIBLINGS: AN UNOFFICIAL BIOGRAPHY

CHAPTER 2: BETTE

As I have hinted throughout this book, Bette Elise McCoy perhaps was not born of this earth. Let's just say Mom and Dad "brought her back from the hospital" in late February. As a baby she was mostly quiet except when she had the thing that babies get when their stomach is always upset. To this day, she will not eat these foods: bananas, lemon or anything that has lemon in it, pineapple, Ritz crackers, oranges, mango, papaya, carrots, pasta, corn, squash, baby corn, and hot dog buns.

Bette used to have an invisible parrot that she named "Barrot." She claims she can talk to birds of every kind. I will point out that most of this claim comes from her running at any group of birds and saying, "Fly, fly." So, yeah, sure, the birds "listen" to her.

Anyway, Bette entered the fourth grade a whiz at math. She also, as you can see, has a strong imagination and is not afraid of what people think about her. Let's say that for many years these two skills do not mix, and maybe Bette will not make a lot of friends. I can say that with a lot of truth because I see a lot of myself in Bette and that's probably why I am so hard on her. I hope she doesn't just spend all her time talking to herself, like me.

But this is my book. So I say that instead of spending her teenage years cooped up studying, Bette will make friends with someone like Maddie right away, and know that she isn't alone, and she isn't the only one.

Let's say her best friend is really good at playing guitar and Bette is great at the words and the math of writing great songs (because a lot of it is math, especially for more windy-long-tons-of-sounds songs, Stuart told me that) and together they form a band called BARROT. HA-HA yes.

So BARROT gets big in the Upper Valley playing gigs and soon they go to New York City. They will blow everyone's heads off with their crazy opera pop. They will do costumes and whole huge sets like *Alice in Wonderland*. They will play in Canada, they will play in Europe, they will play in Africa and India and Asia. They will make music like the two Beatles guys damn damn what are their names except they never break up.

They will live two floors from each other in an apartment building. The two friends, Bette and Whoever, will raise birds of every kind on the roof, and they will write songs and albums together for the rest of their lives.

THE MIRACLE OF SCIENCE

As a tribute to an Elizabeth Warren–esque dedication to straight-talking about my disease, I went to see Dr. Clarkington again with my parents, and asked them to put the specialist on speakerphone. I told both doctors all my symptoms, and how I was writing in this book.

"That's great," they said. "The book is great."

"Do crosswords, too," the specialist said over the phone.

Crosswords. Great.

"And her symptoms?" Mom asked.

"Things sound steady," they said, "but not great."

Steady, but not great.

Great.

The Linds watched the kids while Mom and Dad and I went to Molly's afterward. They told me I could get anything I wanted. This was uncommon. Molly's was usually reserved for birthdays, and birthdays meant pizza, because pizza was cheap. I don't think we've ever been to Molly's and ordered individual dinners.

"Are you sure?" I asked.

"Of course," Dad said. "Hell, let's get a bottle of wine."

"We don't need to do that," Mom said, putting her hand on Dad's.

"I want to," Dad said, forcing a smile at both of us. "Get anything you want, Sammie-bo-bammie."

So I was going to get the fettuccine. Mom was going to get a burger. Dad was getting salmon. It still felt wrong. Like we were celebrating something that didn't warrant celebration.

"Why don't we just get pizza?"

"No," Dad said quickly. "We already chose."

"I was just saying," I said, shrugging. I was just trying to tell them, *Hey, we don't have to spend extra money because Sammie's brain doesn't work.*

"If you want pizza, we'll get pizza," Mom offered.

"I don't want pizza. I was just saying that we *could* . . ."

"Let's drop it," Dad said to me, his voice louder.

Mom turned to him, her lips tight.

"I'm tired, Gia." He turned to me, his Irish cheeks now tinged. He paused. "I just want us all to be grateful we're eating a nice meal."

By "us all," he meant me, I was pretty sure. So I thanked him. I put my hands in a prayer position. "Thank you, Father, for this nice meal."

"Don't give me attitude, Sammie, not after today."

I felt my eyes narrow, automatic, my chest tight.

"What is that supposed to mean?" I asked, but I knew what it was supposed to mean.

He was going to say that he wished I would just shut up about it because they had to bust their ass every day to pay for my doctor visits, my prescriptions, my hospital stays, and he wanted me to be a grateful little golden angel child.

Well, me fucking too. I was trying to be grateful. I was tired, too. "I said we should get pizza! Did you not hear me?"

"That's not the point—" he began, and I could tell he was weighing his words. "I didn't mean . . ."

"Dad, like, you think I want any of this either?"

"I know, but—"

"You think I even want to be in the Upper Valley right now?"

"You want to be in New York. I know." At this point, Dad's eyes were in his palms.

"If I had my choice, trust me, I wouldn't be living on your dime."

"Then go!" Dad said, waving his hand.

"Stop it, both of you," Mom said.

"Gladly," I said. "In fact, I think I'll go to Canada."

"Oh, Jesus . . ." Mom muttered, and flicked Dad in the shoulder. "She's kidding, G."

"I'll walk to fucking Canada," I said, and stuck my straw through a clump of ice. "Stay with Nana. Learn how to fish."

I sat very still, letting hot blood pump through my broken body. We were both kidding, right? But the truth behind all of it hung over the booth.

"Don't joke about Sammie going away," Mom said quietly. "Either of you."

"No, of course not," Dad started, holding out his hand. "Sweetie."

Mom started to cry. She held on to my arm. "It wasn't funny," Mom whimpered.

"I know," I said, and I took Dad's hand.

"I'm sorry." Dad's lip was shaking. "It doesn't matter."

"I know," I said again.

Mom's tears unsettled a big boulder that was sitting in my stomach, and I tried not to cry, but I was leaking them at a quick rate, I couldn't hold them in fast enough, and Dad suddenly spit out air into a sob, and we were all trying to keep it together. We were all trying not to look at the other Molly's patrons, staring at us.

The server approached like she was walking on glass. Dad lifted his palms, imploring. "I'm a full-grown adult," he said, shrugging, sniffling. "What can I say."

The family next to us looked away, eyes on their food, trying to pretend like they weren't staring.

"Whatever," Mom said. "People can cry."

We ordered. We didn't get pizza.

After a while, the heaviness that had been pressing in on us was gone. Instead, the air was blank and clear. Mom and Dad dried their faces on their restaurant napkins. We ate. It was delicious.

Mom told us about one of her co-workers, a pregnant lady named Denise, who had offered to come over and show us how to raise bees.

Dad and I agreed that Davy would be an excellent beekeeper's assistant. Bette would probably set them all free, and Harrison would get bored.

Mom asked Dad and me what we thought about her getting a

tattoo, a hexagon for the six of us. I said no, Dad said yes. Mom said, too late, she already got it, but we knew she was lying because she started laughing before the end of the sentence.

Dad moved to my side of the table, so that Mom and me and him were all in a row in the booth, his stocky legs sticking out into the aisle.

Mom laid her head on my shoulder.

Dad confided to us that he would probably ask Stuart to stop feeding the chickens, since he'd always find the food piled in one place, as if Stuart had ran into the coop, tossed it, and left as quickly as possible. I laughed and told him that'd be a good idea, that Stuart probably liked *the idea* of feeding chickens more than actually feeding them.

Mom said she had a confession, too, that she was a little tipsy. And that her burger had made her fart.

"Gross!" Dad and I said at once.

"But it doesn't smell!" Mom said.

"It truly is a miracle of science," Dad said, cracking up, his face scrunched up with mirth just like Harrison's when farts are mentioned. "That Mom's farts don't ever really stink."

After our bellies stopped shaking with laughter, we sat in silence for a while.

Until I said, "Is anyone getting dessert?"

Dad replied, "I doubt they have entire gallons of chocolate milk, Sammie, if that's what you're asking."

Mom and I snorted. They probably didn't. Dad checked with the server, anyway.

We walked out of Molly's with their arms around my shoulders, my arms around their waists. I had the urge to hang on to them, like I used to do when I was a kid, with my legs dangling as they carried me. But I got the feeling that after what we'd been through tonight, we were all feeling a little too old for that.

THE MCCOY SIBLINGS: AN UNOFFICIAL BIOGRAPHY

CHAPTER 3: DAVY

Surprise! Hahahahahaha. But seriously Davienne Marie McCoy was not a planned child, but I wasn't a planned child, either. All the yellow and orange Bette will never eat, Davy eats it. That is to say not that she has a big stomach but also that she takes in the yellow, you know what I mean? She is happy and sunny and sweet.

Davy is the one of us who I think can be anyone. It's like all the parts of Mom that somehow didn't stick to the rest of us when we came out, all of those parts stuck to Davy. I was not what's the word talking-big-but-not-lying when I said she is popular in her class. Lots of her friends come over. She gets along with adults, too. She and Father Frank are best friends. She and Dr. Clarkington are best friends.

So let's say she is popular all the way up into high school. Let's say that in high school she is so nice to everyone and everyone thinks she's their best friend that she starts to wonder who is actually her friend. Like she has kind of a crisis like maybe no one knows what's really inside her. And I can actually see Davy doing this because I don't know where else such a good-hearted sweetie could go without people yanking her around.

Let's say that she has a vision from God. Okay I know it's crazy but go with me. So like a vision from God, but not God as a white man with a beard, but a force that comes to her in this yellow light and tells her that her purpose is to use her kindness to help people.

So she starts a thing where people can take classes for free if they don't have any money. She uses all her friends around the town who are good at different things and they form sort of a school but anyone who goes doesn't have to pay. Everyone can come and learn about stuff that will help them get a job, but no one has to owe the government money or owe the banks money.

Even when things get harder and harder for people, or for her, because it's not going to be easy, she will be that brightness for everyone and keep them going.

And she will help all the people here that I am usually so mean about, all the people who live here for life, and those people will help each other, too, and no one will ever want to leave because people are learning and growing and being kind to each other all because of Davy.

well today is not a good day because i forgot the names of all our chickens so i feel kinda dumb stuart just left and i hope he wasn't turned off by the way i am sort of swallowing a lot and shaking when i try to reach out for things and i tried to smile a lot and say its okay its okay and he was very nice but of course i was mad that i didn't know any of the chickens names and he didnt know them either so its not his fault

harry and bette and davy came from the woods and davy pointed at the spotted one, the black one, the brown one, the brown and white one, and the white one and we went over and over the names again and maybe stuart got bored

i hugged him a lot before he left i hope he wasn't scared or weirded by me he told me he didn't want to go but i asked him to go because i was not doing great

for future reference . . .

THE SPOTTED ONE IS CLARKY

THE BLACK ONE IS MARGIE

THE BROWN ONE IS CELESTE
THE BROWN AND WHITE ONE IS POOPSIE
THE WHITE ONE IS MOONY

THE MCCOY SIBLINGS: AN UNOFFICIAL BIOGRAPHY
[COMMENTARY BY SUBJECTS]

CHAPTER 1: HARRISON

Ya I'm probably going to be a developer.

Sammie, you also forgot the part where I'm in a helicopter and I, like, drop down on a rope and jump on buildings, and the part where I'm a sucsesful YouTube star and I make a million dollars just because I can make fart noises on my belly. Lol.

CHAPTER 2: BETTE

Hmmmmmmm.

I guess, yes, I am an alien. I keep telling you guys that. Hehe.

My uncle is from Mars.

I like dogs and other animals a lot.

I am always just joking when I say I can talk to birds.

I think that sounds pretty good but I am not a very good singer!!!!!!

Thank you for writing that dear sister.

Will you please teach me how to braid later today?????

CHAPTER 3: DAVY

i like to rite on this cmpoter mom tot me how to do a face :) i dont no how to do captal letters but we are lernng how to in class sammie is the best sister

EVERY DAY THIS SUMMER HAS BEEN SUCH GOOD WEATHER, EVEN WHEN IT STORMS

I wish that Stuart didn't have to leave on such a beautiful day. The sky was practically purple out, and the rain came down in big diamond drops.

"I kept picturing you leaving with a fat stack of papers under your arm," I told him as we stood under my umbrella at the Dartmouth Coach stop in town. He had his windbreaker hood up, and his eyelashes sparkled with moisture.

"You've got a very romantic view of writers," he said.

"I can't help it," I said, and lifted my chin to kiss him.

He only touched me lightly on the lips. "Are you sad?" I asked.

"I am sad," he said, and swallowed. "I don't like to leave you for so long." He would be back in a few days. He was meeting with his agent and his publisher, staying in his parents' apartment.

"I'll be fine," I told him.

"I know. I'm also . . ." he began, and sighed. "I'm nervous to meet with these people."

"But they love you!"

"No, they don't," he said, and looked away.

"Hey," I said, and took his hand. I made my grip strong. "Are you okay?"

"No," he said.

"No?"

"I don't want to talk about it right now." Stuart forced out a smile.

"Okay," I said. "I know this month hasn't been easy. It can't be easy, like when I kind of lost it in front of you." I forced myself to make eye contact. "I know it must be weird."

"It's not about you," Stuart said.

I blurted, "Then what is it about?" and hoped it wasn't as biting as the truth behind it.

"What do you mean?"

I said slowly, "We spend all our time together. I can't help thinking that if you're agitated, it might at least be in part to how much stress my . . . situation has caused you."

"No, no . . ." he began. Always, no, no.

"Yeah, but if you need to, you know, take some space, I understand."

"Sammie," he said, stern. He repeated, "It's not about you," and the sharpness in his voice took me by surprise.

"Well," I said. "I was trying—"

"I'm sorry," he said quickly.

"I don't like to be interrupted," I said. I took a deep breath. "I was trying to find out. But I'm glad I can eliminate our situation as a possibility."

"Yes," he said, his voice softer. "It's just going to be a big reality check. Parents and agent and everyone all in one week." He lifted his hand to my cheek.

I took his hand and kissed it. "Have a milk shake for me," I said.

"I will," he said, and we kissed.

"Tell everyone at NYU I won't be able to make it."

"Oh, Sammie."

"I'm sure they'll be heartbroken. All the people I've invented over the four years I've pretended to live there." My voice cracked. It appeared my brain was cracking, too. Insane to think that if I got on the bus, in eight hours I could be there with him, with everything I'd wanted. What if I just got a job waiting tables? What if I just showed up?

"Hey," he said gently. "We should go sometime."

"But not now," I said, watching the second-to-last passenger board, a college student going home after summer school had ended.

"Soon," he said, and stepped onto the bus without me.

COOP'S GCHAT ATTEMPT TO MAKE ME THINK LOSING MY MEMORY IS NOT SO BAD

Cooper: hey!

Me: Hey

Cooper: hey i was just thinking about you

Cooper: about your npc task force thing

Cooper: and how you wanted to meet someone with npc

Me: Yeah?

Cooper: do you remember my grandma?

Me: I remember she was very nice.

Cooper: yes, she is very nice, but she has dementia, unfortunately, and i was thinking if you wanted we could go talk to her. it's not npc but it is similar and i thought it might be nice for you to see that she hasn't lost herself completely

Cooper: she's still happy, i mean

Me: Yeah, I think that would be good!

Cooper: cool

Cooper: well let me know when you want to go

Cooper: i know how you like to pencil things in :)

Me: Yeah, I do, haha

Me: But

Me: You know what?

Me: How about now?

Cooper: okay!

FRIEDA LIND, 87, AUDIO TRANSCRIPTION FROM A VOICE
MEMO I RECORDED ON MY PHONE:

Frieda: The McCoys? Oh yes, of course I know the McCoys. They've been here for about as long as the Linds have. They came around the same time, migrated from Boston to set up farmland. Our families have lived around the mountain from each other for almost one hundred years. The best story is their shared, well, stewardship of an albino goat named Francis.

Sammie (*snorts, to Cooper*): Is that how you got your middle name?

Cooper: My mom says no but the coincidence is unsettling.

Frieda: I believe this was around the turn of the century. The story goes that . . . let me think. Francis was an albino goat, and he was such an oddity that people came from all around town to look at him, and I believe it was one of the McCoys who had the idea to charge people to see him.

Cooper: Of course it was the McCoys.

Sammie: Hey!

Frieda: A penny a peek or something like that. The difficult part of this was, 'scuse me. (*coughs*) The difficult part about this was that the goats roamed the backyard freely between the two pieces of property. One of the Linds, I think it was Geoffrey Lind, claimed that the McCoys had no right to make money off Francis because Francis was born of their goats. Then Patrick McCoy, of course, said no, absolutely not, Francis was his goat Freddie's kid. What was funny was that Francis wasn't even a kid anymore. He was a fully grown goat! So the whole life of this goat they didn't even care whose he was, but now that they found out they could make money off him, they both claimed him. They were still fighting even when there was a line of people outside to see Francis, and finally Colleen McCoy, who was a religious woman . . .

Sammie: No surprise there.

Cooper: Ha!

Frieda: Colleen McCoy had this high-and-mighty idea in her head that was just like the story in the Bible with the wise King Solomon. You remember that, Jerry?

Cooper: It's Cooper, Grandma.

Frieda: Oh, you look just like Jerry.

Cooper: Jerry's my dad.

Frieda: Of course he is!

Sammie: So you were saying about the wise King Solomon . . .

Frieda: What was I saying, sweetheart?

Cooper: Francis the goat. Colleen McCoy.

Frieda: So Colleen got it in her head that only if she threatened to cut Francis in half, Francis's true owner would reveal himself. She was quite dramatic.

Cooper: No surprise there.

Frieda: Colleen lifted the knife above her head . . . (*feigns lifting knife*) . . . and slowly brought it down, down, down, toward poor Francis the goat, and no one said a word!

Sammie: What?

Cooper: Wait, it gets better.

Frieda: So neither Geoffrey Lind nor Patrick McCoy was the true owner of Francis. For all they knew, Francis could have just wandered down the mountain from someone else. Or most likely they had just forgotten.

Sammie: But did Francis die?

Frieda: Yes, he did.

Sammie: Aw! How?

Cooper: They had a goat roast, because all the town was there anyway!

Sammie: They made Francis into a roast???

Frieda: Yes, and legend has it he was delicious.

KIDS WILL BE KIDS
(THAT WAS A GOAT PUN)

Frieda told Coop and me the "Francis the goat" story two more times, and four or five times, she told a story about how her husband took her out in his car for their first date.

The stories changed each time she told them—not the details, just which details she decided to include. In one version of Francis the goat, it was revealed that they tied a little blue ribbon around his neck. In the other, she told us that after the town ate Francis, Patrick McCoy said no, really, Francis was his goat, and the argument started all over again.

Coop's grandma has dyed brown hair and this soft baby-powder skin and lots of veins you can see, like a map of rivers and tributaries. She and Coop have the same navy blue, dish-plate eyes, though hers are a little cloudier.

"Jerry, I don't mean to fuss, but I recommend you get a haircut," she kept telling Coop, and it was funny to see Coop's cheeks turn pink about his hair, because of the way he's always running his hands through it around girls. I guess his grandma was the only girl who didn't like it.

"I'm not Jerry, I'm Cooper," Coop kept saying. "And this is Sammie."

"Hello," I would say, for the seventh time.

"Is she your girlfriend?" she would ask, smiling at me.

"I'm not his girlfriend," I kept saying. "I'm just his friend."

Every time we'd say it, Coop would mouth *sorry*, but by the fifth time, he was hiding a smile.

When Coop dropped me off, I thanked him for letting me meet her. "Was it good?" he asked, turning toward me in the driver's seat.

"Yes," I said, getting out. "She's a wonderful lady."

Coop looked out over the yard. "She really is. And think of how good she is at telling that story! It's because she tells it over and over. That's not so bad, right?"

As Coop spoke, I noticed for the first time that he had dressed up. He had his now sun-tinted hair pulled back, and he was wearing a polo shirt with a belt and jeans, and he was wearing loafers. I decided not to tease him for dressing up for his grandma. I lingered at the door of the Blazer, resting my elbows on the front seat.

"No, I guess not," I said. I thought about when Coop had seen me forget where I was, or the other day, when I had forgotten the chickens. "But how does she stay so sweet, you know? When I . . . have an episode . . . all I can do is panic."

Coop pushed a strand back that had fallen out behind his ear. "You were nice whenever I reminded you who I was," he said, and looked at me, his brow furrowed.

"Good," I said.

"Maybe it's that your brain relaxes when it's someone familiar."

"I can be mean, though, too," I said, picking at the threads in the seat. "I was kind of a brat to my family."

"Sometimes Grandma can be kind of a brat, too," he responded. "If she's tired, or if she isn't comfortable."

I laughed a little. "I should start wearing a caftan, to guarantee maximum comfort at all times."

Coop nodded in fake seriousness. "It'd be a good look for you."

We were quiet for a bit. "The rain stopped," I noticed.

"Oh, yeah," he said, glancing up through the windshield.

"Do you have to go home now?" I asked.

Coop shrugged, glancing at me, then at the clock on his dash. "Nope."

I looked back at the house. Mom and Dad would be home soon, with all the kids. But I didn't really want him to go, for some reason. I suppose for the same reason I was glad to see him on the roof on the Fourth of July. "Want to stay for dinner?"

Coop unbuckled his seat belt immediately. "Will there be hot dogs?"

"Probably."

"I'll take my chances."

We shut our doors and Coop came around the Blazer.

"I wonder what stories I'll tell over and over," I said.

"Who knows," Coop said, and grinned as we walked toward the house. "But, more importantly, I think we should get a goat."

Me: How'd the meetings go?

Stuart: good

Stuart: how's life back there?

Me: strange and good

Stuart: strange and good?

Me: I'll explain when you get home.

Davy asked me why I wanted to get my teeth so clean. She watched me brush my teeth three times in the span of one hour before bed. I guess I forgot that I had brushed them. So I created a system—I leave my toothbrush on the sink if I brushed them, then Mom and Dad can put the toothbrush away at night after the kids get ready for bed, and then I put a note up that says: "If the toothbrush is on the sink, you brushed your teeth. If it is put away in the cabinet, you need to brush them."

WHEW!

New day. Another cloudy one but the sun poked through by ten a.m. or so and Coop came over with tennis rackets because what else, we were going to try fucking tennis. I don't know why I chose tennis on my NPC Task Force but unfortunately Coop saw it and remembered it, so dear Serena Williams, I ruined your sport.

But you know the studies say people with memory stuff have to learn new things, it's good for them, but I don't know why I chose tennis. Sorry I'm not writing too good my pain medication kicked in but honestly it's kinda like roses writing on the pain medication because I'm not so worried about making it pretty you know?

But I will tell you everything that I remember as always.

But I am a little loopy.

So Coop came up the mountain and I swear I almost lost it because he was wearing these red short-shorts and socks up to his knees and of course the THAT GOOD GOOD tank top and he had his hair in a pony with a sweatband and these aviator sunglasses. When I let him in he saw Harrison was playing Minecraft with headphones on so he snuck up behind him and stood right next to him at the computer until Harrison noticed he was there and jumped a little and took off his headphones and said, "What the hell?"

And then Coop said, "I'm Pete Sampras," in this really low voice.

We found a flat enough spot in the yard and Coop tied a rope he found in the shed between two trees and draped a bunch of mine and Dad's old shirts on it.

"Tennis!" he said.

"I'm not going to last five minutes," I said.

"It's not about how long you last, it's how you do it," he said, or some other joke alluding to sex. "Ready?" He threw up the ball and hit it over to me.

I missed it by a few inches. "I am too distracted by your pale thighs," I said.

"Focus on the tennis ball," Coop said, and I laughed. I was already winded. I kicked it back with a clumsy jerk.

He tried again. I missed again. Coop ran up to the T-shirt net. "C'mere," he said. He smiled at me between one of Dad's gray CITY OF LEBANON T-shirts and my DAN & WHIT'S sweatshirt. He handed me the ball so I could hit first. I smacked it over his head and for the first time that day, I liked tennis.

"Okay!" Coop said. "There she goes," he said, jogging after it.

By the time he got back I was sitting on the ground. My heart was beating pretty fast. "I have a different idea," I told Coop.

"What's that?" Coop said, sitting across from me on the grass.

"It's called femi-tennis. It's where you roll a tennis ball back and forth and quiz each other about accomplished women in history."

I didn't expect Coop to go for it but pretty soon we had made a diamond with our legs and would shoot the tennis ball across the diamond, and the rule was, shins were post-1970, thighs were pre-1950, and knees were wild card. I beat him pretty badly but he held his own, especially about the life of Harriet Tubman, and, surprisingly, he totally stumped me with this radical Japanese artist named Yayoi Kusama. I made him write her name down, turns out she also had problems with her mind and began to hallucinate dots later in life. I told Coop I had not seen dots but I had seen giants, and he also remembered that game we used to play where we built houses out of rocks and sticks and pretended we were giants and stomped on them.

So when the little kids got home from camp we taught Bette and Davy that game, and they built elaborate little houses out of Popsicle sticks, and before they were about to stomp, Davy said, "Wait!" She asked us what the game was called, and Coop and I looked at each other, trying to remember the name, but we both agreed that we were pretty sure we just called it "the giant game." Bette and Davy love it. I mean Bette really, really loves it. Davy I think just likes putting jewel stickers all over the houses.

Then it was Cooper's turn to pick a game but we were both pretty tired so we just lay down out in the yard away from the trees and looked at the clouds.

"That was a good day of tennis," I said.

"Yes, tennis is a great game," he said.

And then god I don't know our shoulders were like inches from each other's and I just needed to tell Coop thank you in some way for coming over and obviously we're just friends but it was a deeper thank-you than just like "thank you for the ride" or "thank you for the food" so I moved my hand until it was on top of his hand, and I held it for a second, and Coop shifted his hand to be underneath my hand and held mine for a second, too, and then we let go.

"You should show them Captain Stickman," I said after a while, watching a cloud shaped like a fish.

"Right now?" he said.

"No, doesn't have to be right now," I told him.

Then Coop said, "How about tomorrow?"

"Yeah," I said and closed my eyes to the sun on my skin. "Tomorrow."

TOMORROW

The days are like this: sometimes I wake up and think, *What's due? What do I have to do today? What must I write? What's next? Who's in my way?* I have to let the stillness of the morning hit me in slow waves. I'm in bed, I think, and I am breathing and some things hurt, some things don't.

First I put one leg out of the bed, then the other leg, and put my feet on the floor. Mom arrives with her basil and air, and Dad with his mint and kiss, and today as I stand in front of the mirror, eating my yogurt and pills, I wonder why there is such pleasure in waking. I wonder how I could have wanted to know so much about everything out there and why, now, everything close to me is so fascinating. I wonder how the brain can work just as well when it moves slowly as it does when it moves fast. A million things happen at once just to make up a house and a yard and a mountain.

Did I ever mention that there is a nest of warblers outside my window?

Did I ever mention that my dad sometimes plays guitar in his room when he thinks everyone else is asleep?

How can one body hold so many different people? I wonder how someone can want such different things in such a short time. I wonder why everyone is so good to me.

Stuart would be home tomorrow. I was trying not to think about it because I didn't want things to go back to the way they were. Not that Stuart had done anything wrong, Stuart was fine, it was just that I didn't know yet where he fit into this magic combination I'd found of Coop and games and all the people around who had helped find this version of me, a person who never existed but might have always existed. I didn't know how much he'd like playing fake tennis or building tiny stick houses. Stuart's girlfriend was Future Sam and Sammie trying to be Future Sam and I didn't know how well he'd like regular Sammie, as I was right now. I was just learning to like me this way. Anyway.

I followed my family outside to say good-bye for the day, waiting on Mrs. Lind, and from far away, I could see Coop making his way toward me, holding a bowl of strawberries from his mom's garden.

"Hello, Samantha."

"Hello, Cooper."

He threw a strawberry at me. I held out my hands and missed, of course. "Oh, Jesus, sorry," Coop said, and immediately went to find the berry on the ground. He rubbed it on his shirt and ate it. "I asked your mom and dad if it was okay that we go on an adventure."

I thought, *one last adventure*, though maybe that wouldn't be true. But I was not getting better. I was getting calmer, but not always better. We both knew that, I think.

"Is that okay?"

"It's perfect." I motioned him to come closer to me so I could have a strawberry. He came closer. We ate the whole bowl one by one, sometimes I turned my neck to look up at him, sometimes I didn't.

"Let's go down to the creek," I finally said, and whistled for Puppy. As the dog rushed toward us, I decided I wanted the grass blades between my toes, so I sat down and slipped off my shoes. It took me a while. Coop threw a stick down the slope for Puppy until I was finished. I reached out my hand for him, and we were ready.

The creek's just across the highway, a little break in the land under bending trees that you can barely see until you're right up close. We sat with our feet in a sunny patch of water.

"I hate being slower," I said.

"Maybe you're not, though," Coop said. "We were both chubby kids, so you're probably just the same speed we both were a few years back."

I burst out laughing, thinking of the two of us bumbling toward the creek, cheeks and hair flying, making *whooshing* sounds. "Running down the mountain really does make you feel faster than you are, doesn't it?"

"It's just gravity!" Coop said, laughing with me. He laughed with his belly and turned to me, the serene smile back on his face, and said, "Yeah."

"Yeah, what?"

"I was just thinking and I said the end part aloud."

"I do that, too," I said.

"Let's go to the general store!" he said. "That was my idea."

"We can stay here for a little while, though," I said. I wanted every part of the day to last as long as possible.

"Sammie. How . . ." Coop started, then said, "Never mind."

"No, what?" I asked.

"What do you think of me?" he said, rushed.

His face had turned back toward the water, so I couldn't see what exactly he meant.

I looked at my feet. "I think you're Coop," I said. "You just . . . are."

"Do you think I'm just here with you because you're sick? Because it's not just because you're sick." He had his hands wrapped around his ankles, twisting, nervous. A funny thing to do with all those muscles, the boy inside coming out.

"No," I said, and he turned. "I just think you've been a good friend to me."

"Yeah, good," he said, nodding.

A bug jumped into his hair. I couldn't get it, quite, but I brushed it out. He touched his hair where my fingers had been. "A bug," I said. "It's gone."

I pushed my glasses up my nose.

"I missed you," he said suddenly, and shrugged like it was the most obvious thing in the world.

"I missed you, too," I said, also quick. But too quick for how big that feeling was, for how long we had stayed away. I hoped he would come back every day from then on, even though he didn't like Stuart, and we could have adventures, or just say hello, at least. I wonder what that meant. I took a deep breath and said, "We were different people for a while, but now we're not. Right?"

"Right. Well, kind of." He was looking at me, but not quite at my face. I blushed.

We stood. The sun had started warming the water, the rocks.

And then we made that circle I talked about, the one we always used to make on summer days like these.

Down the mountain, to the creek, to outside the general store to talk to Fast Eddy (he told us it was nice to see us again, but he had noticed Coop's Blazer speeding several times, he'll let it slide—thanks, Eddy). We had sweat through our shirts by the time we went inside.

There were two Dr Peppers left. "Oh, good," Coop said, opening the cooler door. "We don't have to fight."

"Let me in there with you, I'm burning up."

We stood as close to the racks as we could, our shoulders pressed together, sticking our faces near the sodas.

Then farther down the creek to drink them. Mine had been shaken up where Coop had kept it in his pocket, so when he opened it for me, it sprayed both of us. We used creek water to get the sticky stuff off our skin, then went up the mountain again. Coop gave me a piggyback ride. I laid my cheek on his back. He was sweaty again, but I didn't care.

When we got home, Coop showed Bette and Davy all the wonders of Captain Stickman in the front yard.

He kneeled and handed them both long sticks we found near the tree line.

"I now pass the mantle of Captain Stickman to you, Davienne McCoy, and to you, Bette McCoy. Amen."

"Remember, you can be Captain Stickwoman, you don't have to be Captain Stickman," I told them.

"Friend to all humans and animals," Coop said.

"Amen," I repeated.

"Ayyyyy-men!" Davy said, and took her stick.

"Ay-women," Bette said, and took hers as well.

"Exactly," I told her.

Then we came inside, and after Coop used the bathroom, he saw my note to myself and asked, "What's that?"

I told him the toothbrush trick, and he had an idea, which I think he can explain better himself.

hello esteemed memory book, cooper lind here, ladykiller and connoisseur of dank weed. anyway i was thinking after seeing sammie's pasting of stuff on the wall, her notes to herself, maybe it would be a cool idea to paste things all over her house, to help her remember. not just labeling, but more like a memory book of the house? maybe long term memories will help her better access short term? i don't know, i'm no doctor, but take the bathroom for example: she can have her practical notes to herself, but also a story about a time she had there. like, on the tub, "here's where sammie and cooper once put kool-aid in the tub when they were six, because they wanted to take a kool-aid bath, and they were grounded from seeing each other for two weeks." that kind of thing.

Sammie here again. Here are some of them:

On the fridge door: What time is it? If it's 11:30, it's lunchtime and you can have whatever you want! If it's earlier than that, you already had breakfast. If it's later than that, wait for a bit. Mom and Dad will make you dinner. Chocolate milk: anytime!

Once, Harry used one of Sammie's old chocolate milk cartons to mix wheat paste to use as glue for his "time machine" science project. He had it clearly labeled WHEAT PASTE DON'T DRINK, but Sammie had her nose in a Redwall book and wasn't paying attention while she grabbed it and took a big mouthful of wheat paste! She spit it all over the fridge door. When she went to go get a rag to clean it up, Davy had thought it felt neat and smeared glitter all over it. Fun fact: that's why it looks like a unicorn threw up on the door of the fridge!

Above Puppy's food bowl: Puppy doesn't need food! Harry already fed him this morning, and will feed him later tonight.

Remember when Coop thought it would be a good idea to do a "Puppy Easter egg hunt," but instead of Easter eggs, he used uncooked hot dogs? He put uncooked hot dogs around the house to see if Puppy would find them. And Puppy did find them, except for one, which Mom found later in the washing machine. Coop is sorry about that.

On my mirror: Good morning, Sammie! Mom and Dad will be coming in shortly to say hello.

Remember when you picked out this mirror and dresser when

you were six? You had been sharing this room with Harry, and for your birthday, everyone decided it was time for you to get your own room. So we went to the flea market in Lebanon, just you and Mom and Dad while the kids stayed with Mrs. Lind, and you found this dresser and mirror within minutes of being there. Mom and Dad tried to tell you that it looked clunky and old-fashioned for a little girl but you knew what you wanted, so they trusted you and put it in the back of the truck and let you ride home with it in the back the whole way. Besides your books, it was the first two things in this house that were fully yours.

Now we're just lounging after dinner in my room. Coop's been reading the trainer's manual for his new job fixing equipment during the off-season at the ski resort, which he'll start next week.

He went to get a glass of water from the kitchen.

I didn't forget anything today.

In fact, I've been really good for the past couple of days since Coop has been around.

I feel strange in my stomach, but not a bad kind of strange, sort of, like, butterflies, at the idea of Coop being in my room late at night. How cheesy is that? Okay, he's coming back.

So . . .

so

How's that water?

delicious. want some

Yes.
Thank you.
What's up?

lol

Now you're the one who's typing lol when you could just laugh.

yeah but your parents just came in to check on you, which means we're not supposed to laugh

That's not what that means.

does that mean you should go to sleep and i should go home

No! Don't go yet.

are you going to fall asleep

No way.

you look sleepy

It's because I'm staring at a computer screen, dorkus.

look at me

. . .
See?

nah you look sleepy

I'm wide awake.

what do you want to do now

I don't know, what do you want to do?

how are you feeling

So fresh, actually. Really good.

are you up for another field trip

Where?

guess

Potholes?

duh

Yeah.

are you sure? you gonna be okay?

Yeah, I took all my meds. And you know what to do if I can't remember stuff.

yeah plus i actually am a first responder

What?? Really? You know CPR and everything?

yeah

When did that happen?

i took a class

When?

that night i drove you home from the side of the road your parents told me you weren't supposed to hang out unless it was with someone who was certified. so i took a class. i even have a card! i'm a card-carrying member

I don't know what to say. Thank you, Coop.

:)

:)
Let's go.

you ready?

Yeah.

HIGHWAY 89 REVISITED

I just have to say this one thing while I'm sitting next to Coop in his car and we're on our way to the Potholes, and I'm not sure how to say it, but I'm looking at Coop with the wind going through his hair, and through my hair, and there's no music, just the sound of crickets and leaves and tires on the road, and he's telling me to get off my phone, and I will but just let me write this, I just want you to remember this, Future Sam.

Coop is lying asleep next to me on a blanket on the ground.

We were lying next to each other, telling jokes, and when we ran out of jokes we were both sort of shaky and awkward, not like usual. The crickets were out. Frogs splashed in the water nearby. Coop he asked me if he could tell me something.

And I said yes.

I didn't have to respond, he said, but he needed to tell me, especially with everything going on.

He scooted closer to me and I smelled strawberries. The frogs got louder. I burst out laughing because I was so nervous, and he asked, why was I laughing?

Because I'm nervous.

Why are you nervous?

Aren't you nervous? I asked him.

Yes, but I know why I'm nervous. Why do you think I'm nervous?

I don't know, I said, but I have an idea, because I might be nervous for the same reason.

Well, in that case, Coop said, and he hoisted himself to lean on his arm, looking over at me, and we were no longer just saying words into the sky. He opened and closed his mouth a couple times, and swallowed.

I have feelings for you, he said.

Oh yeah?

Not just a friendship feeling.

How weird it is that you have no idea what love is until it happens, and then you're like that's it, wow, there it is! It was there the whole time. Like a hidden image in one of those optical illusion books. When I took his hand. When he sat across from me in the ceramics studio, his eyes on me. When he and I were giants.

We don't have to talk about it, he said. I just wanted to at least bring it up.

No I'm glad you did.

Coop swallowed again, and put his full hand on my cheek, then took it away. I wanted him to bring it back.

I think I have them, too, I told him.

When did that happen for you? he asked.

In the bedroom just now, I answered. When did that happen for you?

When I was twelve, he said.

And you still have them? I asked, and I moved closer to him.

I still have them, he answered.

And you have them for sure? he asked me.

I have them for sure, I answered.

I love you, Sammie, he said. I've loved you for a long time.

I love you, too.

And by now our lips were basically brushing against each other's as the words came out of our mouths, and we were practically kissing, but when we did actually kiss it felt like I was drinking warm honey right to my gut, spilling out around me.

He put his hand on my stomach, right below my ribs and moved upward and I felt every millimeter and it was another time I wondered how the brain could work so well and move so slowly at the same time.

We shifted my body on top of his and my hair hung on his face, and he brushed it away, and I kissed his neck, and he rolled me on my back and kissed my neck, and then down on top of my shirt, to my waist, and then onto the skin between my shirt and my jeans, and he unbuttoned my jeans, and there was more, there was more.

As Coop was touching me it was like my muscles started climbing big steps, and I was breathing really fast and Coop asked if I was all right, if I wanted to keep going, and yes I wanted to keep going. All of a sudden I was at the top of the steps. I knew I was at the top because between my legs there was something I can only describe as a feeling as strong as pain but the exact opposite of pain, or maybe I could say that Coop's fingers turned my body into a camera flash, hot and fast and bright, something you knew was coming but surprises you anyway.

After, in my mind, there was gratitude that I climbed with Coop, that I found who I was supposed to find, that what we did on the blanket was true and correct and just ours. Just me and Coop's.

This is the story I will tell over and over.

I'm tired but only in my body.

I'm not tired anywhere else.

BAD

I fell asleep next to Coop and it was the stupidest thing to do, well, not what we did before, before that was the best night of my fucking life, but I wish we had gotten in the Blazer right away after, but it was so nice to fall asleep with my arms around his hard warm chest

So I wasn't home when Mom checked on me in the morning, and found an empty bed, she almost fainted she said

She called Coop but of course he didn't answer because we were asleep

So then she assumed I had gone somewhere with Stuart because he was supposed to have gotten home last night

She called Stuart and he said, yes he was home, but I wasn't with him

She called the cops

The cops told Mom they couldn't search for me until I was missing for forty-eight hours, and she couldn't go out to find me because Dad had already gone to work, and she couldn't leave the kids

So she called Stuart again and he went looking for me everywhere, first to Maddie's, then to school, then around town

Meanwhile Coop and I woke up

Well, he woke up, I didn't know where I was

I knew I was at the Potholes, and I knew Coop, but I couldn't remember what we had done at first or how we had gotten there, but I was feeling really good for some reason, I remember, and I gave him a hug, and he tried to bring me back and tell me everything

As he did that Stuart called me and I picked up because that's what people do when someone calls them

I shouldn't have picked up

WHERE ARE YOU

I told him where I was because that's what people do when someone asks them

I was just being stupid, not Sammie, who is usually very smart

STAY WHERE YOU ARE I remember him saying

When Stuart got to the Potholes, Coop and I were sitting on the blanket together and my memory was returning, especially the part where I loved him, and he had his hand on my back, rubbing my back, and everything was good until

We saw Stuart and stood up

His eyes went from us, to the blanket, to our messy hair and our socks and shoes next to us

Stuart made a fist

He hit Coop so hard

He hit Coop so hard in the face that Coop's mouth and nose were bleeding and tears came out of his eyes

Tears came out of my eyes

WHAT THE FUCK Stuart yelled

Please don't yell, I said

Take it out on me, Coop said, come on, bring it again

Don't do that! Don't do that, I said and stepped between them

We can talk, I said, when the details began to hit me

Stuart was breathing heavy

Why? he asked

I didn't answer

What were you thinking?

Why?

Why did you do this?

Because we have feelings for each other, Cooper answered

I asked Sammie, Stuart said

I don't know, I said

And of all the people to do this with, it's the guy who you called a dumbshit? Stuart asked and pointed at Coop

What? Coop said looking at me, wiping blood from his face in a long red smear

Yeah, the pothead who you told me got kicked off the baseball team

Coop narrowed his eyes at me and asked me if I'd told Stuart about freshman year

Yes, but not on purpose, I told him

You told HIM something I told you not to tell anyone

And the way Coop was hunched over and looking at me, I'll never forget

Like I had broken his neck

Like he had put his heart out for me and I had smashed it

He didn't need to say it, we were both remembering that day he told me he got kicked off the team, and how hard I had tried to keep it out of my eyes, but he could sense it, and he had said, please don't judge me

But I did, and he could feel it

So it wasn't the day he asked me out on the date, and it wasn't the day Coop didn't show up to help me babysit

The day we stopped being friends was the day he made a mistake, and the day I had looked down on him for it

And now he was looking at me like he was about to return the favor

What the hell is this, Stuart asked nobody

Fuck you man, Coop said

I tried to take Cooper's hand but he pulled it away, slick as a fish, and walked away

I think you're better than this, Stuart said to me

He sat down on the ground and said, You're selfish, I know that now

Maybe it's not your fault

But you are selfish

You kept your sickness from me because it was easier for you, you decided to break up with me because it was easier for you, and you slept with this asshole because it was easier for you

It's hard for me to know you this way, the way you are now

I was never anyone but myself, I said, I'm sorry for what I did, but it's true

Then I didn't really know you, he said, and I don't want to know you

Stuart stayed where he was until Mom picked me up

Coop left without saying good-bye

Now Coop hasn't responded to my messages in four days

Except to say "maybe you should be with your family and your boyfriend and think about things"

Stuart needs some space, he told me

I don't need any space from anyone

I just need Coop to say something to me

Anything to me

Even if it's just good-bye

BIG WORLD

Had a couple of blank days. Just wandering around, muttering. I don't know how to tell the difference between NPC and just pure sadness. The lack of getting out of bed is the same. The heavy white space of my brain is the same. So is waking up in the middle of the night, wondering what's happening, what went wrong.

Mom and Dad tell me I should forget about Coop and Stuart for now, both of them, and be positive. Coop would be back, they tell me. They also said that neither of them, nor anyone for that matter, could have "fully realized what I was going through." I did, though. I knew what I was doing and wanted to do and felt all those things. Maybe I knew all along that I was trying to speed up before I slowed down.

I just didn't know that slowing down would feel so good. I also didn't know how much it would hurt. Or maybe I did know and I just did it anyway.

Now Mom and Dad stay home from work.

I recorded them talking at dinner the other night, after everyone else had gone to sleep. They were telling me about how they met.

MARK MCCOY, 45, AND GIA TURLOTTE MCCOY, 42,
TRANSCRIBED AUDIO RECORDING:

Mom: We were working at the ski resort after high school graduation. Dad went to West Leb, I went to Hanover.

Dad: And there was this five-star cutie running the coffee stand.

Mom: And you didn't even drink coffee!

Dad: I started that summer just to have an excuse to talk to (*makes rainbow hand motion*) Gia.

Mom: Anyway . . .

Dad: So. We're crazy about each other. Can't get enough. We move to New York City after six months. Guess what I wanted to be? Sammie will never guess.

Mom: I'm actually curious if you'll guess this, Sammie. Not a city maintenance guy.

Sammie: A clown?

Mom: What? Ew.

Sammie: Just tell me.

Dad: I wanted to be (*makes air guitar strum*) a punk rocker. I even lived in Brooklyn, back when it was cheap and dirty.

Mom: So I moved there with him shortly after but the city is cruel and we could never stay long in one borough, let alone one apartment, for one reason or another. We didn't have real jobs and we weren't sure we wanted them.

Sammie: But living in New York together must have been fun.

Mom: Mmm. We were always so sad. And when we got sad we were too dependent on each other.

Dad: And then that cat ran away.

Mom: Our buffer cat.

Sammie: What?

Mom: We found a sweet little cat and gave it milk and whenever one of us was mad at the other we would find the cat and give it to the other as a peace offering.

Dad: It was an ugly feral cat. Let's be real.

Mom: But it always worked to calm either of us down.

Dad: That buffer cat was our only friend. We couldn't find a real community. We ended up hating it there because we hated the selves we had turned into.

Mom (*in a fake punk rocker voice*): Smokin', drinkin', stealin' records.

Dad: Your mom worked in a movie theater and we used to steal popcorn from the concession stand for dinner.

Mom: I stole the popcorn.

Dad: Yes, yes, Gia stole the popcorn.

Mom: Anyway, we had this huge fight. Like a massive, massive fight. I still can't believe it.

Sammie: What was it about?

Dad: Hmmm, nothing.

Mom: I can't remember, either.

Dad: And the cat was nowhere to be found.

Mom: Oh god, Sammie, your dad looked everywhere for that thing. He was gone for three days straight, only coming home for some food, and then he'd be back out again.

Dad: And the worst part about it was the cat had no name. So I was just yelling, "Kitty! Kitty!" hoping it would come out.

Sammie: Why didn't you name it?

Mom: You know what I think?

Dad: What? I'd actually be curious to hear that.

Mom: I think we secretly didn't name it because we knew it wasn't ours. Like we didn't want it to be ours, because that meant we were there permanently.

Dad: All I know is . . . (*eyes well up*)

Sammie: Aw, Dad!

Dad: That stupid cat made me realize that I wanted to marry Mom. And that I wanted to have children with her. You know, out on the streets of Brooklyn for three days, and you ask yourself, what are you doing here? And you realize . . . (*sniffs*)

Mom: He just wanted someone to love. People to care for.

Sammie: So you came back?

Mom: He wrote a lot of songs about that cat.

Sammie: I want to hear Dad's punk rock songs.

Dad (*composing himself*): So anyway, we came back and settled here, among familiar faces.

Sammie: Wait, wait, going back. Is that why you named Puppy just Puppy?

Dad (*buries his face in Puppy's fur*): Yuuuusss.

Mom: Let's see . . . when we got back and moved into this place, Cooper's mom and dad were here, and Father Frank was just Frank, he hadn't gone to seminary school yet, and Mrs. T was working at a preschool actually . . .

Sammie: Mrs. T?!

Mom: Beverly, yeah.

Dad: It was strange at first, so tight with people we knew but so much space at the same time.

Mom: But your dad got a job right away because he knew a guy working for the City of Lebanon, and that gave me time to get my associate's degree, and then you came along! I mean, I wonder, Sammie, with all of your talk about getting out . . . You think we only stay in the Upper Valley because we don't have enough money to leave?

Sammie: I don't know. I guess so.

Mom: We're lucky to be here. Maybe it's because the mountains are bigger than everyone, they give people perspective. Listen, you can go anywhere you want, you can conquer the world, you could have gone to New York and been incredibly successful, and I know you would have been. (*breaks in voice, sniffing*) But the more you win, the more people you might have to beat out, or have to leave behind, the smaller your world becomes.

Dad: That's absolutely right.

Mom (*points out to the yard, to the mountain*): We've got a big world here, Sammie.

Sammie: I know. I know now.

A LETTER I HAVEN'T SENT

Dear Coop,

I might forget some words so just read as you go and try to make sense. First I'm sorry Stuart punched you. I hope your nose and mouth are okay. I haven't been able to think of much else since the other morning. I mean, more than just your nose and mouth, but you do have a very handsome nose and mouth and I hope they are not destroyed.

Most of all I hope our friendship isn't destroyed. Remember the day we became friends? It was probably when we were five or four. I saw you a lot and I remember staring at your hair because you had the loudest color hair I had ever seen and you were always naked running around in your yard. Maybe not the right moment but there was a time when you had run all the way from your house to see how far the garden hose could go. You ran all the way yanking the green hose and right when you got to our yard you stopped. I think I was probably catching those little yellow butterflies between two cups like I often did. Anyway I looked up and there you were holding the hose, pulling it, trying to get it to go farther but it wouldn't budge. So you set it down and ran away back to your house. You left the hose and I just stared at it and all of a sudden water started trickling out of the end. It was magic. I had no idea how you did it or if it was you that even did it. I walked up closer to the hose and watched the water flow out, harder and harder, and then you came running back. You were laughing because it was amazing. You picked up the hose and waved it around and I went and jumped in the water with you and I think we played together ever since.

I've been wondering where that person was for the last four years when we could have been friends. The person who noticed little things like that and thought they were special. I was so busy thinking about how I could be better than everyone that I stopped seeing anyone else at all. I thought I knew what I needed and perhaps I did need some of it. I am happy I worked so hard in school. I am happy I got to be in debate and give a speech. But now what does that mean? What about the space between the things I checked off my list? What about when the list has to get thrown out?

What I mean is we could have had four thousand and sixty days instead of just fourteen or seven or the six hours we had by the Potholes. I will be sorry for the rest of my life if we can't have any more days together.

I'm sorry I told your secret. I don't judge you, and I don't think I'm better than you, and anyone who thinks they are can suck it. I was trying to be a better version of myself but didn't care who I was stepping on to get there. I was trying to pretend I had a future that would never exist, and never will. But I would have rather gone back and had you with me, no matter what my future was.

I've lived with you right now and those right nows are everywhere, every time, in my house, in your house, on the mountain.

I love you. Home is where love is. You're my home.

Sammie

PS And I don't think you're a dumbshit

PPS At least not all the time

STUART SHAH,
NEW YORK TIMES BESTSELLER

Stuart and I met in the early morning before he caught a bus back to New York. He came over and we sat on the plastic lawn chairs. He was wearing all gray again, a stuffed backpack strapped to his back. The echolocation between us was gone, replaced with a sort of pillow that seemed to muffle everything. I took tea, he took coffee, and we looked at each other with puffy eyes. He came on a good day.

"You look nice," Stuart said.

"Don't lie," I said, and smiled at him with a mouth that didn't go all the way up on one side.

"I'm not," he said. "How are you holding up?"

I did not expect him to be so civil. But I guess he had gotten all his anger out. "I'm okay. How are you?"

"Back to the city life."

"I'm happy for you," I said.

"You shouldn't be," Stuart said, almost bitter.

There it was, the anger. "I'm sorry," I said, taking a deep breath. "I said it before and I still mean it: I'm sorry for what I did."

"It still baffles me," Stuart said. "How far I was willing to go for you, and you threw it away."

"I never . . ." I searched for this word, I remember, and was embarrassed. "I never understood why you were willing to give me yourself so fully without knowing me that well."

"I like you! I was trying to do the right thing!"

"I know. And I like you, too. That was always true."

"Maybe you liked the idea of me." He did the thing in the air, where he pointed at nothing. "You liked the idea that you had always wanted me, and now you had me, and you liked that I was going to be a powerful writer."

"Mm . . ." I said.

"Admit it."

"That was part of it. But there's more, too. The part of you that reads poetry out loud when you're drunk and pets every dog. And then another part of you I just straight up wanted . . . to . . ."

He waved his hand. "I get it."

"So prudish these days!"

He burst into a laugh, but it didn't last long. "These days! It's been a week."

I had to keep joking or else I would lose it. I had hurt this person beside me, I could feel it in the air, just as I used to feel his connection to me. And I had hurt myself. I wished I could take it all back, but I had wished that so many times in the last few months the words meant nothing to me anymore. I had no tears left.

"It feels like forever."

"Because you want me back?" Stuart said. I couldn't tell if he meant it. He was still looking down the mountain.

"Why, do you want me back?" I teased.

"I don't know about that. Not that you aren't . . . I just . . ." he said.

"I was joking. I wasn't easy. Even before NPC."

"You will be the first and last girl that I will ever let drag me into a boyfriend/girlfriend conversation over goddamn text message. You have the patience of a goldfish."

I spit back, "Yeah, no duh."

"Oh! Well!"

Mom walked out in her clogs, threw a towel over one of the empty chairs, and walked back in.

Stuart put his chin in his hands. "It was just . . . terrible timing."

"Ha!" I let out. "Preaching to the . . . the, uh . . ."

"Choir."

"Choir," I echoed.

He exhaled. "I guess I'll just say it. My agent dropped me. That's why I was in New York." He stared at the ground.

"Oh."

"I hadn't done a single page of writing while I was here."

"I'm so sorry." So that's why he never wanted to talk about what he was working on. His future didn't exist as he thought it did, either. "What about the piece you wrote for Mariana Oliva?"

"That was old. Already published in a tiny journal in Portland."

I looked at him, his head lowered. Stuart continued. Apparently, he only went to New York to beg his publisher not to cancel his contract. He was so ashamed.

And he shouldn't have lied to me, he said.

"It's okay, Stu," I told him. "Are you writing again?"

"I'm trying."

"I remember the story you read with Mari's piece, and the ones that had gotten picked up before this. I even reread a few recently, even after you and I fought, and the stories still struck me. You're talented."

"I don't know about that," Stuart muttered.

I almost laughed. "Remember how young you are? There's a reason you're doing what you're doing. You've got to keep going."

Finally, a smile. A real smile. The first one I had seen on him in a long time that lit up his dark eyes.

"You can argue with me all you want, you can give me excuses, but you know I'll win," I told him, smiling back.

"I know," he said.

The words hardly came from my mouth, more from my chest, exploding. "I wanted to give more to you, to everyone, I just didn't know how," I said. Stuart's eyes filled up, and so did mine. "I am learning how to be less selfish now, I really am. I just want you to know that, even if it's too late."

"You don't have to be anything right now except yourself."

"Sometimes myself is too much to handle." My lower lip was shaking. "I wanted everything all at once."

Stuart reached for my hand, like he always used to. I felt the sobs subside a bit. "You have a terrible disease. Smaller things have turned people into ego monsters."

I let out a laugh.

He added, "Being born turns people into ego monsters."

We laughed together, in between sniffs.

He stood up, helped me stand, and we faced each other. We hugged for a long time, ribs shaking against each other as we wet each other's shoulders, and I moved my fingers to his spine.

He looked at the time.

"Time to go?"

"Time to go."

"You meant so much to me," I told him.

"Don't speak in past tense like that," he said, his voice breaking.

"You mean so much to me," I corrected myself, because he does.

"I think we would have been good, if things had been different," he said into my ear.

"I know we would have." But things were. There's no "will be" or "could be" for me anymore. Things just are.

"Tell me if you ever need anything."

"First thing I need."

"What is it?"

"Keep trying."

We let go. "Okay," he said, nodding. "Okay."

MASS

I went to mass at Our Lady of Perpetual Help with my parents for the first time in six years

I didn't talk to God, but it was a comfort to hear the voices together, their chanted prayers so deeply memorized they don't even have to think

I cling to every memory now so hard

I'm glad Harry and Bette and Davy have something that can dig deep traces in their memories, and it's something beautiful, something outside themselves

Mom and Dad took my hands on either side

When I got home I asked them to help me do something

I had a little money set aside from my grandparents, a little from Mom and Dad trying to help me go to New York, and most of it's gone now to the disease

I asked that if all of it wasn't gone most of it should go to my siblings' college of course

But if at least a hundred or something was still left over

Mom and Dad can call the NPC Clubhouse, you know those kids in the tropical shirts, and buy each of them a book, whichever book they wanted

Stories are good at times like these, to tell them, to hear them

I thought of Coop and the notes we made around the house

Stories are always good

I WISH I HAD DONE THIS
FOUR YEARS AGO

It had been almost a week and I was fed up

I kept making excuses to walk Puppy down to the highway to see Cooper's house, even when it was almost too hard to walk

Mom and Dad got me a wheelchair but I don't like it

Coop's truck would be in his driveway, but he'd never come out

I don't know when he came or left

Maybe he didn't

Maybe he was staying at Hot Katie's house

Or maybe he had gone away to another city, too

Every possibility made my bones feel like sawdust

The next day I think it was the next day we piled into Dad's car to go to the ski resort for oh, no reason, you know, just to stop by, no I begged them please, please, and eventually I just showed Mom the letter to Coop, which I still hadn't sent because I was too afraid it wouldn't make a difference. I told them I missed him like I was missing one of my senses, a sixth or seventh sense that I didn't know I had until it was gone

I didn't even know if he was working so we noodled slowly from the parking lot to the lodge

Dad asked Mom, bring back memories?

They remodeled, Mom said, and for some reason they both looked at some sort of storage locker thing at the edge of the parking lot

Ew

But so I went into the lodge and there was a man scraping grime off the countertops with a metal blade

Excuse me sir is Cooper Lind working here now

He's on the lifts, the man said without looking up

My heart jumped into my hands

Can I speak to him?

You can call him on my walkie and he'll come down here

Or maybe he wouldn't if he knew it was me

I had to try

The man handed me the device but I had trouble keeping it in my bending hands so Harrison steadied them and I was about to press the button when Harrison pointed to a switch on the side

The switch read "announcement"

We looked around and saw a white speaker horn attached to the edge of the building

Identical speakers lined the poles all the way up the slope, to the top

Harrison mouthed *announcement?*

I looked at the man, who was still scraping his grime, and nodded

Harrison flicked the switch

I cleared my throat, and the rumbling went straight from my

mouth up the mountainside, echoing so loud that every person working nearby looked up

None of them were Coop

So I said, as clear as I could, trying not to laugh, WOULD DUMBSHIT PLEASE REPORT TO THE LODGE

Harrison erupted in a fit, Mom covered Bette's ears, and Dad covered Davy's, but we were all doubling over

DUMBSHIT TO THE LODGE PLEASE I repeated

The man scraping grime shook his head and held out his hand for the walkie

I watched the slope

Three figures had been working, and they kept working

Maybe he wasn't coming

Maybe he thought I was trying to humiliate him

I thought about grabbing the walkie again and announcing I LOVE YOU, COOPER LIND, I'M SORRY, PLEASE COME BACK TO ME

But then a figure came out from behind the base of the chairlift, holding a wrench, flipping it like it was no big deal, walking slow, like he was coming down for lunch break

He was wearing a ball cap but I knew it was Coop, he took it off, and his hair fell out

I came out of the office, my family stayed inside

I realized I had been holding my heart in my hand the whole time so I put it back in my chest where it started ticking again

When he saw me he started walking faster

And then running

He stopped himself, pausing for just a moment, and I reached in and stopped my heart

Coop, I called, and I have never been so happy to see someone in my entire life

His face broke into a smile and he ran the rest of the way down hello memory book it's cooper lind. i just wanted to let you know that sammie mccoy is the love of my life and i was dumb to spend more than an hour apart from her. i was afraid that she and stuart had gotten back together. even when i received her texts i got this sick fear that she just wanted to meet me to tell me that it was over, that she was caught up in the moment, or that she had made a mistake. i shouldn't have been afraid. in fact i didn't even know what fear really felt like until the last eight hours i've spent awake in the waiting room of dartmouth medical center.

sammie had a seizure that sent her into shock. she's in stable condition now, but she wasn't before, and if she had gone that quickly, without me even getting to say goodbye, i would have wanted to lie down in the street. she's awake now and talking to her family.

a few days before the seizure sammie and i were lying in her bed and she gave me permission to read this. i suppose i want to explain myself a little bit. i mean not how sammie saw me, because these are her words and she gets to write her story, so i won't address anything she brought up. but i would like to tell you, future sam, why i never told her i loved her until now:

no fucking clue.

trust me, i have had eight hours to mull this over in my head, but i still don't know.

my best guess is that i am human

she gives herself a lot of credit in the brains department, as she should, but i don't know what she was thinking when she said she was not attractive. girls like sammie confuse the average man. girls like sammie befuddle anyone who is used to being told a certain type of woman is the best possible looking woman, because she's not that, and yet she is undeniably a knockout. sammie has these pale pink delicate lips, light brown eyes that change color in the sun, this crazy head of hair, and the way the top of her moves from the bottom of her could give a guy motion sickness. she started exhibiting these traits, or at least i started noticing them, when she was 12 and i was 12. but all of those are not what makes sammie attractive to me. you could point out a million girls with those traits. what it is, is . . .

i guess it's for the same reason i didn't tell her i loved her sooner. it's because she has a light behind her coming from somewhere mysterious that only very strong people can take without feeling intimidated or jealous or wanting to suck it up for themselves. like confidence or something. and maybe that light is just love, and that's what makes her so attractive to me, this endless loop of love and desire, love and desire, but i don't think it's just that.

so i admit it, i was kicked into gear when i saw that a disease was going to try to eat away at it. and then it was a real kick in the ass when i thought someone else was trying to take on that light. because i was stupid, and i always thought she would go somewhere, and when i was ready, whenever that would be, maybe at fuckin 50, i don't know. but when i was ready, i would just happen to get a job nearby and we'd reconnect and we'd spend the rest of our lives together. i was "saving" her for later. like a fucking asshole.

i regret that. i regret that with every fiber of my being. i'm ready now. i was always ready.

Hey Cooper Francis Lind-

Thanks for sleeping here with me. I'm going to the doctor's. You're the best. I think there are some breakfast hot dogs in the refrigerator that as you know are just normal hot dogs that you eat at breakfast time. I love you.

-Sammie

sammie darlin-

i have to go to work today but i will be back this afternoon to walk puppy with you if you'd like, or at least you can sit outside with us and play captain stickwoman. be aware though that davy is really into turning me into a whale lately and it is not a flattering impression. no legs will be broken though. i think.

i love you.

-cooper

to the doctor's again coop. i hate these early appointemtnts but i love you.

samantha,
it is i, francis the goat! i have returned from the dead to express my undying love for you.
don't eat me,
francis

cooper lind is in my bed? i think i am having a dream but i should probably wake him up
i haven't seen him since last year
i wonder if he came over after a party or something
did cooper lind come over?
i should sleep on the floor

SAMMIE! MY LOVE! always wake me up. always, always, always wake me up. i know it's not that easy for you to remember but i thought i would at least type it here in case you decide to write at night again. i'm your boyfriend now. always wake me up, always wake me up, always wake me up.

COOPER. FRANCIS. LIND.
did you smoke a j in my shed before work????
i seriously hope i am not imagining that smell
either that or we have skunks

guilty

sammie,

i hope you slept okay after last night. i have to go to work but if you're feeling a little tired, just know you had a little episode. you did fine.

i love you.

coop

Coop I don't know what I would do without you
I'm really happy
-Sammie

Hi, Zam Zam! My favorite memory of us would have to be the fall of junior year when you started wearing this very strange, cheap kind of Chap Stick, which you applied normally at first, and then it was like your lips got addicted to it and you didn't realize. Remember? And this was before we were friends, so I didn't know if I should say something or not, but it was like, you would come to practice, and as you were making an affirmative speech, you would be putting on this Chap Stick without even realizing it, pacing around, and your lips started to get tinted this bluish purple. I think when Mrs. Townsend stopped you in the hallway and asked you if you were cold, you realized you had to stop. You came up to me like a heroin junkie and handed me the tube and you were like, Maddie, HIDE THIS FROM ME. That's when I knew: you were not just a nerd with vicious cross-examination skills, you were a weirdo just like me. And you will always, always be in my weirdo heart where you belong. You pushed me to be better in every single way because of your strength and ferocity and your pure grip on every moment.

You're true blue, Samantha McCoy. You changed my life. I'm going to try to call you tomorrow without losing it. Thanks to your mom and your lovely Cooper for reaching out to me down here in Atlanta. (By the way, COOPER LIND? Your neighbor?? I knew it! Did you know he used to come to all the debate tournaments we had in Hanover? I was always like, who's that stoner bro in the back of the room?)

I will love you always.

Your partner forever,

Maddie

Hi sissy,

Mom is typing for me since I want the words to be right. My favorite memory is when you watched *The Princess and the Frog* with me and we sang "Almost There" together. I will see you at the hospital and give you every jewel.

I LOVE YOU.

DAVY

Hi sissy,

My favorite memory with you was probly something you might not think of. It was actully very close to now when you were not doing so good but you were ok. We were in the yard and you started to look around and I knew you were not remembring. Then I took your hand and took you to the hummingbird feeder and said hey sissy look remembr. You said oh good Bette its hummingbird season. Then you said shhhhh and pointed and we watched. It is my favorite because it didn't matter that you didn't remembr that it had already been hummingbird season but it was just nice that you were excited and wanted to share them with me! And that is my sister forever! I love you very much.

Bette

Hi Sammie,

I can't do this very well. I asked Dad if it would be ok if I told you in person because it just doesn't feel good to type it. I know you liked typing on this but I type a lot (haha) and I'm on the computer a lot (haha) so I just want to tell you in person. I'll see you.

I love you,

Harry

Hi sweetheart,

Harry and I are in kind of the same boat. The best moment of my life was when I held you in my arms for the first time. I'll talk to you soon.

Love,

Daddy

My first baby,

Words cannot capture my grief at watching you fall away little by little. But I suppose in losing some layers, your golden core came out. You are loving, compassionate, driven, talented, and beautiful, and you will be that way forever, whether in body, in our memories, or in this book.

My favorite memory is so hard to choose, because I have loved every waking minute of our lives together, from the minute you kicked me inside my stomach to this very moment, when I am watching Daddy hold your hand.

I remember when you were eleven, at your first spelling bee in Grafton County. You beat out thirty middle schoolers, and I was so proud. You came running off the stage and you were absolutely beaming and your arms were held wide open. I know not everyone will relate to this, but in a mother's life, there always comes a time when "I love yous" become scarce and weird for both parties. Sometimes you're scared your kid is only going to say it because they want something, or they're doing it out of obligation, or they hate you, but in that moment, when you ran toward me and the first words out of your mouth were "I love you, Mama!" my heart almost burst with joy.

That I should be so lucky to be the person you want to be with and express affection for in the proudest moment of your young life. I was just as bursting at every single one of them, and I know I would have been present at thousands more.

I hope this time is one of them, too. Because I am full to bursting for you, and you should be so proud of yourself for how gracefully you have walked this long road.

I love you, I love you, I love you, infinity times.

Mama

hey sammie

you have just gone. my favorite memory is this whole book because it is you. thank you for recording your life. it was supposed to be longer. i guess you should know that before you passed, at sunrise, you asked to be moved to the window so you could see your side of the mountain. you said, "so i can see home."

i love you,

Cooper

ACKNOWLEDGMENTS

Oh, man. This book means so much to me. Whether they know it or not, many at Alloy—Joelle Hobeika, Josh Bank, Sara Shandler—have seen me grow up. Five years ago I walked into their old offices fresh from sleeping on a couch in Brooklyn, wearing a T-shirt with pit stains. I had no idea what I was doing. I've got to admit: for all the flailing melancholy I bring to their incredible stories, I am always pleasantly surprised when they keep me around. Designers—wow, three for three. Stephanie Abrams, for answering all of my panicked, broke emails. Romy Golan, for your fine-tooth comb. And the standing ovation goes to my editor, Annie Stone. Annie, thank you for allowing me to stretch your story, for letting Sammie be as weird as she needed to be. On the sea of writing, your creativity and sharpness and *patience* were anchors and lighthouses and the storm, all in one. (You would probably cut that sentence.)

Pam Garfinkel, what a pleasure to work with you twice in a row! And how strange to gain so much insight from someone I've never met. You packed the foundation of this story, and you never let me get away with anything. That's invaluable. Thank you.

Leslie Shumate, thank you for running with me in the final stretch. And to all at Little, Brown—Farrin Jacobs, Kristina Aven—Poppy has gained a dedicated fan for life.

To the fine folks who reside in the very real, very green Upper Valley, thank you for letting me wander through and romanticize. Thanks, Charlie—yeah, bud.

Mandy, Emma—you, too, plus everything. For being there at the best and worst. Minnesota, my sweet, unexpected home. Anthony, Hannah, Ian, Luke, Patrick, Ross, Sally—I'd lasso the moon for you, you know that. Sometimes I wish we could all live in connected caves and gather berries for food and stay up all night telling stories and jokes.

To anyone who has had to suffer through a terminal disease like Niemann-Pick (or anyone who is related to someone who has), thank you for the liberty to live in your shoes for a few hundred pages. Forgive me for inconsistencies and exaggerations. If the way I told Sammie's story doesn't feel right, write to me. Or better yet, write it the way you would like to see it.

Grandma Sally and Grandpa Buck, Grandma Hazel and Grandpa Bill, and Great-Aunt Margaret, for telling the stories that matter. Lastly and never leastly, Mom, Dad, Wyatt, Dylan, Puppy, and Lucy. Thanks for letting me go off to build my little worlds, and for being there when I return.

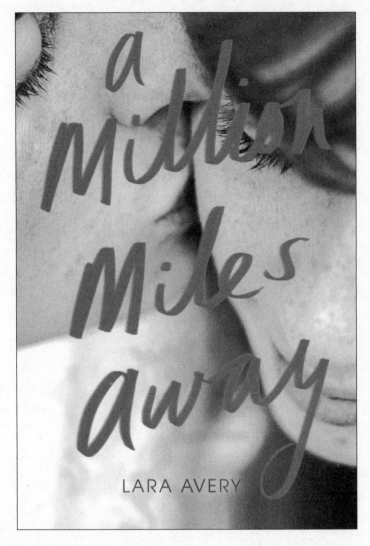

a million Miles Away

LARA AVERY

CHAPTER ONE

"Cops?"

"Where are my shoes?"

"Turn the Beyoncé back up."

Just a few blocks from Massachusetts Street, under the branches of century-old oaks, across a yard full of dozing sunflowers, silence fell over a peach-colored house with a wide porch. This was the Maxfield house. It had been the Maxfield house ever since Rob and Melody Maxfield returned from their honeymoon thirty-odd years ago, and filled the rooms with two daughters.

It was Friday night, and their Subaru was absent from the redbrick driveway. Inside, a hush had fallen over the room, punctuated by the static of girls laughing behind the shoulders of their friends, while plastic cups of Bud Light were emptied and tossed aside.

Kelsey Maxfield moved through the crowd, holding the

sweaty hand of a younger girl not so different from herself when she was that age—no hips, no boobs, body-glittered and hair-sprayed. Kelsey had been the one to turn down the music, and with a reassuring glance back at the nervous girl, who was still wearing her Lycra dance team uniform, she cleared a space around a silver beer keg resting in a bucket of ice.

"Y'all," Kelsey yelled. She gave them a Crest-commercial smile.

Kelsey's husky voice carried through the house. Her dark eyes changed color in the light from the kitchen. Her hair— not quite blonde, not quite brown—was pulled into a high, tight bun, left over from their halftime performance at the final football game of the season. The younger girl beside her adopted Kelsey's hand-on-hip pose, following her captain's lead.

"Hannah T. here has a proposition."

A few catcalls from the male voices.

"Shut up," Kelsey said, flipping the bird with a blood-orange nail. "As I was saying, Hannah thinks she can break my keg-stand record. Twenty-four seconds. You know it's twenty-four, right, Hannah T.?"

Hannah whooped, and a chant began, building volume.

"Hannah, Hannah, Hannah . . ."

Hannah gripped either side of the keg, while Gillian and Ingrid took her legs.

"You ready, Hannah?"

"Ready," Hannah's small voice called.

"Go!"

Kelsey could picture the beer, flowing steady from the keg into the spout, into Hannah's mouth, into her stomach, probably full of lasagna and Gatorade from the pregame dinner.

"Three . . . four . . . five . . ." the onlookers chanted.

Funny, Kelsey had always been the one to do the first keg stand. She felt kind of nostalgic. They used to count for her.

But she was a senior now. She was cocaptain of the dance team. She had to be responsible, or, you know, as responsible as possible. She had put the jade Buddha statues from the living room under her bed, pulled down the wooden Venetian blinds, and then called her mom and dad to make sure they wouldn't be coming home early after another pointless argument with their friends over sauvignon pairings. (All had seemed well, or well enough, on the only vineyard in Central Kansas. They wouldn't be home until tomorrow afternoon.)

Kelsey had also promised her sister she would lock her bedroom door. Michelle didn't want anyone spilling beer on her paintings. *But wouldn't that give them more character?* Kelsey always joked. Michelle didn't find it funny.

"Ten . . . eleven . . . twelve . . ."

Oh, shit. She'd forgotten to lock Michelle's door.

"Thirteen . . . fourteen . . . fifteen . . ."

Hannah was really getting up there. Close to Kelsey's record. Too close. Kelsey looked at Hannah's concentrated, upside-down face. "You had enough, Hannah T.?"

Hannah responded by continuing to swallow beer.

Kelsey knew how to deal with Michelle. She imagined her sister's fist forming when she saw her sticky stereo equipment. They were a couple of punchers, the two of them. What did their parents expect, making twins share a room most of their lives? No head shots, no kidney shots, but the rest was fair game. The fights usually ended in split lips. *It's how they show affection*, their parents had told suspicious teachers when they were younger. It's healthy.

"Eighteen . . . nineteen . . . twenty . . ." Shoulder to shoulder, red-faced partygoers crowded the keg, getting louder.

Kelsey forced herself to chant with them. She started to plan her concession speech. And so the time has come. I must pass the keg-stand mantle. . . .

But right at twenty-three seconds, the younger girl lifted a finger, the universal Lawrence High keg-stand symbol for defeat. Guiding Hannah's skinny legs back down to the floor, Kelsey allowed herself a celebratory swig and a couple of fist pumps.

"Don't worry, Hannah," Kelsey's cocaptain, Gillian, said. "Kel's keg-stand record is higher than her ACT score."

"Shut up," Kelsey said. "Nice job, Hannah T."

Hannah made an elaborate, tipsy bow, and accepted a glass of water Gillian had gotten her from the sink.

Ingrid draped a long arm around Kelsey's neck and spoke in the terrible British accent she always adopted when she had been drinking. "My deah, I see an extremely attractive college fellow in the corner. I believe he belongs to you."

Kelsey searched the dim room. Davis's parted sweep of dark hair was towering above a couple of baseball players and the yearbook editor.

She could hear snatches of his baritone. "And I was, like, gimme the hammer. You've obviously never held a hammer in your life. . . ."

Kelsey maneuvered toward him. Michelle's security emergency could wait.

Everyone was down here, anyway; even Michelle's friends, who were standing in the corner, looking like anthropologists studying a youth species from under their asymmetrical haircuts.

But no Michelle, nor her boyfriend. Not boyfriend. More like object-of-temporary-and-obsessive-lust. Kelsey had even offered to pick Michelle and what's-his-abs up after the game, but she never answered. Because of him, Michelle didn't even respond to the Facebook invite for a party at her own house.

Davis caught Kelsey's eye, flashed a smile. "And then I walked out of there with a free shelf. Hello."

He bent to Kelsey, all other conversations now over.

"Hello, handsome," she replied. She took his face in her hands and kissed him. His skin smelled like he'd been partying. "When did you get here?"

Davis lifted her up and pulled her into a piggyback. "Just now. All the frat row parties were, like, if you don't have a girl, you can't come in. So."

"Lucky for me!"

"Lucky for you." Davis advanced, causing her to accidentally kick a cheerleader or two.

"Where are you taking me?"

"To Beer Land!" Davis called.

Hannah T. stood swaying near the keg, sipping water. She looked at Kelsey on Davis's back, to her arms around his solid chest, and back to Kelsey. "Who is that?"

Kelsey laughed and took on a late-night radio DJ voice. "My lover."

Hannah T. shrugged, half of her mouth lifting in a lazy, incredulous smile. "Why do you have, like, the best life in the world?"

"She bought it on sale at Sears," Davis said.

"Please don't tell people I shop at Sears." Kelsey slid down to the floor, winked at Hannah, and gave Davis her Solo cup. "Refill me, please? I have to go do damage control."

The sisters' rooms were a recent addition to the Maxfield house, after Michelle had given Kelsey a bruised rib, fighting over the remote when they were fourteen. As soon as their parents were sure Melody was tenured and Rob's second restaurant was going to survive, they had knocked off the back upstairs wall and built the girls adjacent dwellings, complete with locks on the doors and a back porch. Kelsey used her side of the deck to tan; Michelle, for drying the hyperreal paintings she did of their neighborhood, perfect replicas except for the colors: Everything was neon or reversed or slightly out of focus. Kelsey didn't get it, and she liked it that way.

Once at Michelle's room, she would have to lock her sister's door from the inside, exit through her balcony door, and climb through a barrier of small trees that acted as a "fence" between the two sides.

But when she got to Michelle's door, it was already locked.

"Yo!" Kelsey called, banging on the still-unfinished wood.

No answer. Movement. Laughter. It sounded as though someone was using Michelle's room as a temporary brothel.

Kelsey banged on the door again. "Hello! It's Kelsey."

More laughter. Still, the door remained shut.

"Hey!" Kelsey called. She jiggled the handle.

Lost cause. This would have to be a rescue mission. She stepped through her own dark room, over piles of discarded leggings and sports bras, and opened the screen door to her side of the deck.

Light poured onto the wood on Michelle's side of the

porch. Slipping between the trees, Kelsey looked through the glass to see her sister stretched out on the bed. A sandy-haired dude in jeans sat in her desk chair, bent over a book. He was reading aloud.

Kelsey yanked open the screen. "Oh," she said loudly. "Interesting."

Michelle turned her head, brushing the same lumber-colored hair out of her eyes. "Oh," she said, echoing Kelsey. "Hey."

Michelle's new boyfriend closed the book and smiled at her. "Wow, you guys really are identical."

"Yeah," Kelsey said, still looking at Michelle. It was prob-ably better she didn't see his face up close, as she was going to have to forget it anyway. "Come out in the hall for a sec, please."

"Okay." Michelle was doing that thing where she talked and moved slower than necessary just to piss Kelsey off.

When Michelle emerged, Kelsey closed her sister's bed-room door with a bang.

"Is he sleeping over?"

"Yeah, he has to. He's on his way to ship out from Fort Riley. Can you believe it?"

"I don't know! Why didn't you respond to my texts?"

"I was busy."

"You could have at least come down and said hi. Some of your townie friends are here—"

"Hi!" Michelle said, giving Kelsey a double wave. Her dark eyes lit up with fake enthusiasm. Something was different about her sister. She was wearing mascara. Kelsey's mascara. "Can I go now?"

"Don't be a bitch."

"I'm not. Thank you. I'm sorry. Whatever you want to hear. I haven't seen Peter for two months, and he's about to be halfway across the world."

"So? You'll just find another, like, film school student or something."

Or a Brazilian on KU's soccer team, Kelsey thought. *Or a theater major who looked exactly like a brunette version of Woody Allen, or a record-store employee who had to wear prescription yellow-tinted glasses.*

Kelsey was there for all of them. She knew how to listen politely to Michelle over the dinners their father cooked, as she went on about how each one was "love at first sight," and to watch her get in their cars after school, sit on their motorcycles, balance on their handlebars. Then, to watch for the silent signals that her sister had stopped caring— the drifting eyes, the legs crossed and recrossed. Last, she would stand on the deck with Michelle, composing the breakup texts for her, because Michelle was terrible at typing anything less than a novel. And then they would walk back to Massachusetts Street, where it would start all over again.

But none of that had happened with this one. Kelsey shot him a quick glance through the door, his toned, pale arms resting on his knees as he flipped the pages of an Andy Warhol coffee-table book.

Michelle sighed. "Peter is different. You haven't been paying attention at all, have you?"

Gillian came up the stairs and yanked at Kelsey's arm. "Time to get back. Who's that?" she said as she glanced through Michelle's cracked door.

"Don't know," Kelsey said, letting out a snort. "It's kind of hard to keep track."

Suddenly, Michelle's fist shot out. Right to the solar plexus. Kelsey seized up in pain as Michelle went back into her room. "A soldier, huh? Don't get syphilis," Kelsey choked out.

Kelsey straightened, rubbed her stomach, and made her way back to the party with Gillian.

"He's cute," Gillian said.

"Whatever."

Michelle hadn't even introduced them.

On the stairs, Kelsey stopped to survey the crowd congregating around the beer, the coupling off, hands in the air bouncing to the music. Ingrid was doing a handstand against the wall. Davis was surrounded by girls in UGGs. He found her gaze and beckoned.

Kelsey took another step down. "Hey!" she yelled. Heads

turned to behold her tanned arms lifted, her legs silhouetted in tight jeans. The world's eyes were on her. Well, her world's eyes, at least.

"Who wants to see me break my own record?"

Jeremiah Satterthwaite

LARA AVERY

is the author of *A Million Miles Away* and *Anything But Ordinary*. She lives in Minneapolis, Minnesota, where she is a contributor to *Revolver*. You can follow her on Twitter @laraavery or find her on Facebook at facebook.com/laraaverybooks.

Get swept away by Carrie Firestone's
stories of love, friendship,
and finding yourself.